Praise for *Bloody Av*

'A truly special novel. A delight fror
pain of being a teenager perfectly. I
Jennie Godfrey, author of

'In a perfect balance between levity and sadness, Andrev Walden depicts
a boy's attempt to come to terms with a life where fathers are constantly
replaced. *Bloody Awful in Different Ways* is a humorous examination
of a different kind of childhood, which, despite the pervasive blackness,
is portrayed with an inexhaustible warmth and presence'
August Prize Judges

'Walden makes both trivialities and atrocities sparkle'
Aftonbladet, Sweden

'If there is such a thing as an absolute literary ear, Andrev Walden has it,
because throughout the book he hits every single note right and that is
something very unusual – 5/5'
BTJ, Sweden

'An incredible account of growing up'
Ann-Helén Laestadius, author of *Stolen*

'Through Walden's precise and evocative language, we are invited into
a young boy's observations of the world and his journey into manhood.
A sharply critical view of the male-dominated world is interwoven with
tender portrayals of how a person is shaped by their relationships. It
becomes unmistakably clear how vulnerable and strong we are in relation
to one another. I laugh, I ache and I reflect as I read Walden's book'
Lisa Ridzén, author of *When the Cranes Fly South*

'This is a childhood story of the humorous kind, which occasionally
resembles a fairy tale – but also has a core of seriousness and
sadness, through its portrayal of men's violence against
women and children . . . A remarkable achievement'
Svenska Dagbladet, Sweden

'Walden impresses greatly with his thoughtful storytelling
and unique filter against reality'
Göteborgs-Posten, Sweden

'A gripping coming-of-age novel with a playwright's confidence and lin-
guistic flair . . . Brilliant'
Verdens Gang, Norway

'Bloody good!'
NRK, Norway

'Elegant and distinctive . . . It's painful, it's strong, but it's also really funny'
Adresseavisen, Norway

'Bad fathers, great novel'
BOK365, Norway

'Marvellous'
Dagens Næringsliv, Norway

'Outstanding literature. Shamelessly entertaining'
Sydsvenskan, Sweden

'A little treasure of a book. Hilarious but vulnerable, clever but raw, and pure joyous storytelling on every page. You'll come for the laughs, but you'll stay for the love letter, from a grown man to his boy self, promising everything will be all right'
Fredrik Backman, author of *A Man Called Ove*

'I challenge you not to fall in love with Andrev as he thrashes doggedly through life – perpetually hopeful and inept. This is a small gem of a novel, with an irresistible voice and a teasing sidelong wit'
Meg Rosoff, author of *How I Live Now*

'What a book! I laughed, cried, despaired and hoped for this young boy negotiating seven fathers in seven chaotic years, taking us with him for the wild ride. A story that reads this easily with consummate fluidity, pace and comic timing deserves the widest audience possible'
Jo Browning Wroe, author of *A Terrible Kindness*

'This tragicomic account of a boyhood is at once sitcom, circus and extended nightmare. As Andrev learns about masculinity through a series of hapless and sometimes toxic "dads", his memorable and wildly vivid voice persists as a form of hope'
Clare Pollard, author of *The Modern Fairies*

'A hair-raising story, formidably told . . . I would sacrifice blood for his language'
Dala-Demokraten, Sweden

'The new Knausgaard . . . Witty and insane about lousy stepfathers and the innocent but brutal eighties'
Dagbladet, Norway

Bloody Awful in Different Ways

ANDREV WALDEN

Translated by Ian Giles

FIG TREE
an imprint of
PENGUIN BOOKS

FIG TREE

UK | USA | Canada | Ireland | Australia
India | New Zealand | South Africa

Fig Tree is part of the Penguin Random House group of companies whose addresses can be found at global.penguinrandomhouse.com

Penguin Random House UK,
One Embassy Gardens, 8 Viaduct Gardens, London SW11 7BW

penguin.co.uk

First published in Swedish as *Jävla karlar* by Bokförlaget Polaris 2023
First published in Great Britain as *Bloody Awful in Different Ways* by Fig Tree 2025

001

Copyright © Andrev Walden, 2023
Translation copyright © Ian Giles, 2025

The moral right of the copyright holders has been asserted

Extract on p. 242 from *Dagens Nyheter*, edition published 20 January 1956

The cost of this translation was supported by a subsidy from the Swedish Arts Council, gratefully acknowledged.

SWEDISH ARTS COUNCIL

No part of this book may be used or reproduced in any manner for the purpose of training artificial intelligence technologies or systems. In accordance with Article 4(3) of the DSM Directive 2019/790, Penguin Random House expressly reserves this work from the text and data mining exception.

Set in 12/14.75 pt Dante MT Std
Typeset by Jouve (UK), Milton Keynes
Printed and bound in Great Britain by Clays Ltd, Elcograf S.p.A.

The authorized representative in the EEA is Penguin Random House Ireland, Morrison Chambers, 32 Nassau Street, Dublin D02 YH68

A CIP catalogue record for this book is available from the British Library

ISBN: 978–0–241–72028–8

Penguin Random House is committed to a sustainable future for our business, our readers and our planet. This book is made from Forest Stewardship Council® certified paper.

For Mum

(NB: not in a passive aggressive way)

Once upon a time, I had seven dads in seven years. This is the story of those years.

If anything sounds made up, then you can be sure that it is true – like the thing with the rat and the hamster. Or the girl with the barbecue spice clown lips. I don't intend to make up anything in particular, because the particulars stick in the memory and don't need making up. If I do make anything up then it is tucked away in the most mundane parts – like the colour of a cushion on a sunlounger in a fisherman's hut where something of note took place.

PART ONE
The Plant Magician

In which:
Santa is beaten,
a secret comes out,
and
men and stones change names.

He crouches down and looks me in the eyes.

'You have two noses,' he says.

I check, as if it is necessary to refute the assertion. I don't understand what he means, but I do understand that he is going to explain because I can see a smile creeping about in his beard.

He's beautiful when he smiles. Those pale greyish-blue eyes don't appear to belong to the rest of his head because they're fitted inside a frame of black curls. But the colours don't clash. On the contrary. He is the light in his own darkness. His gaze sparkles like a salmon's back in a seaweed forest, lending him the ability to enchant. And once again I am enchanted.

'Follow my lead,' he says, raising a hand in the gap between our faces. There is sap on his cuticles. He's going to teach me one final thing before we part for ever, and I follow his lead but take care to hate him. It's only been a few months since I learned that I've never been his son and sometimes I forget that I've been liberated from the obligation to love him. When it comes to hate, I'm still on my L-plates, but I'm starting to get really good at it. I have found the keynote and allow it to resonate within me as I raise my hand and place it in front of his.

The Plant Magician is going to teach me one final thing, but I shouldn't start there. (I have most assuredly already done so, but I think the attempt should remain, given its aptness as a bridge to a dramaturgical arc.)

I want to begin with the day when he stopped being my dad, because it was so odd and I have such vivid memories of the oddness.

But first, I suppose I need to explain what a Plant Magician is.

I fear that your mind's eye may already be lingering upon some kind of druid clad in a wadmal tunic, but he didn't dress like that. The man I called Dad wore blue dungarees and gloves of earth. In the summer, he wore nothing else. In the winter he donned Graninge boots and a vegetable-dyed woolly jumper worn over the braces. My mother had dyed the wool.

While you repaint the picture in your mind's eye, I want to emphasize the bit about him being beautiful. You've got to make him beautiful – otherwise the logic around him falls apart. He was the kind of man that beautiful women knit woolly jumpers for. He was the kind of magician who gets laid. That much I know for sure, because I saw him do it.

'Love shouldn't be hidden from children,' he said, letting us tumble about the bed while he had sex with our mother.

I scrambled to the foot of the bed and listened to their breathing. I didn't like it; he made her sound like a witch. I was afraid that she would have a witch's face if I looked, so I didn't. Instead, I allowed my gaze to roam over the walls.

There was a peculiar painting hanging over the bed. *The God of Seasons.* He had peapods for eyelids, corn cobs for ears, spring onions for shoulders and a whopping big squash in shades of grey and green for a chest. He was formidable to look at: an apple-cheeked demon. But the Plant Magician swore he was good. When the witch sounds had fallen silent, he stood up and touched the frame – as if thanking the demon – before stepping into his dungarees and disappearing into the garden.

He always had plenty to be cracking on with and his mission on Earth was important – so important that the state paid him a wage to devote himself to it. The man I called Dad was a state-remunerated Plant Magician.

You don't have to be of a conservative disposition for that sentence to take your breath away, so before your lips turn blue I'd like to add that the state didn't really know what my dad did. And that he would probably have got the sack from his job as a state-remunerated Plant Magician had the state discovered what he spent his working days doing. Or indeed, had the state even found out that his days were spent working. You see, somewhere in the drawers of state there was a piece of paper stating that my dad was unable to work and needed to be paid not to do so.

He was an invalid – although only on that piece of paper. In reality, he was remarkably frisky. One morning, he awoke with a sudden desire to run to Västervik, so after breakfast he set off. At the time, we lived in Gamleby, but it was still a long way to Västervik and he made it almost all the way. Towards the afternoon, a stranger from Hermanstorp called and said there was a man lying in his garden and that we had to come and get him. Mum and the stranger helped to carry him to the car. He couldn't walk, but he was beaming away like a winner.

The Plant Magician often beamed like a winner because he was a winner. He had outsmarted and defeated the system, and his contentment at this victory was always more powerful than his fear of being caught out and about. He was a proud and incautious member of the resistance. As soon as he found an ear that hadn't yet heard the story about what happened when he defeated the system, he would take a deep breath and tell it.

Now, you quite probably want to hear that story and find

out more about the magic itself – and rightly so, given that you (or at least your parents) funded it – but I'll have to slip all that in along the way, because what the story needs right now is to be enriched by movement and direction.

So let me tell you about the day when I ceased to be his son.

The snow is falling like in a fairy tale that day. Flakes as big as hornets swarm silently over the woods and lake at Vrinneviskogen, but vanish as soon as they reach the bare ground of the gardens. It looks strange – as if the wintry sky were pasted over the landscape. There is only a week or so left until Christmas 1983, and the day that is to be my last as the Plant Magician's son is almost over. It has already begun to get dark when I open the bathroom window and stick a leg out into the chill.

The Plant Magician is pounding on the bathroom door yelling that the food will get cold. It's only the second time that he's told me, but his voice is already smouldering. I cover my mouth so that he won't hear the laughter but he hears it anyway.

'What are you laughing at?' he bellows through the wooden door, his voice now full of fire – but I can't turn back. Both feet are already on the ground and I'm too small to climb back up. I just have to hurry and then the fire will go out. He'll laugh when he realizes.

I'm wearing a Santa hat. No one saw me take it into the bathroom; I kept it hidden under my top before putting it on my head and clambering out. I'm also carrying a small cloth bag in my hand. It's filled with building blocks and is meant to look like a sack of Christmas presents.

Now I need to run around the outside of the house to ring the doorbell. 'Are there any good boys and girls here?' I'll ask when the door opens, and then he'll laugh. And when he laughs, Mum will laugh too. Little Sis won't even wait for his laugh before she lets rip with her own, because she doesn't know the rules and laughs at everything I do. Little Bro only laughs if you tickle him, but Santa can arrange that.

I round the first corner of the house, moving carefully along the gable end to avoid slipping down the slope towards the outbuilding. The outbuilding is the Plant Magician's workshop. It's where he sometimes locks himself away to eat mushrooms and smoke henbane. He does this to open doors into other worlds, and he writes down everything he sees in big notebooks with black covers.

When he goes to the outbuilding, he can be gone for hours. I like those hours because then you can laugh and behave however you like up in the house. Then you can eat sandwiches between mealtimes and chew with your mouth open, and I reckon we'd be allowed to watch TV too if only we had one.

But those carefree hours come at a price because sometimes he opens the wrong doors down there. Sometimes he returns from his workshop harried by creatures only he can see, before crashing about naked on all fours in the kitchen, howling in terror.

'Help me!' he'll wail, glistening with sweat and tears. And then Mum has to hold him in her arms until he calms down. Not even a state-remunerated Plant Magician can open doors any old way.

It's so dark that I have to grope my way along the wall to stay on course. I can't fathom how it got so dark so quickly, but all I need to do is get around the house and ring the doorbell, then we'll laugh together. It ought to be quick, but everything slants out here. The whole village is built on a slope down towards Lake Ensjön in the bowl bottom of the valley, and our garden has no terracing. The house is just about the only thing that doesn't lean, and the grass is now as slippery as snot because winter has got stuck.

I slip on the slope and slide into the darkness. Away from the house where the nettle soup is cooling on the kitchen table.

A knot forms in my stomach, because I really don't like the dark. I'm scared of everything since I believe in everything, and everything I believe in hides in the dark.

I believe in vættir, gnomes, elves, trolls, werewolves and witches. Especially witches. And I believe in God and other gods and the devil. The hulder. The nixie. The kelpie and mylings. I'm a miniature encyclopaedia of various beings. A monster watcher. Some I have seen with my own eyes, although only when I have a fever. I always run a high fever when I'm ill – so high that I see things and scare Mum.

'He's burning up,' she usually says, while the Plant Magician applies an onion dressing and strains hot water through coltsfoot leaves. I burn and I see witches. And men with peapods for eyes.

'There are no monsters,' she says, but I know that there are. I've seen my dad howl in terror as they come after him.

I crawl back up the slope and grasp the drainpipe at the next corner of the house. I'm soaked and probably filthy, but the Santa hat is still on my head and soon everyone will laugh. I gaze into the darkness. Beyond the hayfield, the windows glow in the house where my only friend lives. He's called Blomma and we usually play in the forest.

I hug the drainpipe and catch my breath. There's only a minute or so left of my time as the Plant Magician's son.

I carry on, laughter once again rising inside me. They won't believe their eyes when the boy who went to the loo is suddenly standing outside the door, transformed into Santa. I squeal with laughter as I climb onto the porch.

I'm not clueless; I realize that it may have been too long and that he may be angry by now, but at least he hasn't been drinking. One Christmas, he drank all the booze in the house and nothing went right. Mum had invited her siblings to celebrate with us and she'd bought bottles for Christmas dinner. The Plant Magician was only going to taste them, but by the time they arrived he'd tasted the lot. He ran out onto the road and chased them off before they'd even got out of the car. Mum cried. The house smelled of cleaning fluid and cinnamon.

I ring the doorbell and inflate my chest as the door is opened.
'Are there any . . .'
I want to say it with a Santa voice, but I can't. I'm laughing too much. The words seem to be whistling out of me, and I have to inhale again. I'm only seven years old and barefoot in the winter's night. It would be asking a lot for me to be able to talk too.
'. . . good boys and girls here?'
He looks puzzled. That's good. What expression would he otherwise wear, between fire and laughter? And now I say it again for safety's sake. Well, I shout. It's not even a question any more.
'ARE THERE ANY GOOD BOYS AND GIRLS HERE!'
I shouldn't have shouted – the fire feeds on shouts. He doesn't even remember to open his hand properly before he strikes. That's new. Different anyway. The blows usually burn my skin – like a thousand needles, but to the cheek. Now I break, and it almost feels nicer than the needles. Like when water blisters burst.

Of course, it looks worse. Blood gushes from my face.

Mum screams. That's new too. Not the scream – but the tone. Something is happening to her. She isn't backing away like usual; she's approaching him, chin held high. Into the flames. The sun had set before this day stopped being an ordinary day, and now it can't get enough of being new.

'He's not your real dad!' she screeches. 'A real dad would never do that to his child.'

He lets go of me at the very moment she utters the incantation, as if stripped of his powers.

And it only takes a few moments for me to realize that it's true. I've never thought the thought, but as soon as it takes hold of me I know. I don't look like him, and I don't look like any of my younger siblings either. I don't have their grey-blue eyes. Don't have their sandy curls. Don't have their freckles. And they rarely have my bruises. Of course it's true. The Plant Magician has never been my dad.

I run upstairs, my feet strangely light, lie down on the bed and suck the towel my mum gave me. They're clattering about and loudly bickering, but I can't hear the words. I'm filled with something else. At first I don't understand what it is, but my mouth is grinning, living a life of its own in the folds of towel. I'm fizzing. It seems as if . . . I love not being his son.

Yes. I can feel it in my whole body. A great thrill – as if an adventure has begun. As if I'm the boy in a book about a boy who finds out his dad is the king of a magical and distant land.

Am I going to be plucked up by the genie now?

I briefly pity my siblings who still belong to the Plant Magician, and I pity him. He was so overwrought and powerless when she said it. I saw him shrink away, as if the words had pierced holes in him.

The house falls silent.

She sits on the edge of the bed and promises it's over now. 'We're not going to live here any more,' she whispers while I fiddle with the lattice front of the bedside lamp. She promises to take me away from here.

I don't ask about my real dad, but she tells me about him anyway. Just a little. She says he lives in a land far away and that he has long black hair – like an Indian. She makes a sign against her elbow with her hand so that I understand. Then she says nothing more about my real dad, but that's enough.

An Indian in a land far away.

That's the best thing I've ever heard, and now all I want is to fall asleep so that I can cross the hayfield and tell Blomma.

Mum turns off the light as she goes. I turn it back on once she's gone – it's what I always do. She says there aren't any monsters, but that doesn't help. We have a credibility problem in the house. There's something moving in the shadows.

I tuck the duvet under myself and pull it over my head. I seal off every way in, leaving only a narrow tunnel through which to breathe. The air gets hot and heavy in there, but it's the only way I can fall asleep – in a cocoon where I can guard the only way in.

In the morning he says sorry. He hit too hard. It didn't go right. He was unfair, which isn't like him.

'I'm usually fair,' he says, which feels like a question, so I nod, because surely that's the answer.

He puts his arms around me and promises that no one is moving anywhere. Then I feel sorry for him again – doesn't he know that Mum has already promised we'll move? That she promised first?

'Now let's celebrate Christmas.'

He says it as if he liked celebrating Christmas, but he doesn't. He doesn't like celebrating anything except his own birthday. I'll never meet another person who takes their own birthday as seriously as the Plant Magician.

When Mum had Little Sis in her tummy and was thirteen days overdue, he was in a state of despair because he'd promised his friends a big party on his birthday. The birthday came but Little Sis didn't. He tucked me and Mum in upstairs while downstairs was filled with people and music.

'Just lie still and take it easy,' he said, and then the party raged on all night. An orchestra formed, with the Plant Magician on vocals. He sang 'Heart of Gold' and tooted on his harmonica while Mum lay beside me with her hand over my ear. She drew long breaths through her nostrils, but her breathing became shallower towards dawn. Little Sis was almost born in the car because he was so plastered that he had to drive to the hospital at a snail's pace. He was there when she was born, but when he saw her he became so pirate-king happy that he had to drive home to breathe new life into the birthday celebrations. The next morning, he returned to the hospital with the whole orchestra in tow. They played 'Heart of Gold' to Little Sis and he tooted on the harmonica and then they were chucked out.

The Plant Magician loves to celebrate as long as the dance revolves around him. He can't countenance dances around anything else – in his house, he's always the Christmas tree.

But now he sits on the edge of my bed and says that we're going to get a tree from the woods and that there will be parcels underneath it. He's making it up. On his way out of the room, he turns around one last time. The salmon back can be glimpsed through the seaweed.

'I'm still your dad,' he says, before adding something about it not mattering much whose balls you come from.

He's trying to take the fizz away from me – he's nuts.

My dad is an Indian and now I'm going to tell Blomma this.

Sometimes you can see a glowing point at the edge of the trees or a wisp of smoke between the trunks, which means you know he's there. But it's not him I'm looking for. Not yet. I'm looking for his little brother, the one who is my friend, and I find him down by the lake.

'Does he have a horse?' Blomma asks. He's standing by the water's edge, slashing at the reeds with a knife.

'I don't know.'

'If he's a real Indian then he has a horse,' Blomma says, and I'm obliged to tell him about the long hair. I make a sign against my elbow with my hand so that he understands. Blomma stares at my elbow and looks like he's understood, but then his gaze roams up to my face.

'You don't look like an Indian,' he says.

'I think he's got a horse,' I say.

'We should tell my brother,' Blomma says. 'He's an Indian too.'

So we go to find Blomma's big brother. He's tall and he's smoking in the woods and it's not hard to find him because that's pretty much all he does: stand in the woods being tall and smoking.

The Plant Magician says that Blomma and his brother aren't real brothers but that they were adopted from the same country and that country is called Chile. The Plant Magician likes Blomma. When we are playing in the hayfield, he sometimes looks up from the garden and waves, but he waves in a weird way. He raises a clenched fist and says 'Allende!' when he sees my friend. Maybe he thinks that's how they say hello in Chile, but it probably isn't since Blomma looks confused each time he does it.

I don't like the Plant Magician trying to share a secret language with my friend, and it feels just as good every time it fails. Blomma is mine.

He's actually called something else, but he says he's called Blomma and it's not something I'm going to argue about – not with my only friend. He probably just wanted to be called something Swedish without really knowing what you can be called in Sweden, so he went with the floweriest word he could think of.

I'm called Andrev, and you can't be called that in Sweden either, but Blomma never makes a thing about it – not like the other kids.

Apart from me and my younger siblings, there are only four kids in the village, which isn't really a village at all – it's more of a built-up corner in the woods on the road between Norrköping and the bathing spot on the shore of Lake Ensjön. The four kids are Blomma and his older brother, and two girls. One of the girls lives further along the curve and is a teenager – and thus unresponsive – while the other lives right across the road and is my age, but I once broke her arm so she doesn't like me.

I only have Blomma, but I have him as if he's in a small box because neither of us has a real dad in this country. Now we're both waiting to be plucked up by the genie and I can feel how it bonds us together. We're the boys in a book, I think, as we cross the hayfield on the lookout for the glowing spot at the edge of the forest.

'You don't look like an Indian,' Blomma's big brother says, exhaling smoke at me.

It's the first time I've heard him speak. He has a brown quilted jacket with Larch Bolete yellow cuffs and a helmet of thick black hair. I'd like a quilted jacket with cuffs too, but quilted jackets are made from synthetics and we don't like synthetics – we like vegetable-dyed wool.

'I'm only half-Indian,' I say.

'Want to see my cock?' he asks. Apparently he's not all that interested in Indians.

I shake my head, but Blomma says I've got to see it and he gestures with his whole arm as the fly is opened.

'There it is,' he hoots, as if it were hard to see. It most definitely isn't, but he probably just wants to introduce it – like a circus director.

'Is it real?' I ask.

'It is,' says the owner, as if the question weren't strange at all.

Then he pees so that I understand, but it still takes me a while. I thought I'd seen all the sexual organs there were, but it's like looking at a new and hitherto unknown body part – a third sex. It's huge – much bigger than the Plant Magician's. I get a nosebleed and go home.

The Plant Magician pushes me down onto the sofa. 'Pinch here,' he says, guiding my fingers to the bridge of my nose as if I didn't know.

He stays there, stroking my forehead. He doesn't usually do that. All that usually happens when I get a nosebleed – which happens almost every day – is that he gets annoyed. I don't even have to bump into anything for my nose to bleed. Not any more. It's enough for me to get angry or scared. I can get nosebleeds from feeling too much – a pointless superpower that I developed in the summer of 1983.

Well, it's not completely pointless, because I've noticed that the nosebleeds can look pretty bad and it's got harder for the Plant Magician to slap me about for no reason at all. He likes to administer slaps at the dinner table – quick blows to the back of the head with his open hand – and if you start to cry then he tells you right away that it's only a slap, and that's nothing. But the blood is something. Especially if you wait to pinch your nose and just let it flow down onto the plate. That throws him off-kilter – it's like red tears that I can't stop and no one can take them away from me.

(That's not quite true, because one day my mum will take me to a doctor with a soldering iron, but I don't know that yet. That will be later on when we live in town. Right now, we still live by a lake in the woods, and I have nosebleeds almost every day and my dad is an Indian.)

From the kitchen sofa bench, everything looks the same as ever. The old cabinet stripped of paint that you can hide inside and the Dr Westerlund geraniums in the window. Mum has a towel wrapped around her head, and I know what the scent means: she's mixed henna dye in a steel basin and smeared it on her hair. She wants it to be fiery red when Christmas comes. Everything is as usual, and that usualness makes the day before seem like a dream. It's as if we're not going to move away from here at all.

I know Mum is susceptible to the calm of contrition – I am too. It's so nice when the Plant Magician is full of regret and his hands become soft. On days like that I can love him, and I catch myself doing it again. Although he's not my dad any more. I love him for a while and remember that he wants the best for me.

He wants me to learn to live in this world – or something like it, at least. It's as if he's preparing us for a poorly advertised ice age or possibly a war. As if he knows something the rest of us don't.

He's taught me everything about the mushrooms that grow in the woods and fields – which ones you can eat and which ones will kill you (unless you're a Plant Magician). He's taught me to tell the difference between the parasol mushroom and the panther cap, and he's taught me that russula aren't russula if they've got socks. Sometimes he hits me to make sure I remember, and when he does that I hate him but the hate burns very fast and sometimes all he has to do is take my hand for it to go out.

He showed me the morels and we knelt in the moss and laughed – they looked like small, homeless brains.

He taught me how to start a fire using tinder, how to tap birch sap in the spring and which roots you can gnaw on. There's one that tastes like liquorice which I like.

He taught me how to poo like an Indian, clambering up onto the toilet seat to demonstrate by squatting over the ring and drawing a line across his tummy. 'When you poo like an Indian, it straightens out your insides and helps your bowels to work properly inside you,' he explained. Since then, I've always pooed like an Indian. I was pooing like an Indian even before I knew that I was an Indian.

He taught me that large stones in the woods are called drift boulders and that they were dragged here by the inland ice ten thousand years ago.

He taught me to play chess, but he never lets me win. I once threw him off balance with an opening that's apparently called the English Opening, but he still won in the end and, besides, the English Opening was an idiot move and I ought to always play the King's Pawn like Bobby Fischer.

He taught me how to make yarrow tea and how to make another sort using camomile (which resembles ox-eye daisies and scentless mayweed – just use your nose if you're not sure).

He taught me to use the casting rod and I caught a pike. 'Take the pike home. I'll stay a while longer,' he said. The sun had set when he returned from the lake having caught an even bigger pike, although unfortunately it had got away at the last second, but he showed us how big it was with his arms. Bigger. That much was apparent to all. We ate my pike and talked about his.

The Plant Magician always wins.

And with his fingers in my hair, I realize that he's won again. He means to keep me – no one is going to move anywhere. No genie is coming, and now we're going to celebrate Christmas.

It's 1984 and Blomma has been given a pair of mini skis. I'm ill and I can see him from my window. He's going back and forth across a patch of snow down on the hayfield. I suppose he's waiting for me to get better. I want mini skis too, but mini skis are made from plastic and we don't like plastic – we like long, wooden skis that you can take corners on.

Mum has been given a knitting machine, and from down in the kitchen comes the sound of the rattling carriage crossing the bed. I will soon discover that the knitting machine is a powerful blow against my desire for modern clothes. The knitting machine is the industrialization of my patheticness.

At night, I burn. Mum is there with a wet towel.

'Take away the sound,' I say, and Mum blows out the candle in the angel chimes.

I like the angel chimes and the shadows that dance across the wall, but not when I'm burning. The chimes hurt my ears. The shadows exhaust me. The cherubs become witches and the trumpets brooms.

The fever dissipates during the day and I sit at my desk looking out of the window. Blomma is bored on his own down there, and I like that.

The Plant Magician seems to be bored too. He's tinkering with the car but can't get it to start. He doesn't know much about cars. He doesn't even have a driving licence, although he still drives. That's the only thing he knows about cars: how to drive them. Now it won't start and he's standing helpless in front of the silent chasm of the open bonnet.

We have a big car that looks like it was made up – like a child's drawing of a car. It's tall and wonky and only barely coloured in between the lines. No one else on our road has a car like it, but once there were men who came and climbed the telephone poles and they had one like it, although it was orange. And better drawn.

Our car is red like a barn, and painted with a brush. If you go up close you can see the strokes. It looks crazy, but I didn't realize that until I got up close to other cars. Our neighbours' cars don't have any brushstrokes – it's as if the paint has been breathed onto them.

Our neighbours' cars are straight and shiny. Ours is lopsided and dull. And as of a few days ago, dead. It's unclear why, which makes the Plant Magician twitch as he stands with his hands by his sides, glaring down at the engine.

The calm of contrition has lingered after Christmas, but there is something creeping within him. I can feel rising unrest and I think Mum can feel it too.

The Plant Magician frequently says that he can't die, that he's going to live for ever thanks to the power of plants and monthly enemas using lavender water, but for a man with all the time in the world he is curiously restless.

He rules over a small kingdom, but carries the keys to a larger one. He is the chosen one, although what for he isn't sure – sometimes he tries changing his name to be more certain. That's going to happen again in a few days' time, although we don't know that yet. Perhaps he doesn't even know it himself.

The approaching transformation is still just a movement under his skin.

Blomma's big brother has got himself a girlfriend. I can't understand how – all he does is stand in the woods smoking. But maybe he found her there – in the woods.

'This is my girlfriend,' he says, pointing at the girl.

The girl makes no objection.

I recognize her. She's the teenager who lives further along the curve, in one of the houses with straight cars parked on the drive. She smokes too. The cigarette wanders back and forth between Blomma's big brother and his girlfriend.

'Want to see us shag?' he asks.

We do.

He leads us further into the woods before stopping by a rock that comes up to his hips. He tells us to turn around while they undress. I turn around slowly – I don't want to get a nose-bleed. The only sound audible is the whisper of quilted jackets, then nothing – just the breathing of the treetops and the odd twig snapping as the spirit of the forest creeps closer to catch a glimpse.

And then: a faint gurgling sound.

'Now you can look,' he says, and we look. She's lying on the rock with her trousers rolled up to form a cushion under her head, and he's standing between her knees pumping with his hips.

The scene is something of a disappointment because he's holding up her white quilted jacket like a surgical drape in front of the only thing we really want to see. With his other hand, he's smoking. He really does love to smoke. She must do too, because she now extends two fingers towards him and he slips the cigarette into the crevice between her fingers. It's as if they're made for each other. But she drops the cigarette and his hips stop. Everything stops.

I look at the cigarette and wonder whether to go over and pick it up for him, but he's already lit a new one and I suddenly understand why there was a fire in the Vrinneviskogen woods back in the summer of 1982.

The whole country was on fire that summer, and I asked Mum whether you could see the fire from space and she said you probably could. They were talking about waterbombing on the radio, and I hoped there'd be a fire in our woods too because I really did want to see a waterbomb. And then there *was* a fire in our woods, and I was standing there watching for the waterbombers when a man stepped into our garden. The man spoke to the Plant Magician and said that someone had seen two little boys playing in the woods and now he wondered if I was one of them. Well, he wasn't really wondering – the village only had two boys that size. He was accusing.

'I expect they were playing with matches,' the man said suggestively, which made the Plant Magician furious and he bellowed that his son hadn't even been into the woods.

That wasn't quite true – we had been in the woods – but right then I liked being his son. Not even for a second did he hesitate to lie on my behalf.

The man apologized and left, but the suspicions lingered on in the air, and there they have remained ever since. For a year and a half, the men with straight cars on their drives have been casting narrow glances at Blomma and me.

'It was you,' I want to say to Blomma's big brother, but I don't. This isn't the right moment. Perhaps another time, when he isn't shagging and smoking at the same time.

'Get lost,' he says.

On the way home, I tell Blomma that the rock they were doing it on has been in the woods for ten thousand years and that it was dragged here by an ice sheet several thousand metres thick.

'It was a drift boulder,' I say.

'Now it's a shagging boulder,' Blomma says.

The Plant Magician has changed names – he's now called Nicodemus. He wants us to call him that and he says that he's taken the name from the disciple that Jesus talked to at night.

He likes his new name. He hums it. It unlocks something in him, and his evenings in the outbuilding grow longer. He is on the verge of seeing through everything. You can hear it as he delivers his keynotes in the kitchen. There's wine in small glasses that get bigger, and candles that burn down and new ones that are lit as the words pour out of him. Little Bro falls asleep in Mum's arms while Mum has to listen and the hours pass and eventually she cries and says she can't take it any more. Says she doesn't understand what he's saying. It's not her fault that she's stupid, but he gets angry anyway.

I hear him hitting her down in the kitchen.

Well, I don't suppose I actually do, because the sound of a blow can't pass through walls and floors. What can be heard are the felt pads on the feet of the furniture moving and small, muffled cries that are cut off on their way up out of the throat. Witch sounds. Sometimes I don't know whether he's hitting her or having sex with her, but this time I know for sure because I hear a sound I recognize. I know how this goes.

The Plant Magician has a particular blow that leaves you speechless. He aims for the tender flesh just beneath the ribcage and completely winds you. Then you sound like an idiot if you try to talk. One word at a time and with that laboured breathing.

That's how she sounds now – like an idiot. And I know what

she's thinking: What if the wind doesn't come back? What if I suffocate and die?

When it's over, she comes and sits on my bed.

'We're not going to live here any more,' she whispers, and I wonder whether she'll remember this tomorrow when he's filled with regret and his hands are soft.

The calm of contrition will descend. The Plant Magician is restless and inflammable. He looks tired, and I think he's hungry too because he hasn't eaten since he changed names. He's fasting.

'Don't take that tone,' he says when Mum suggests that he should lie down for a while.

That's what he usually says, and it means that you have to be quiet. 'Bullshit' is another thing he usually says, but you don't have to be absolutely silent because it's only a first warning. 'Don't take that tone' is the final one. After the bit about tone, you'd better chew with your mouth closed and think about your attitude. You mustn't slurp or glower or anything else. I'm bad at all that stuff. Especially the nothing bit. Sometimes, the final words need to come out because it's not right that he gets to have the last word just because he's big.

But after the bit about tone, it's as if he's a trap ready to spring. His hand appears to be resting on the table, but if you look carefully you can see that it isn't touching the surface – it's hovering in the air, vibrating. Crescents of earth under scratched fingernails. Earth in the creases at the knuckles. A carelessly rinsed root vegetable come to life.

Mum's better than me at the nothing bit. She can sit as still and quiet as you like. She can turn into a piece of furniture when she has to – but this morning she doesn't want to. She takes that tone and the root-vegetable-come-to-life rises from the tabletop.

Again, I think. Hit her again so that she doesn't forget. And fix the car so that we can put the old cabinet in it and then drive away from here.

I know the cabinet is hers because the Plant Magician has said that everything else is his. I know she inherited it from her grandmother, and I remember the smell when it was stripped of paint and the warning not to go near it. It's one of my earliest memories – possibly my first – and it must mean that I don't have any memories of the Indian, because it was the Plant Magician who was stripping the cabinet.

In the borderland between the lake and the hayfield, there is a floor of brittle ice. Although it's not a floor really, it's a roof – you can see that if you make a hole and get down on your knees to peer through it. There's no water under there, and there's nothing else either. The ice seems to be suspended on the blades of grass, and beneath it small creatures can walk upright without humans even knowing. I wonder whether that's what our world looked like in the Ice Age – whether there was an air gap between the ice and the ground where some lived in darkness, or whether everyone moved around in the light up on the surface.

'Are you going to live with your real dad now?' Blomma asks as I stare into the underworld.

'Maybe,' I say, and it's not a lie because I haven't heard anyone say that I'm not going to.

Mum hasn't said a word about the Indian since she told me that he exists, and I've swallowed every one of my questions. Nor has she said a word about the move. I don't even know where we're going to live, or whether Little Sis and Little Bro are going to come with us, although I guess they will. I can't imagine a household in which the Plant Magician takes care of two children without anyone taking care of him. He knows practically everything, but he probably doesn't know how to be a mum.

Sometimes I wonder how he learned all the other stuff. I've never heard him talk about school – only the Coastal Ranger Company and May 68.

In the Coastal Ranger Company, he learned to hold his breath for a long time and climb trees with a bicycle strapped to his back. I'm not quite sure what he learned in May 68, but it must have been something remarkable. 'You know I was in May 68,' he often says when talking to other grown-ups, at which point the other grown-ups usually lean into the conversation. It's like a ruse of his for restoring himself to the centre of attention in a room that's begun to buzz too much with the words of others. 'You know I was in May 68,' he says, and silence falls. I don't know what May 68 is or where it is, but I assume you must learn a lot there.

'Is your stepdad going to stay here?' Blomma asks.

'I don't know.'

'When are you moving?'

'Soon.'

'When's soon?'

Blomma is full of questions, and I shush him. There's something moving in the darkness beneath the ice.

'I think someone lives here,' I say, pointing into the underworld.

Blomma falls to his knees and looks. We agree that there are small creatures living there, and then Blomma decides that the underworld must be destroyed. I don't agree, but I help him nonetheless and we trample the whole roof to pieces.

'Sorry,' I whisper each time I stamp my foot, and I regret revealing the secret of the underworld dwellers to Blomma. He seems completely unfazed by their fate – it's almost as if he hates them. He stamps and stamps, his lips pursed in an expression of determination.

'You should take my phone number,' Blomma pants once the underworld is devastated. 'Have you got a pen?'

I haven't. Blomma fetches a stick and writes the number in the snow. He can remember all the numbers. We help to break the snow free from the ground whereupon the number falls apart. Blomma pats down another tablet of snow and writes the number again. I take the tablet home but on my way through the garden – the one that slopes everywhere – I slip and the number breaks.

That night, I cry under the covers, although not for the numbers spilled onto the slope. And not because of the argument raging in the kitchen below. I cry for the underworld dwellers. What if they were good beings? What if they are swarming up from the hayfield under cover of darkness to mete out God's punishment?

They must have been wicked, because at dawn there comes a reward: the Plant Magician has approved the dissolution of the family. Just like that.

And quickly too. A strap is placed around the belly of the stripped cabinet and the kitchen is filled with banana boxes. The Plant Magician helps to pack. He appoints himself foreman and moves with an urgency that puzzles me. Not until much later will I learn that it is the haste of someone seeking to own their defeat.

Blomma is prowling about the hayfield – I wave from the porch and he waves back. The Plant Magician steps outside, a banana box in his arms, and stops next to me. Blomma raises his arm again, but this time he doesn't wave. The arm is still and his fist clenched.

The Plant Magician rests the banana box on the porch railing to free his hand, which he clenches into a fist and raises to the sky, not shouting as he usually does but instead whispering:

'Allende.'

He's clearly moved by the fact that the little Chilean has suddenly remembered how they say hello in Chile.

One day I'll write about this in a book, at which point I'll marvel at which images the brain chooses to retain and which it dispenses with. I will descend into the memory of Blomma's clenched fist down on the hayfield and turn my head to the left, towards the road, to seek the answer to the question of how we left there. I won't find it. I won't remember whether the cabinet was lashed onto the Plant Magician's roof rack or whether it was perched on a trailer hooked up to someone else's car. But I will remember the last thing he teaches me – the way he crouches on the gravel and looks me square in the eyes.

'You have two noses,' he says.

I don't understand what he means, because I've only got one. He raises a hand in the gap between our faces and tells me to do the same. He crosses his index and middle fingers, and then puts the crossed fingers to the bridge of his nose. Then he draws the crossed fingers down his nose and when I do the same I can't help smiling.

'You have two noses,' he says, and I nod, because I do.

He knows so much, but I'm almost never going to miss him.

Blomma, on the other hand, I am going to miss. We shall never meet again, but one day almost forty years after he clenched his fist on that hayfield, someone who knew him later in life will tell me that he was probably adopted from Thailand.

PART TWO

The Artist

*In which:
the mums become brown,
the kids become Nazis,
and
a treasure is found.*

They say he's an artist and I ask whether he can draw an Indian.

'I'm not good at people,' he says, I suspect with false humility because a moment later his ballpoint pen clicks into action.

He draws quickly and his hand looks light and supple. It dances across the paper, making me envious. When I draw, my hand is heavy and stiff. My fingertips whiten around the pen, forcing me to pause and shake off the numbness. It can take me half an hour to do a knight.

The Artist's Indian is done in half a minute.

'Pooh! I don't know,' he says, pushing the sketchpad across the pub table.

'You have to sign it!' Mum bleats, touching the Artist's arm.

'Yes, you've got to get it signed!' bleats the Artist's sister, who has just returned from the bar with a clutch of bottles.

'You've got to keep that, because one day it might be worth a pretty penny,' rumbles the man at the end of the table, who once sang on television.

The women bleat and the men rumble because everyone is drunk, although not in the dangerous way. I gaze at the Indian and it feels as if everyone is waiting for me to say something, but I don't know what to say. It's a shit Indian. It wasn't false humility. My judgement was misplaced. But I don't want to say that the Indian is poorly drawn.

'He doesn't have a horse,' I say, whereupon everyone laughs and it's apparent from their tone that they think I'm a little cheeky to sit there finding fault with an *artist*.

The Artist laughs too, but then he turns serious and taps the drawing with his fingertip.

'Did you know that the Indians never clapped eyes on horses until the Europeans arrived? There were no horses in America – we were the ones who brought horses there.'

Everyone's mouths become circles – including mine. Right away, I want to call Blomma to tell him that the Indians got their horses from the cowboys and that proper Indians didn't have any horses, but then I remember that I don't have his number and that I can't find it in the phone book since I don't know his last name (or his first name, for that matter).

'And thank fuck they didn't have horses,' the Artist adds, glancing at Mum, 'because I can't draw horses either!'

She's overcome with wild laughter and touches his arm again.

The others are laughing too. They seem to love the Artist even though he's so bad at drawing. I wonder whether he's simply made up that he's an artist, because he's no better at drawing than I am.

I know the guy sitting at the end of the table is a singer because everyone knows that. His daughter is in my class and the other kids say her dad won at Melodifestivalen song contest. He's popular, and you can tell. He slips in and out of different parties in the pub, and now he's slipped into ours, but waves from other tables indicate an eagerness for him to slip onwards. No one waves to the Artist, and as I look at the drawing I can understand why. He draws like a child, just a little faster.

The Artist signs the Indian and I tuck it into my pocket.

As I tuck the Indian into my pocket, I don't know that the Artist is going to be my dad. I haven't learned to see when love begins to take effect. I don't know how dads begin and end, but I'll soon come to realize that the boundaries of the family are loose and that dads can percolate in and out in just a short time.

The Artist will no longer be my dad by the time I next take the Indian out of my pocket. And the time spent in my pocket will be so brief that the paper won't even have got dog-eared.

When one day I come to write about the Artist, my mum will dismiss the decision to count him as one of the dads, but I'll stand my ground because I'll remember that I had enough time to wonder whether I ought to call him Dad. And I'll remember that I saw him in her bed. Three times I shall see him there, and one of those I will recall with acuity: the morning when I run into her bedroom to tell her the Prime Minister has been shot. It's a morning that everyone will remember, but no one will remember it like me.

The Artist is going to be counted among the dads, but it's mostly his sister I want to tell you about. We spent longer living with the Artist's sister than we did with the Artist, and I learned a great deal about monsters during the time I spent on her sofa.

It's actually rather unfair to call her the Artist's sister. She was more than a walk-on. I'll call her Little Cloud.

Little Cloud smokes almost incessantly. There are building-block towers of cigarette packets on the draining board and even though she hunches underneath the cooker hood, mist drifts throughout the flat. She smokes as if seeking a golden ticket to the cigarette factory.

In the living room – where the mist is at its lightest because it is as distant from the kitchen as you can get without leaving the flat – there is a leather sofa, and sitting on it there are two boys but no dad because he doesn't live here any longer. The boys are older than me and when I enter the living room they greet me in the way older boys do: with a narrowed gaze and a silent twitch of the head. I do the same but forget to tilt my head back down, and end up standing there with my chin pointing at the ceiling.

'We're going out soon,' Mum calls from the hall.

It's a weird thing to call out because we only moved in a few minutes ago. I return to the hall. The mums are standing there making themselves pretty in front of the mirror and I'm informed that it's Little Cloud's birthday.

'It's as if we're her present,' Mum says, although apparently that present isn't enough because now they're off down the pub.

'It's only around the corner – why don't you hang out with the boys for a while?' Little Cloud says with a nod towards the living room.

I become anxious.

'They have a television,' Mum says, at which point the anxiety goes away.

I start grinning like an idiot when I realize that for the first time I'm going to live in a home with a television. When we left the Plant Magician, I thought every other home had a television and that the door to this strange dimension – populated with gods such as Stenmark, Borgmcenroe, Eee-Tee, Carola and Rummenigge – would immediately be opened to me. A year has now passed and these gods remain no more than words in the mouths of other children and on magazine covers by the checkout queue.

First we lived with a mum who had a girl my age, and I was happy there but there wasn't a television and one day I forgot to lock the bathroom door and was walked in on by the girl's friend while I was pooing like an Indian. She saw me perched on the toilet seat, crouching with my feet on the outer edges, and she laughed so hard she had difficulty breathing. We're in the same class now and I'm pretty sure that all the girls have heard about how I do my poos.

Then we lived with another mum with another girl, and there wasn't a television there either, but at least I didn't forget to lock the bathroom door.

Little Cloud is the third of Mum's friends that we're to live with, and it is here that a lifelong desire will be satisfied.

Little Cloud pilots me back into the living room and now I see it. It's opposite the sofa, across the glass coffee table that the boys' feet are resting on. She tells the boys to make room on the sofa and put on a film. When I hear the word film, my gaze falls to below the television and I realize that the altar upon which it stands conceals something more. My hands are clasped in my lap. I'm sitting there as if I'm on a church pew, my back straight and both feet on the floor. The mums make their exit, leaving only boys behind.

(You may be wondering: what's become of my younger siblings? You may even find that question more interesting than my first encounter with the television, but this is my story and right now you don't need to know any more about theirs except that they are pootling back and forth between the Plant Magician and Mum. If there's any schedule for said pootling then I'll never understand it, but it seems at any rate that I've underestimated the Plant Magician because he always manages to keep them alive until it's Mum's turn again.)

The boys on the sofa aren't much alike. The elder has short, dark hair. The younger has blond hair down to his elbows. The elder has a face covered in spots and a somewhat despondent and frozen air about him. The younger is so supple and smooth-skinned that he resembles a girl, but only facially. His arms are muscular and bulge out from a T-shirt with a monster on it. The elder is wearing a jumper with the sleeves pulled down over his hands.

'Do you like Lucio Fulci?' asks Frozen Boy.

'Come off it,' laughs Girl Face, but his brother doesn't come off it. Instead, he just grins and crawls up to the altar.

We watch a film about a group of beautiful people who sail to an island with palm trees where the dead come back to life and rise from their graves to eat the entrails of the aforementioned beautiful people. The beautiful become fewer and fewer in number but soon learn that the dead can be killed again by smashing their heads. They smash a lot of heads, but the film still has an unhappy ending. The undead flood into a city with skyscrapers and it's apparent from the music that the whole world is about to end.

As the credits roll across the march of the undead on civilization, I'm shivering with horror. This I will do many times on that sofa, because Little Cloud's sons are engaged in their own small-scale entrepreneurial venture at that altar. They know a man who imports uncensored and sometimes outright banned films, and using the machine in the altar they copy the films and sell them to other boys. All of this is explained to me by Frozen Boy while I quiver.

I want the mums to come back and I want it so much that I don't even bother feeling ashamed of it.

'Aren't they coming home soon?' I ask.

'Not a clue,' says Girl Face. 'Where were they going?'

I say they went out to celebrate Little Cloud's birthday, whereupon the boys look at each other. Frozen Boy looks horrified.

'We were supposed to sort out a present!'

Just a few minutes later, the brothers are gone and I'm alone in Little Cloud's flat. I turn on every single light I can find and build a pillow fort on Little Cloud's double bed. I sit inside the fort quivering, wondering whether to call the police and tell them Mum has gone missing. Or whether I should get dressed and go outside to look for Mum. After all, Little Cloud said it was only around the corner.

I leave the pillow fort and have already put on my shoes when I change my mind. It's so dark out there, and what if I go around the wrong corner? What if the undead have reached this town?

I return to the pillow fort. I think as hard as I can about Mum, so that the thought reaches her and pokes the back of her neck like an invisible stick. Then I think just as hard about the Indian and I can picture him before me: slumbering beneath a starry sky in a country far away and waking up with a start when the thought reaches him.

'My son!'

If he intends to show up at any point (or send a spirit) then he'd be most welcome to do so right now.

It feels as if I sit there all night, but suddenly I wake up even though I haven't fallen asleep and find myself lying between Mum and Little Cloud. They're sound asleep even though the room is bathed in light. The morning sunshine is penetrating through the curtains. Mum's hair smells of smoke.

I slither out of bed and go out into the hall. The mist is gone. The boys appear to have returned during the night because their bedroom doors are closed. There is a red drip trail on the hall floor and when I examine it more closely I'm almost certain that it's blood. The trail extends from the front door to the bathroom.

I go into the kitchen. Standing in the centre of the kitchen table is a sewing machine, and in front of it a handwritten note.

'Happy birthday Mum!'

In an hour or so's time, Little Cloud will stumble into the kitchen and be happy even though the sewing machine is missing its pedal – but so far I'm the only one who is awake.

I make a sandwich with ingredients from the cupboards. The flat is still quiet when I creep back down the hall and into the living room, where I switch on the television. I watch a programme about migratory birds.

Two more things about Little Cloud: she has a daughter and she has a hole in her head.

The daughter is a year or so younger than me, and like my siblings she is pootling back and forth between two households. We've been there for a week when her dad shows up to drop her off, and for a while I hide in Little Cloud's bedroom because I'm not sure what kind of dad he is. I've heard Little Cloud crying and swearing when she talks about him. They're fighting over the daughter. He's won parts of her, but he wants more and he's good at making war. His dad was once the Prime Minister. Twice, in fact. He knows words that Little Cloud doesn't, and it makes her furious. She hates him because he's trying to ruin her life, but he wasn't the one who made the hole in her head. That was a different man.

I've never seen the hole, but I know it's there. I've heard Mum talking about it, and I've seen her indicate the size of the hole with her index finger curled against her thumb. The hole is as big as a one-krona piece and hidden under her hair. I know how it came about and I shudder when I think about it.

It wasn't Little Cloud's fault – she never asked for any holes – but the man who's good at making war tries to turn it against her. He says that a mum who lets men make holes in her head can't take responsibility for a daughter.

The daughter doesn't have any holes, but she has a palm that is completely smooth and I've seen it. I can't stop looking at it, even though it makes my own palms crawl when I do.

I learned the story of how the palm came to be smooth

without having to eavesdrop because Mum poured it straight into my ears in a moralizing tone. And one day, when I have children of my own, the story will ring in their own ears every time their small hands fumble about in proximity to hotplates.

I'll get down on my knees and tell them about a hand that had to be prised loose using a spatula, and the skin that was left on the hob.

One more thing about Little Cloud: she has a half-body solarium on wheels. Mum gets to borrow it as often as she wants, and she wants to borrow it often. Every day she lies on Little Cloud's bed and sunbathes in just her knickers and a small pair of rimless sunglasses that look like beetles' backs. Every time, she falls asleep and sometimes I sneak up close and take a look even though she says doing that can make you blind.

Things change colour in the glow of the solarium. Breasts turn purple and nipples turn black. It's somehow supposed to make her brown. I've never seen it happening, yet happen it does: she becomes browner and browner.

She becomes just as brown as Blomma – a shade you want to bite into, since it's the colour of the soft, thick Skåne gingerbread in the packs with the stork on them.

But she wants to be even browner, and carries on until she's as brown as Little Cloud.

A few weeks after Little Cloud's birthday, it's my turn to get a year older and a package arrives with worn edges and many stamps.

'It's for you,' Mum says, but there's still a hesitancy in the way she hands it over.

My gaze drops to the last line of the handwritten address, where an unexpected statement of the obvious makes my fingers tighten around the package.

SWEDEN

My gaze climbs in reverse up the address and finds my name. But it isn't mine – it's only close.

ANDREV IGOR DELHAYE

I recognize the first name, as well as the loathsome middle name that I'll never learn to live with, but the last name doesn't even bear a resemblance to mine.

'That was your name when you were born,' says Mum.

'Is it from my dad?'

She nods. 'I sent him letters and said that he's welcome to get in touch with you now.'

'Wasn't he allowed to before?'

Mum puts her hands to her head. There are curlers in her hair and she now realizes they have been in for too long. She goes to the hall mirror and begins to tug at the pins. I follow her, the package in my hands.

'When you were little, parcels came more or less constantly,' she says. Loose coils of red hair fall down across her face. 'It was your grandmother who sent most of them.'

'I have a grandmother?'

'Of course you have a grandmother. That's obvious.'

I suppose it must be, but I'm still taken aback.

My mind's eye has never seen the Indian in the company of anyone else – he's always alone on horseback. I insert an old Native American woman into the image, adding feathers in her hair. The feathers make her look like an ancient bird, and I immediately like her better than my last grandmother. The Plant Magician's mum didn't like children and she didn't even want to be in the same room as us when we came to visit, and that made it difficult for me to form any opinion of her at all.

'Your grandmother lives in Tucson, Arizona,' Mum says. 'In the desert.'

'And she used to send parcels?' I say.

'Big parcels,' says Mum. 'Everything's big in the USA.'

I look down at my parcel. It isn't big.

'Your dad lives in Belgium these days,' says Mum, as if apologizing for the size of the parcel.

I ask why my grandmother stopped sending parcels and Mum is quiet for a while before explaining that they made the Plant Magician angry and sad.

'I had to ask her to stop,' she says. 'I *had* to.'

When I realize that the Plant Magician has cost me multiple big parcels, steam practically comes out of my ears. And while I open the small parcel from Belgium I can think of nothing but the big ones that have been lost.

Inside the parcel there is a box, and inside the box is another box. The present is getting smaller and smaller as my ears grow hotter. But when, at last, I find myself clutching a small compact camera made from blue-and-yellow plastic, I calm down. The camera makes me happy even if it seems strangely plasticky for a present from an Indian.

One evening, the mums want to join in watching a film. Little Cloud's sons suggest films mums might like but the mums haven't heard of any of them. Then Frozen Boy remembers that mums like Charles Bronson and we watch a film starring him. I have to lie under the glass table because not everyone can fit onto the sofa and armchairs.

The film begins with a man who isn't Charles Bronson taking off all his clothes, which makes the mums purr with delight. Then the man runs into the forest completely naked and begins stabbing people to death, which makes the mums shriek. I look over my shoulder and through the glass tabletop I can see Mum covering her eyes.

'Blokes,' Little Cloud says, and Mum laughs and then they go into the kitchen for a smoke.

We watch the rest of the film without the mums. The killer can't get a hard-on, which is why he's killing. He's killing instead of shagging. I don't understand how the desire for one can be sated by the other, but I know for sure I can get a hard-on because sometimes I do and that's for the best because I definitely don't want to be a murderer. I don't want to shag either, but if this is the fork in the road that awaits me then I'm prepared to rethink.

The mums are laughing in the kitchen and now they must be drinking wine too because the laughter grows louder and louder until Girl Face has to go and shut the living-room door.

The killer strips naked every time he's going to kill and the police can't catch him because they never find any blood on his clothes. In the end, Charles Bronson has to cheat and kill the killer, and the boys on the sofa clap. So do I. It was a good murder, and we clap together.

I'm drifting off under the glass table when Frozen Boy switches tapes.

A village is being ravaged by men with snakes on their helmets and a mum is brandishing a sword to defend her son. Immediately, I perk up. It looks like an adventure is about to begin. The boy is holding his mum's hand. A baddie with a kindly face cuts the mum's head off and the boy loses his grip of her hand as her body falls. I crawl out from my hidey-hole beneath the glass table and sit up. The boy looks down at the hand that was so recently holding his mum's and then at the kindly face and I realize it's going to be a saga of revenge.

The boy, who is called Conan, grows up to be big and strong and moves through a world with rules I don't recognize. It's a world where evil can hide behind kind faces, where a thief can be a hero and where the woman the hero is going to live happily ever after with can die.

At the moment when Valeria has been hit by Thulsa Doom's snake arrow and is lying poisoned in Conan's arms, I have to bite my jumper.

'Kiss me. Let me breathe my last breath into your mouth,' she says, before dying. Then I get a nosebleed.

Moments later, Conan has beheaded the baddie and I'm hurrying to the kitchen to recount the whole tale but the mums don't want to listen to me. There's a male figure in the mist of cigarette smoke and they're fully occupied listening to him. He's telling a story about the time he passed wind loudly at the pub and the mums are laughing so much their eyes are filled with tears.

'This is my brother,' says Little Cloud, pointing to the man. 'He's an artist.'

One summer's day, the mums cook up the idea of going to Germany. Little Cloud has just got a car. Or perhaps it was Mum who got it – I won't get to the bottom of who the car belongs to before it falls apart, but right now it's the summer of 1985 and the car is in one piece.

Before the car is picked up, I hear Mum say that it's called a Saab ninety-five and I wonder whether it's a car built for the future. When I see the car, I stop wondering. It's clavaria yellow with flames of rust around the wheel arches and shaped a lot like a fish. It's from the past.

There are four of us in the car as we trundle out of Norrköping: Mum with her hair freshly hennaed, Little Cloud with her hole in her head, her daughter with her scary hand and me with a hole between my feet.

Little Cloud is driving and each time she has to smoke she rolls down the window but only a few centimetres to make sure there's suction. I don't understand how that can work, but it does. The tendril of smoke undulates but hangs in an almost straight line between her hand on the wheel and the slit to the outside world.

Mum is in the passenger seat with a tape recorder she's been lent by Frozen Boy, and each time she plays Mike Oldfield's 'Moonlight Shadow' she's compelled to shout about it.

'It's insane that a song can be this good!' she yells, and Little Cloud agrees. 'It's insane!' they yell in chorus and once they've done it a few times, Scary Hand and I begin to agree too. It really is insane that a song can be that good.

'IT'S INSANE!' we all yell, and the car speeds along contentedly.

Scary Hand is sitting behind her mum with a Barbie doll on her lap, whose hair she proceeds to brush all the way to Germany. I'm sitting on the other side of the back seat fiddling with my camera. I still haven't taken a single picture because I don't want to waste film until I find a subject that it's appropriate to immortalize.

Occasionally, I bend forward and lift the newspaper that Mum has laid out on the floor. She put it there to plug the hole between my feet. The hole is around the size of a fist and when I lift up the newspaper I can see the asphalt racing by beneath the car. I don't want to stop looking, but as soon as I lift the newspaper the scent of petrol seeping into the inside of the car betrays me and then Mum puts her chin on her shoulder, getting wind of it.

'Is the newspaper still down?' she asks, at which point I immediately let go of it and say it's still down.

In Germany, everyone has new, straight cars and they can't believe their eyes when they see the old car that looks like a fish in the inside lane. On the Autobahn we're constantly being overtaken and I see children hurling themselves at side windows to point – as if they really have just seen a big fish rolling by on land.

One more thing about the car: it has a feature known as freewheel. Each time we reach a downhill stretch, Little Cloud can 'freewheel' and it's as if the car switches itself off and just whizzes along silently. The mums think freewheeling is fun, and I don't really understand why, but it's fun when the mums are having fun.

'FREEWHEEL!' they yell in chorus, and we soon learn in the back seat that it's time to yell every time the car falls silent after the crest of a hill.

'FREEWHEEL!' we all yell as the car whizzes along, feeling wonderfully proficient.

Somewhere outside Lübeck, the car begins to make a wailing sound and we have to crawl our way to a mechanic's. The mums are worried that the car is going die, and it is – but not yet. A man in blue overalls offers the mums beer and repairs what is broken, but as we're about to climb back into the car he issues us with a warning.

The mums don't understand what he's warning us about, but it must be something – that much is obvious from the index finger raised as he speaks.

Mum once spent a summer at a stud farm outside Frankfurt am Main (which just so happens to be where we're heading) but the German she learned that summer stretches only to her saying that she understands what he's saying. Had she spent more than a summer at the stud farm, she might have learned enough of the language to understand what she says she understands. But it was only one summer in the end, and all we take away from the mechanic's is a car that's moving again and the feeling that we need to be careful with something if it's to carry on that way. But no one in the car knows what.

'FREEWHEEL!' we yell in chorus, whizzing down the slope of the world.

We're met in the yard by the Slut and the Farmhand. The Slut embraces Mum and then the Farmhand tries to do the same but his arms end up hanging in mid-air.

At first I think they look like they're from a different era, but then I see that the whole farm appears to be from a different era, so in fact we must be the ones who look like we've come from a different era. The fish car has carried us backwards in time and we are now surrounded by small half-timbered houses and big stables with cobbled aisles running between the stalls.

The horses inside are wild and crazy and we have to watch out for their hindquarters. I make myself thin as we walk between the rear ends of the animals. Mum explains that the horses are wild because they're young, and that wildness needs to be tamed before they're sold.

'But you mustn't completely extinguish that wildness,' she says. 'They just have to learn to focus the wildness in one direction at a time before they can run *die Galopprennbahn*.'

She says the last bit in German and I can tell she's happy. She becomes tall standing there and she knows things as she gazes at the backs of the horses that are still being wild in every direction. But when I ask her whether she can ride she seems to shrink down again.

'No, I don't like horses,' she says with a laugh. 'I find them scary.'

That I can agree with – the horses *are* scary. But the Farmhand is scarier. He's old and incurably filthy – as if he's been buried in the ground and recently risen to devour the living. At any rate, he appears to want to devour the mums because he glances at them hungrily and is keen to get close to them with his sour-sweet scent.

The Slut is also old but she's clean and odourless. She's the owner of the stud farm and I know what her real name is because in the final hours on the Autobahn the mums couldn't say her name enough.

'SELMA SCHLAMP,' they said in chorus before we all laughed. Now they're calling her the Slut, though not so she hears it.

The Slut escorts us to a huge bedroom upstairs in her house where we're left to unpack before dinner. Little Cloud opens a window and smokes three cigarettes in a row by way of apology to her body for the careless smoking in the car. She sucks hard on her cigarettes – sucks the life out of them. The glow creeps quickly towards her lips, the white butts becoming soft and speckled with grey before crumbling away.

I ask Mum whether the Farmhand is the Slut's husband and she tells me that the Slut's husband is dead and that the Farmhand is just a farmhand from Saarbrücken who's sort of disgusting and thinks everything has gone to the dogs since Hitler died.

'Is he a Nazi?' Little Cloud asks from her spot on the windowsill.

'Shh,' Mum says and then they laugh.

Smoke billows from every opening of Little Cloud's face, as if her entire cranium is filled with smoke. I squint at her hair and think I can make out a tendril of smoke escaping from the hole in her head.

The Slut is serving hotpot. I don't know whether I like it, because the Farmhand is sitting at the table and his scent floats across the plates, making everything taste as if it's been buried in the ground.

After the hotpot comes a dreadful jelly dessert and then the Farmhand wants to show us the sausage pantry. It sounds like a good pantry to me but only until I get to see it. They're not good sausages. They look nothing like any sausages I've ever seen before. They're pale and lumpy and I can see their insides because the skins are translucent. I know sausages are intestines stuffed with meat and entrails – everyone knows that – but this is the first time I've seen sausages that aren't trying to hide the fact.

The Farmhand draws a knife and points at these authentic sausages with the blade. He seems to be wondering whether there's anything the mums would like in particular. I can tell from the mums that their particular wish is to be spared the sausages altogether, but the Farmhand doesn't see that. He cuts down a few sausages and lines them up on the table while the Slut tops up the wine glasses. I get very fed up looking at the sausages and I ask Mum whether I can go upstairs to our room. She says yes, whereupon Scary Hand gets tired too and comes with me.

The last thing I see before we leave the Slut's kitchen is Mum raising a piece of sausage to her lips. Her eyes are shiny and her other hand has already encircled the wine glass. On my way up the stairs, I wonder whether she's going to wash down the sausage without chewing and the thought worries me until I realize we're a long way from the Plant Magician. You were never allowed drink when you had food in your mouth in the vicinity of the Plant Magician. If you drank before you'd chewed and swallowed your food then a slap would come flying across the table.

I'm lying on the bed fiddling with my camera. Down in the kitchen, the wine has amped up the mums' voices. Scary Hand is bored and vanishes into a huge closet. When she emerges again she's wearing a cream-coloured dress.

'There's fancy dress in there,' she chirps, shuffling towards a mirror on the wall, the fabric of the skirt gathered up under her arms. The dress is old-fashioned with fabric-covered buttons down the back and it's much too large for her small body.

I get to my feet and take a look in the closet. It's full of dresses, hat boxes, high heels and boots. There's also a grey uniform with resplendent markings on the sleeves hanging up. And on the shelf above the uniform's hanger is a peaked cap that appears to go with it. I pull on the uniform jacket and place the cap on my head before exiting the closet to examine myself in the mirror.

'There's a skull on the hat,' says Scary Hand, and there really is. It's made of metal and is attached to the fabric above the rigid peak. Above the skull there is an eagle extending its metal wings.

I lean closer to the mirror. The eagle's claws are gripping a wreath and inside the wreath there is a symbol I recognize from some of the many films I've watched with Little Cloud's sons. It's the baddies' symbol.

Scary Hand is going through the boxes by the mirror and finds a few pearl necklaces as well. The pearls don't go very well with the uniform, but I snatch one of the necklaces and put it around my neck. Scary Hand puts on the rest of them and we rattle as we descend the stairs to show the grown-ups that we've dressed up.

Little Cloud has apparently obtained the hostess's permission to smoke at the table because there is now a mist throughout the kitchen. Scary Hand struts into the mist like a princess. For my own part, I march in as loudly as I can and when all eyes gazing through the mist have found me on the threshold I come to a halt and give a salute.

The Slut puts both hands to her mouth but that doesn't seal it because I can hear a whimper escaping between her fingers. She looks like she's seen a ghost. The mums' mouths are wide open, but there's not a sound coming out of them. Only the Farmhand doesn't allow the presence of the ghost to worry him. He puts his dirty hands onto the table and makes all the wine dregs slop about as he braces himself to stand up.

For a moment it looks as if he's going to return the salute, but he stops short when the Slut bursts into tears.

I take just three photographs in Germany: one of an unusually small man, one of a horse and one of a cage that people used to be hung upside down in until they died.

I take the first photograph at the Frankfurt race course where the Slut drives me and Scary Hand in her Mercedes so that we can watch a horse that was once hers be ridden by an unusually small man.

He's so small he doesn't look real.

'Is that a dwarf?' I say.

'Maybe,' says Scary Hand.

I want to ask the Slut but I don't know what the German for dwarf is.

I don't know what the German for anything is. I might possibly be able to ask whether he is a car or a potato.

When the man who might be a dwarf mounts the horse I raise the camera to my eye and watch him through the viewfinder. In there, everything is very small and it's not quite obvious that the man on the horse is smaller than everything else, so I try to get closer. The Slut places a hand on my shoulder and pinches it. I hesitate but at last I press the button. I feel a pang in my stomach. An imperfect subject has been immortalized.

I take the second photograph between the slats of a fence surrounding one of the stud's paddocks, where the Farmhand is piloting a stallion towards a mare. The horse's cock is like a shin, and I think of Blomma's happy dance at the edge of the forest when his big brother showed off his human cock.

Blomma would probably be three to five times happier than that if he saw this, I think to myself as I press the button.

I barely hesitate, but I still ache inside. There's something disagreeable about eternity. I don't like the responsibility.

I take the third and final photograph from the top of the walls of an old fortress that we find on the way home. The fortress is on a hill that the fish car manages to ascend by the skin of its teeth. Suspended on a chain from an overhanging tower there is an oblong, rust-brown cage. Mum reads a plaque and tells me that there was a time when criminals were hung upside down in the cage until they died.

'Did they die from hanging upside down?' I ask.

'They probably died of terror before they died of anything else,' she says, glancing over the wall. I also peer into the abyss beneath the cage, but she holds me tightly by the collar. We're so high up that the forest down on the slopes looks like moss.

The abyss doesn't fit into the viewfinder – the cage might just as well have been 2 metres above the ground and I feel that ache in my stomach before I've even pressed the button.

'FREEWHEEL!' yell the mums as we whizz down the hill, but this time I'm silent because I'm thinking about the criminals who died of terror. I picture that cage for the rest of the day and all evening until I fall asleep in the car.

The last thing I'll recall about Germany is Mum waking me as the car barrels through the night.

'This is where your dad was born,' she says, pointing. I sit up. There is a city sparkling out there in the darkness and Mum says it's called Hamburg. I don't understand. Indians do not come from Hamburg. My mouth wants to ask what she means, but the rest of my body is too tired and has already settled back down again.

Little Cloud's daughter is lying curled up behind me. Our upper bodies are sharing the space in the middle. There's a broad PVC reinforcement strip along the front edge of the seat and I rest my cheek against it. Mum thinks I should use a folded jumper for a pillow to avoid being poisoned by the plastic, but that makes my head slither about. When my cheek is directly on the plastic my head stays still.

It's cosy sleeping in the fish car. The faint smell of petrol from the hole in the floor. A temperate draught on my arm from Little Cloud's cracked window. The rattle of the car's interior and the mums' laughter in distant outer space.

There's a calm there that I'm going to learn to love. I already like it, but I don't realize that it's an exception – that women and children belong to one species and dads to another and that the two species are fighting a millennia-long, intricate war where the only rest is in the gaps between the battles.

I still think I'd like to have a dad, and preferably my own. The one who's an Indian in a land far away.

I must have misheard. There are no Indians in Germany, I think to myself as I fall asleep again.

The next time I awake we're in Sweden and the car is broken. I won't be able to recall where we leave it – only that we take the train home and never see it again.

One evening, Little Cloud's doorbell rang. She looked through the peephole. Standing on the landing outside was a man who no longer had his own key to the door. She didn't want to open up because he was drunk but he said he just wanted to talk and eventually she opened up anyway.

She didn't see the hammer until the door was open. He didn't want to talk. He didn't even want to come in. All he wanted was to hit her on the head with the hammer and that he did, wordlessly. That's how she got the hole in her head and learned to hate men.

'Bloody men,' she usually says somewhere towards the end of each conversation with Mum. Or at least towards the end of each conversation about men – but almost all of them seem to be about that.

Mum says it too.

'Bloody men,' she says with a shake of the head.

They take turns saying it – sometimes laughing, sometimes in tears. They say it on the sofa and they say it under the cooker hood.

They hate men. Especially Little Cloud. When they talk about men, she sometimes stubs out a cigarette after just two or three drags before squashing it in the ashtray.

'Bloody men,' she says, breaking the cigarette's back in three places.

She hates them so much it makes her jerk and click.

Unfortunately, she now happens to have fallen for one of them, so we have to move.

I didn't know homes this small existed. To get from the hall to the interior of the flat you have to climb over the bed. There aren't any closets, so clothes have to be left in banana boxes that are stacked all the way up to the ceiling. Running between the bed and the wall of banana boxes is a pathway of bare floor from the kitchenette to a cubbyhole referred to as the bathroom, although it's only big enough for a small bird to bathe in. The only window in the flat is above the hotplate in the kitchenette, which is where Little Cloud is standing and puffing smoke over Trädgårdsgatan.

'Come on, you can't live here,' she says, laughing.

'It'll be great,' Mum says, but it isn't.

The flat gets smaller and smaller each time Little Cloud's brother comes up from the street with a new box. He's an artist and his arms are weak, so the flat shrinks slowly.

The Dr Westerlund geraniums are standing in the dark of the hall preparing to die. The old cabinet stripped of paint is still out on the landing. It won't fit and the Artist has said it can go to his studio for the time being.

I ask where my siblings are going to sleep and Mum says they'll be staying with the Plant Magician full time until we find a bigger flat. I ask where I'm going to sleep and she says we'll top and tail. The Artist asks where he's going to sleep and Mum laughs.

I think it's a strange question because I don't know how dads begin and end, but one day I'll realize that kind of joke is part of the human repertoire of mating calls.

Once the last box has been incorporated into the box wall, we head down to Café 12 and eat prawn sandwiches, surrounded by taxi drivers eating prawn sandwiches. The Artist's hands are small and stained. They're like the hands of a child who's been painting with watercolours. On the backs of his hands, the stains bulge like different-coloured broken scabs, while inside the hands the stains are smooth and slightly translucent. Each time he puts down his coffee I look for fingerprints but he doesn't leave a trace. He's dirty and clean all at once.

After our prawn sandwiches, we walk to a pub called Peter's and there the Artist draws an Indian with a ballpoint pen. It's a shit Indian but I don't let on.

There's a wall of lilacs around the school playground, and inside the wall we find treasure. It can't have been there long because we would have found it sooner – we're there every break, running at a crouch through the tunnels and chambers of foliage. The lilacs are a land to which boys are drawn by instinct and where branches can come to life and entangle a boy and then the other boys have to hit the trunks with their swords until he's freed.

There are four of us boys in the lilacs when we strike treasure: Saga, Mouse, Cyclops and me. It's Cyclops who sees it first, even though he only has one eye. He used to have two but the doctor forbade him from using the best one and taped over one of the two windows in his spectacles. We follow Cyclops's cry and find him hunched over the treasure. The bad eye is staring down into a box. The box is under the outermost branches of the bushes, right by the road beyond, and I get the feeling that it was carborne before it was hidden.

'That's porn,' says Mouse, and everyone agrees with him. 'We should show it to the teacher,' he adds, but no one else agrees.

'Don't show Dad,' Cyclops says. He's usually careful not to say dad because while everyone knows that he's the teacher's son he wants us to forget about it. In the classroom he addresses his dad by name, but in the glow of finding the treasure he grows careless.

There must be twenty-five to thirty magazines in the box.

They're higgledy-piggledy and the covers form a patchwork of naked bodies.

Saga falls to his knees beside Cyclops and starts to flip through them without saying a word. This is the boy who usually talks constantly, especially in the land of the lilacs. He's the narrator of the game and when surrounded by monsters he can account for everything that is happening on the battlefield, but faced with naked bodies he is mute.

I too fall to my knees but I can't flip through them myself because I've got a nosebleed and need to pinch my nose. I put my chin on Saga's shoulder and let him show me.

Only Mouse is left shifting his weight from side to side. He is a child in the service of the grown-ups. Once, the class got to borrow a computer from Mouse's dad, who works with computers. The idea was that we'd learn how to use a computer, but Cyclops's dad didn't know anything about computers so Mouse had to be the teacher instead.

'This is the ball mouse,' he said, clicking on a small puck tethered to the computer by a cable. All the kids laughed and many of their faces turned red.

'Perhaps we should call it something else,' Cyclops's dad said, but it was already too late.

Now he leaves us to inform the grown-ups. Soon Cyclops's dad will march into the land of the lilacs. Warnings will be issued and the box carried away to the school's bin store. Then the mums and dads will be notified of the fact that there was an open portal to hell and how it was closed. They'll inhale and then exhale.

But the boys who stayed when Mouse ran off will know that the box in the school bin store weighs less than it did when Cyclops found it.

I'm sleeping well in the flat on Trädgårdsgatan. It doesn't matter that Mum turns off the light because there aren't any nooks for monsters to hide in. Not even under the bed, because that's where Mum has stuffed all the fabrics we currently have no use for: bedless sheets, tableless cloths, windowless curtains and all the rag rugs apart from the blue-and-white one, which lies on the pathway between the bed and the box wall with one end rolled up against the skirting board. Slotted in between the wallpaper and Mum's legs, I don't need to build a cocoon with the duvet to fall asleep – the whole flat is like a cocoon.

Mum isn't sleeping so well. Her legs are hot and restless. Sometimes she has to get up and open the front door to create a cross-breeze, and then I wake up but I'm not afraid because she's standing in the hall guarding the opening onto the world while the lukewarm night is sucked through the dormer window in the kitchenette.

Mum loves cross-breezes. It's such a big part of who she is that it's what I might start with if anyone ever asked me to tell them about her. Or would I start with the hair, because that's what you see first?

She has red hair and she loves airing a room. That's how I'd start. And since the hair thing doesn't require much by way of explanation, I'd then carry on by telling you about the airing.

She can't help herself: not even when it's below zero outside. In the house by Lake Ensjön she'd open two or three windows at the same time even though it was the middle of winter. My siblings and I had to swaddle ourselves in a heap of blankets while she tramped about with the vacuum-cleaner hose in her hand and the wind in her hair. At the flat in Gamleby, where we lived over a travel agent's and had a tower room with three windows overlooking the square, she could achieve a cross-breeze at height. She would put the Dr Westerlund geraniums down on the floor of the tower room and open the windows as much as the stays allowed before running downstairs and opening the door to the inner courtyard. Then there would be a vacuum and the stairwell would be transformed into a precipitous wind tunnel where children had to cling onto the railing to avoid being blown off their feet.

She loves a good cross-breeze, but she can't have that at the flat on Trädgårdsgatan – there's only a gentle breeze and as soon as she closes the front door the draught stops again. She shoves a shoe into the letterbox before returning to bed.

Now neither of us are sleeping – we're just lying there like two sardines in a tin listening to the night. There are echoes of laughter and the creak of bicycle pedals and the rattling each time the number two tram trundles past.

I've got her to myself and I like that but she doesn't. She's crying because she can't get a cross-breeze. Or she's crying because she misses the children that won't fit in here. She doesn't want to be a sardine.

'We can't live here,' she says, and a few days later it's been decided that we're to move again.

The Artist's arms aren't made for carrying but now they are carrying stuff once again. This time it's only up one flight of stairs to the flat we're going to live in, but he gets tired out anyway and has to sit down at the kitchen table to rest his worthless arms. The mums disappear into the stairwell while the Artist and I drink bottles of Loranga. On the table between us are the Dr Westerlund geraniums. His bum is a long way forward on his chair but he is reclining back, his gaze fixed on the ceiling. I'm slumped over, my view filled with the foliage.

There are still a few months left until the morning when I'll run into Mum's bedroom to tell her the Prime Minister has been shot. I still haven't seen the Artist and Mum in the same bed, but clearly I must sense something because I'm wondering what he's good for.

His arms are good for nothing – that much I know because they can't draw Indians or carry cabinets. But his mouth is funny and now it's moving. The mums have returned from the street with a banana box each and the Artist presumably feels he has to do something. So he does the only thing he's good at and starts talking.

'Did you know I used to be a policeman?' he says, shooting a glance over the geraniums.

Apparently he's talking to me. I shake my head because I didn't know. But I immediately think better of him because I'm almost certain that I like policemen. The Plant Magician didn't like policemen; he called them the custodians of the system, but I've got nothing against the system. I'm not exactly sure what the system is, but it seems to embody meticulous order. Pay package, colour television, boys with their own rooms and dads who go to work in straight cars. I want to live in the system, and it feels as if the new flat on Gamla Rådstugugatan belongs to the system. Everything in the kitchen is new and straight. The whole building is new and straight and no one has lived here before. The flat is more than 70 square metres and one of the rooms is going to be mine. My siblings are going to share another when they're here.

'I was a policeman for several hours,' the Artist continues, now grinning. 'It was a film shoot. I played a policeman in a film with Thommy Berggren. Do you know who Thommy Berggren is?'

I don't.

'Per Oscarsson was in it too. Do you know who Per Oscarsson is?'

I don't.

'He played Borka! Surely you've seen *Ronia, the Robber's Daughter*?'

I haven't, but I've grown tired of being stupid so I nod anyway. I do, at any rate, know who Borka is. The Plant Magician read the book to me about a year before he stopped being my dad.

'Anyway, I was a cop in this film. A detective. Do you know what my character was called?'

I don't. How on earth could I? I'm angry because he's making me shake my head yet again. I don't like him any more. But the mums do. They've caught wind of his story and now they shimmy towards him, solarium-tanned and denim-jacketed.

'One of the detectives!' says Little Cloud, pointing a finger-pistol at her brother.

With her other hand she flicks on the kitchen extractor. She hasn't had a smoke in *minutes*.

'Wrong,' says the Artist. 'A different bloke played one of the detectives. I was . . .' He falls silent for a moment and then aims two finger-pistols at his sister. '. . . *the other* detective!'

The mums laugh so hard they have to lean on the surfaces where they have been unloading things. I can't understand what they find so funny about the Artist but I like it when Mum laughs.

When we were in the fish car on the Autobahn I heard Little Cloud say that her brother was a proper ladies' man. As if he were a bit of both things – like a centaur or a griffin. At the time, I didn't understand what she meant, but now it's starting to dawn on me. A ladies' man isn't a mythical animal – he's not a blend of woman and man. He's just a man who can make women laugh. And since I like it when Mum laughs, I change my mind again.

I decide to like the Artist and I laugh out loud so he understands that. A ladies' man is exactly what she needs.

'What was the line again?' says Little Cloud.

'You had a line as well?' says Mum.

'Yes, he bloody did,' says Little Cloud. 'He was the detective who brought in Thommy Berggren's character – he was standing outside Thommy Berggren's flat talking to him!'

Mum looks at the Artist, impressed. He meets her gaze and clears his throat, assuming a policeman's voice.

'Are you Kristoffer Collin?'

There's silence for a couple of seconds before Mum realizes that's the whole line and then she begins to laugh again. So do I.

'By the way,' the Artist exclaims, cutting short all the laughter with a snap of his fingers and a serious expression, 'I was checking the names on the board down by the main door. Do you know who lives in the flat above?'

He points towards the ceiling as he says that. No one knows.

'Harry Brandelius!'

Another name I've never heard of, but I can tell from Mum that this is remarkable information.

'For real?' she gasps.

'No,' says the Artist. 'But almost.'

The mums look puzzled.

'It's his daughter who lives here – her name's Harriet Brandelius. But if you say Harriet Brandelius quickly then there's almost no difference. Listen: Iamneighbourswithharrietbrandelius.'

The mums laugh again. The Artist draws breath and begins to sing. He sings well.

He sings loudly and Mum rushes past the kitchen table to close the balcony door. She holds her breath while grappling with the small plastic latch at the top of the handle, but as soon as the door is shut the laughter bursts out of her again.

Granny has turned sixty and there's going to be a party with a thousand cousins. On the train to Stockholm, Mum tells me that she and her siblings have bought Granny a moped and that the whole moped is going to be swathed in wrapping paper. She indicates with her hands how big the package will be: as big as a moped.

I also want to bring a present. Mum thinks I should do a drawing and gets out a pad of paper and a pencil from her bag.

'Draw Granny,' she says.

I'm trying to draw Granny but I can't remember what Granny looks like. I've barely seen her. When we lived with the Plant Magician we almost never went to Granny's and when we stopped living with the Plant Magician we couldn't afford to.

There's an abandoned weekly in the seat pocket in front of me and I begin to flip through it, looking for something to copy. Mum's trying to sleep with her head leaned against the window so she won't notice if I trace a picture.

I can't find a good picture but I do find an amusing poem. It's about dancing the Hambo and kicking up your heels, and every line rhymes with the last. I copy the poem, word for word, and draw a simple flower beside it.

Granny's eyes moisten when she reads the poem – or perhaps they're already moist because she got a moped. Anyway, she reads it aloud in her kitchen in the cottage on Väddö. Then she crouches down beside me, puts an arm around me and says:

'Andrev, you're going to be a writer.'

She smiles at me and it's very agreeable. A little earlier, she told me off for playing with her hurdy-gurdy. I thought it looked like a machine gun and got it down off the wall when no one was looking. I pulled the shoulder strap over my head and stood in front of the hall mirror, feet wide apart like Rambo on the poster in the window of the video-rental shop. I was making muffled gunshot sounds with my mouth while imagining the muzzle flashing when she caught me.

'That's not a toy,' she said sternly.

Now her voice is soft and she thinks I'm going to make something of myself.

All of a sudden, I have a hamster. Mum has got a job at the county hospital that's being built in the borderlands between the town and the woods at Vrinneviskogen. She's cleaning up the new, straight corridors in the wake of the builders and earning so much she can pretty much buy as many hamsters as she likes. My little sister gets one too.

My hamster is brown like a turban fungus and I name it Hampus. My little sister's hamster is chanterelle-coloured and she gives it all sorts of names. It only has one name at a time, but as soon as I've learned what it's called it has a new one.

All of a sudden, we also have a television. The doorbell rings and I'm the one who gets it because Mum tells me to. She smiles as she says that and when I see the television I realize why. It's on the landing outside and behind it is Little Cloud's eldest. He greets me with a silent head twitch and I twitch back.

He's out of breath but looks just as frozen as ever. Mum gives him a few hundred-krona notes and then he makes himself scarce. It won't be the last time that Frozen Boy stands there and gets a few hundred-krona notes because he's good at finding stuff, but he'll never again stand there with anything better than this.

Now we've got a pay package and hamsters and colour television. It's apparent that we're on our way into the system.

My little sister and I watch television with the hamsters in our cupped hands. Mum is on the sofa too, the smell of henna coming from the towel turban on her head. She has henna in her eyebrows too because she needs to be properly redheaded – then everything will be perfect.

Most people believe she's red-headed, but her hair's actually mousy. That's how she describes her true hair colour, and she hates it. She pulls a face when the mousiness starts to show at her roots. In our new bathroom, in which no person has bathed before us, there's a fluorescent tube on the ceiling and beneath that all is visible. She pulled a face as soon as she went in there, but now she's going to be beautiful again.

Once she got elected as a municipal councillor in Västervik because she had such beautiful hair. That was when we lived in the flat with the tower. The Green Party wanted a red-headed woman on the poster and somehow that ended up with Mum becoming a local politician. She panicked. She had to ring up and confess all: how she knew nothing about politics and that she wasn't even a real redhead. And then the council relieved her of her office.

Everything is on the way to being perfect when the doorbell rings again. This time it's Little Cloud standing there. She's upset and her shoulder hurts and she needs to sit at a kitchen table and say 'bloody men' to make it better again.

And then they sit at the kitchen table all evening.

They take turns saying it – sometimes laughing, sometimes in tears.

I can still hear them talking in the kitchen when I'm lying in my bed. The hamsters run in their wheels and the mums say 'bloody men'.

Their mantra makes me anxious – after all, I'm going to be a man. It's as if Mum can hear my very thoughts because when she comes to tuck me in she says I shouldn't take it to heart.

'You'll never be that kind of man,' she says. 'You're so in touch with your female side.' Her hair smells powerfully of carelessly washed-out henna, and sitting on the edge of the bed she takes on a red halo in the glow of the streetlights beyond the window.

'You're soft,' she continues. 'It's almost as if you're a girl in a boy's body.'

These words make me even more anxious because I definitely don't want to be a girl in a boy's body.

'You're on our side!' Little Cloud calls out from the kitchen.

The mums laugh. The hamsters run. It turns to winter.

Every Saturday morning, I switch on the television at eight o'clock because that's when a programme called *Good Morning Sweden* begins and during that programme there are always a few minutes of cartoons. Sometimes I switch on the television a little earlier to stare at the clock counting down the seconds. I've missed so much television in my life and I require no more than that movement on the screen to feel something within me healing.

One winter's morning, Olof Palme has been murdered. Under that clock it says he's been murdered and that there won't be any *Good Morning Sweden*. This chills me. I'm not exactly sure who Olof Palme is, but I've been waiting a week for Woody Woodpecker and now there's going to be a special bulletin instead.

I run towards Mum's bedroom, my mouth full of disappointment. I wrench open the door and get ready to deliver my complaint, but the words remain in my mouth.

Mum is sitting astride the Artist with her back to me. She's leaning forward and my gaze is drawn straight to her bum. She's seemingly slotted onto the Artist, stretched and close-fitting like the cap on a bike tyre valve. It looks like something in the magazines we found in the land of the lilacs.

It's the Artist who spots me standing there and he gasps as if he's just seen a ghost in uniform. Mum tumbles off him and there's time for his cock, red and shiny, to wobble where she was sitting before she throws a blanket over him.

Is he going to be my dad now? I think. But I don't say that.

I say that Olof Palme has been murdered and then it's Mum's turn to cry out. Blanket wrapped around her body, she runs through to cry in front of the television.

I suspect she's putting it on so that I forget what I saw.

It's Saturday 1 March 1986. It's a little after eight o'clock. The temperature is minus 7.2 degrees Celsius and the wind speed is 5 metres per second. Depth of snow: 330 millimetres.

Twice more I see the Artist in Mum's bed and then he's gone.

Not long after his disappearance, I find his drawing in the pocket of a jacket I haven't worn since the autumn. It's still a shit Indian and I throw it in the bin under the kitchen sink.

One day, when I come to write about the Artist, I'll ponder whether it was a mistake to throw away the Indian. I'll ponder this until I'm anxious and contact an auction house and receive a reassuring response. Not even in death will the going rate for his art on a square-inch basis come close to that of televisions.

Then I'll snap my fingers and feel a different kind of anxiety. Because men can be bloody awful in different ways and I'm going to be reluctant to step back into my memories of the summer of 1986.

But in the context of the chronological direction of travel, it looks nothing but balmy and auspicious. We have hamsters and colour television. Mum is red-headed all the way down to her roots and I've been given a guitar! The Indian sent me a proper guitar in the post when I turned ten, and Mum has booked me lessons so that I can learn to play it.

The buttercup anemones are in bloom. The stage is set for the summer of 1986.

PART THREE

The Thief

In which:
three omens are wasted on the unsuspecting,
the unsuspecting are saved by old souls,
and
a woman has clown lips made from barbecue spice.

It begins with a rat. It appears as an omen, but I don't know anything about dramaturgy so all I see is a rat. It's there on the kitchen floor when I get home from school. Black and white. Its body is as long as my forearm, a stiff and hairless tail trailing behind it.

'Look at this,' Mum says, crouching down beside the rat. She puts a hand on the floor and the rat runs towards it. The skin on my back tightens because it looks like the rat is going to attack her – but it doesn't mean her any harm; it just wants to get up. It uses Mum's arm as a gangway and runs up it in a flash before perching on her shoulder.

She gets up and stands there with the rat on her shoulder.

'It's friendly,' she says, but I can see her shivering and I can tell from her voice that she doesn't know for sure.

I approach cautiously. The rat has two greyish-yellow front teeth that are too long to fit behind its upper lip. The teeth look disgusting and dangerous, but the trembling whiskers are cute.

'Did you buy it?' I ask.

'I was given it,' Mum says.

She explains how the man who owned the rat used to wander the town streets with the rat on his shoulder, but how he's dead and the rat is sad.

'Is it going to live here?' I ask.

'No,' says Mum. 'We're just going to keep an eye on it for a few hours.'

I extend a hand towards the rat to pet it, but the rat only sees a new gangway which it traverses in the blink of an eye.

I shriek and flap my arm. The rat lands on the draining board with a thud and then sits there glaring at me until I say sorry.

Not long after that, I'm marching around the flat with the rat on my shoulder and it feels as if it's going to whisper to me in the language of humans any moment now. It's so big and heavy that it must surely have a soul. I'm the boy in a book about a boy who can talk to animals.

'You can stay here if you like,' I say to the rat.

'No,' Mum calls out from the kitchen – and quickly too, as if the rat really can talk and has to hear this before it has time to cut any deals.

'We'll see,' I whisper, examining the rat boy in the hall mirror.

He looks clever. Like he knows how to do something. The feeling is a new and dizzying one, because I can't usually do stuff. I'm not good at anything, and that troubles me.

In fairy tales, the weak boy always possesses some hidden talent that can be discovered and cultivated – those who aren't strong are instead wise or magical – but I don't seem to be concealing anything. I'm a boy without any attributes. I've taken five lessons with the guitar teacher and can still only just about grope my way through a twelve-note tune about Spain being a country where they dance the tango. I can't play football because I'm scared of the ball and tug the other kids' shirts. At school, every subject except drawing is difficult, but deep down I know that the feeling that I can draw is really just the feeling that I wish I could draw. It would suit me to be able to draw. Sometimes I trace nice drawings out of books and pretend that I've drawn them myself and Mum does her best to believe me.

In my class there's a little Spanish boy who can draw and it's awful to watch him when he does. The pencil is light in his hand and to make matters worse he's as cute as a button and can run really fast. It's not right. He should be ugly but he isn't.

The girls are crazy about him. He has attributes – more than he needs – and sometimes I want him to die.

The boy in the hall mirror has begun to smile because he's had an idea. The animal on his shoulder is going to go to school with him. He'll cross the playground with the rat on his shoulder and drive the girls crazy. The boys too. Everyone will go crazy at the sight of the rat boy.

Then I have another idea and I go to my room.

'You're going to meet a friend of mine,' I say, kneeling in front of the hamster cage.

The bit about a friend isn't just something I'm saying. Hampus the hamster has become a friend – possibly the best one I've ever had. At any rate, there is no one on Earth who knows more about me than him.

He usually goes still when the finger claw comes sidling across the bed of sawdust, but this time he's trying to escape. The rat seems to make him uneasy. I corner him and tell him there's no need to be afraid. His little body is pulsing like a hirsute heart in my cupped hands.

'This is Hampus,' I say, holding up the bowl made from my interlaced fingers.

The rat contemplates the small head protruding between my thumbs. I can feel the mighty body stiffen on my shoulder but I don't have time to wonder why. The rat hurls himself at my friend and bites him on the head.

Mum runs towards the scream and finds me standing on the bed with my hands cupped around my friend. I can feel him moving in there but I don't dare look. Mum'll have to do that.

I close my eyes as she prises open my fingers but I can hear that it's bad. She sucks in air through her teeth, which is a terrible verdict because I know Mum will say anything to preserve the mood in a room. She can't stand other people's anger and sadness. She'd tell someone who'd been cut in half that they were going to be all right just to avoid the look of anguish in the besouled half's eyes. If air through her teeth is the best she's got for me then the patient must be doomed.

Finally, I take a look for myself. In the middle of his head – between the adorable little ears – there is a gaping white opening in his fur. The white is his skull. He's been scalped.

I cry for my friend, but the hole in his head doesn't seem to be bothering him. I put him down in the cage and he roots about in the sawdust for a bit before he begins to groom himself. He doesn't exactly look like he's dying, and I reflect that if Little Cloud can live with a hole in her head then so can a hamster.

That very evening, the rat is collected by a man whom I never see since I refuse to leave my room to say goodbye. All I hear are heels on the hall floor and then in the stairwell and then finally outside in the street. The footsteps ring out like when shod horses walk on asphalt, and it takes a while for them to be completely engulfed by the night.

I've made up a bed on the floor by the hamster cage to keep a vigil over my friend.

'He looks like a tiny monk,' Mum says, and we're finally able to laugh.

We laugh until we're snotty and out of breath, because each time we look at the hamster we start all over again. In the end, our laughter is almost silent – and those are the best kind of laughs. The ones that come in jolts of seemingly hoarse silence that mean you can do nothing but lie on your side and chew air while you keep your hands on your tummy.

That's how we laugh and the summer once again becomes balmy and full of promise.

An omen – the first of three – has been wasted on the unsuspecting.

If you lie on your back and wriggle underneath my bed you can see wooden slats, foam rubber and a woman kneading her own breasts. She's ashen grey and wrinkled because when we found her in the land of the lilacs, I didn't have a mattress of my own to hide her under. Saga and Cyclops were able to take their magazines back to houses in Kneippen and Röda Stan, but I was forced to hide my share of the loot behind an electrical cabinet and there it remained for a whole winter before I brought it home.

It was admittedly a good thing it was behind that cabinet because it meant there was nothing to find in my room when Saga's mum found his share of the loot and rang around everyone else's mums. I was easily able to dismiss the accusation because Mum's search of the house would never extend to the crevices behind the electrical cabinets on the way to school.

Once you've been singled out and then acquitted, you're basically shielded from all suspicion for a while. The peace of mind that a guilty conscience brings with it is empowering, and also shields what must be shielded. What's more, I have – to Mum's puzzled satisfaction – started making my own bed.

Only when she vacuums and mops do I become anxious. She's so thorough as she trudges about in the cross-breeze with her hair tucked under the cornflower-blue headscarf of big cleans. And I don't dare suggest that I vacuum and mop my own room because she'd see straight through something that mad. She still wouldn't let me do it anyway. She takes cleaning very seriously.

But does she take cleaning so seriously that she'll ever lie on her back underneath my bed, I wonder as I lie on my back underneath my bed.

I'm home alone and trying to think like a mum.

Then I try to think like a mum trying to think like a son, but I just end up being myself and I prise the magazine free to flip through it for a while.

A storm is coming. On the television they say it's coming from Finland, although not really. The storm took shape by the Black Sea before heading north. It was on its way somewhere else, but when it caught sight of Sweden out of the corner of its eye it began to lurch off course and now it's headed straight for us.

Mum's pulling out all the plugs and putting stuff in front of the sockets. She saw a flash of ball lightning as a child.

I'm standing with my forehead against the window, waiting. The thunder should start soon because there are already skirts of rain hanging beneath the streetlights, and down in the darkness of Strömparken the willows are moving like agitated trolls on the riverbank. The raindrop-smeared glass is undulating in the wind and a strange longing for destruction rises within me. I enjoy standing here. It's like having the storm inside an aquarium. Like a dangerous but beautiful snake. Or is it the storm that has me inside an aquarium? Like a hamster.

At any rate, that's when I see him for the first time. Tall and lean in a short leather jacket and skin-tight jeans. Crow-like. He arrives on a stormy night because the universe can't get enough of warning me, but on this occasion I'm once again too stupid to spot it. All I see is a stranger waving, so I wave back. And when he calls out Mum's name, I go to fetch her.

She runs downstairs to open the main door and then I hear him in the stairwell. His steps clack on the stairs and I withdraw to my bed while leaving the kitchen door ajar. I turn off the light to make myself invisible and monitor the strip of light.

The clacking steps move from the hall to the kitchen without turning into sock-padded thuds en route. What kind of man is allowed to wander around inside in his shoes when it's raining? And what's that clinking in time with the footsteps? Why is he making so much noise? The approaching racket comes in four parts: apart from the clacking of the heels on the linoleum and the peculiar clinking, I can hear the creaking of the leather jacket and a mouth talking too loudly. Mum shushes him but her admonition is watered down with laughter and means nothing.

He sits down at the kitchen table and through the glowing slit I have time to see that he is tall and beautiful like in a film before Mum blocks my view.

'It's just a friend. He's leaving soon. Now go to sleep.'

She closes the door.

I get out of bed and onto my knees. There's a crack between the door and the threshold that's big enough for hamsters and gazes to wriggle through.

One day, when I come to write about the Thief, I'll be in two minds about the description of what I see when I press my cheek to the floor. I'll ponder whether it might not be a little too convenient to the story that the Indian boy gets to see a pair of cowboy boots under the kitchen table . . .

But I'll make up my mind that the Thief should wear the boots he wore. He'll even get to keep his spurs. It's not my fault that he couldn't dress credibly.

He arrives on a stormy night with spurs on his boots. Yet another omen has been wasted on the unsuspecting.

There's another boy in my block who's found a way into the town hall on the other side of Drottninggatan. He tells me about an unlocked basement door and I say I want to see it.

The door really is unlocked. We slip inside and along the passages beneath the huge building, where we find a keyring with a lot of keys on it. At least a hundred. Maybe two hundred. We don't count them. Instead, we take the bunch of keys off the hook and return to ground level.

'These are the keys to the town,' he says, shaking the metal ring and making them jangle.

We're sitting in a bush in our inner courtyard and it feels as if I'm a boy in a story about a boy who meets another boy – an orphan run wild who shows him the way into a secret world.

Each key is attached to a small ring and all the small rings are in turn strung onto the big one. There's also a name tag with a typed code on it attached to each small ring. We agree that the town will be ours just as soon as we've worked out what the codes mean.

We spend three days walking in ever-wider circles around our own neighbourhood testing the keys in different locks. The keys don't seem to fit anywhere but we decide to try again after the summer holidays. He's going to Öland with his parents. He's not an orphan – only wild.

We bury the bunch of keys beneath a bush in the park.

'See you,' he says, but I never see him again.

A package arrives from the Indian – it's unclear why. It's been almost two months since my birthday when I got a proper guitar, and there's never been a name day in my honour. Not in Sweden anyway. Perhaps there is a day in honour of my name somewhere else in the world?

The package contains a handwritten letter and a book titled *Capablanca's Best Chess Endings*. The book is full of chessboards and tables and in the letter – which Mum translates from English – the Indian suggests I devote my summer holidays to it. Apparently I'm supposed to play through a dead man's chess matches, move by move, alone at the board.

It's the worst present I've ever been given. Mum thinks so too. She sighs at the unsuitability of the gift and explains that my dad has played chess his whole life. He's crazy about chess.

'Although he does also play the drums,' she adds, as if burnishing his reputation. 'He's a chess player and drummer.'

The picture in my mind's eye is repainted once again. For a while, he becomes grotesque. In the beginning, he was just standing on the prairie with a bow and the odd feather in his hair. Then he acquired a horse but it was stolen by an artist and now he's sitting behind a drumkit with all sorts in his hands. He's got four arms, like an Indian god. He looks mad.

I'm not going to play some dead man's chess matches, but I decide to put the book in my schoolbag when the autumn term begins. I'll let it fall out onto my desk occasionally and when the other children ask what kind of book it is I'll show them the tables and explain. I'll fold down a few page corners too, so that it's obvious that I've got favourite matches played by this Capablanca guy.

I ask Mum who would win if the Indian and the Plant Magician played each other at chess. She snorts. The thought of these men hunched over the same table seems to disgust her, but then she says that my dad would win and I'm satisfied.

That night, I lie awake fantasizing about a chess game between the Indian and the Plant Magician. The Indian moves his pieces without pausing for thought. The Plant Magician tears his hair out and topples his own king with the back of his hand in that way he always used to say I should do to spare myself the humiliation of the final moves.

Maybe this game can be played when the Indian comes to get me?

When is he coming, by the way?

She's never answered that question. It's as if she thinks she doesn't have to answer the question because I've never asked it.

A third and final omen: the Thief's needles.

In the cupboard above the hob there's a shelf with assorted odds and ends: matches, painkillers, a box of buttons and rubber bands, a few sparklers, Blutsaft liquid iron formula, coffee filter papers, a kitchen mortar and the jar of Trocomare herb salt that's too tall to fit in the spice rack. It's the herb salt I'm looking for. Mum has put a vegetable on my slice of Saltå Kvarn raisin bread – and my sandwich now needs salt because vegetables are inedible if they still only taste of vegetables. But my gaze slips off the Trocomare jar and tumbles into the darkness behind it. There's something glistening down there. Something that doesn't belong with the rest of the stuff in the cupboard for assorted odds and ends. A spillikins-like heap of big needles, each one with green plastic casing at one end.

'What's this?' I say, holding up one of the needles in front of the bathroom mirror. Mum darts a glance through the jaws of the eyelash curler and snatches the needle away from me.

'You don't have to touch things just because you can!' Her voice is sharp and brittle at the same time, the way that mums' voices get when you fiddle with electrical sockets or death cap mushrooms.

She rushes into the kitchen. The needles are moved and I am made to promise not to touch them again. She explains that they belong to a friend who is ill. I ask whether it's the man with the cowboy boots and she laughs.

'Yes, it is the man with the cowboy boots. He's got spurs too.'
'I know. Does he have a horse?'

She laughs again. 'No, he's just a little special. But he's kind and I'm trying to help him to get better.'

'Did he get ill while he was out in the rain?'

'No, he's not ill like that.'

'Then how is he ill?'

Unfortunately, she doesn't have time to answer that. We have eyelashes to curl and sandwiches to eat. We have a tram to catch to Norr Tull.

Mum has something important to do and it's been decided that I'm to stay with the Plant Magician for the weekend. He's now in a flat on Stockholmsvägen, in one of the blocks clad in yellow corrugated metal beyond Marielund.

I don't want to sleep there but I failed to say so when I had the chance. She asked if it was all right and all I did was shrug. Why do we do that?

The flat is smaller and darker than Mum's and the air is thick with garlic, camomile, pipe tobacco and a number of fainter scents jostling with the more dominant ones. The Plant Magician is living here in exile, banished to one of the system's many small linoleum-lined cells with their aerial sockets, but he has brought the raw ingredients of magic with him.

Yarrow, nettles and bearberries are hanging in the kitchen drying, while in a dark corner he has stacked herb-drying racks made from old window frames with fine-meshed chicken wire attached to them. There's nothing to separate the layers so he's inserted paperbacks between the frames to provide ventilation in the stacks.

I crouch beside them and allow my eyes to grow accustomed to the dark. Lying on the wire are the kinds of things a plant magician needs: juniper berries, coltsfoot leaves, wild thyme, long strips of alder buckthorn bark, Iceland moss that's already brittle. There are other things too. Roots and small mushrooms that I don't recognize. Who knows what worlds you might see if you simply ground it all down and poured the mixture into a Trocomare jar?

He asks how my chess is, now that I'm living with such a simple person. I tell him that it's going well and that I'm reading a book about grandmaster Casablanca.

'You mean Capablanca?'

Yes, he's the one I mean.

'José Raúl Capablanca – from Cuba.'

Exactly.

'Capa.'

Shut up.

The Plant Magician suggests that we play. My siblings say they're hungry, but that will have to wait. He wants to see what I've learned and it's too late to admit that I haven't read the book and that I haven't played a single match in two years.

Luckily, I get a nosebleed. He pushes me down onto the sofa and says that my nose would stop bleeding all the time if I rinsed it with a decoction of field horsetail and tormentil. I agree because I would rather suck stuff up my nose than play chess, but unfortunately he doesn't have any tormentil in. He promises to get some in for next time.

Next time?

He asks how Mum's getting on and I say fine but he doesn't really seem to believe me.

'All bloody chaos, I suppose?'

I shrug.

'Is she seeing any men?'

I pause for breath to oxygenate a no, but I'm too slow to deceive him. He shakes his head and gets up to go into the kitchen, where he rattles about for a while. My siblings pad after him, lured by the sounds of feeding time. I remain in situ with my head tilted back. A plug of clotted blood comes loose and goes down the back way into my throat, forcing me to swallow hard, but it doesn't matter because I secretly like the warm, salty taste of it.

There's a gaze tickling my cheek. I tip my head to one side and meet it in the gloom beyond a curtain of wooden beads. He's hanging on the wall above an unmade bed. Peapods for eyelids, corn cobs for ears, spring onions for shoulders and a whopping big squash in shades of grey and green for a chest.

My siblings return from the kitchen with topping-covered sandwich wafers, and even though I pinch my nose, I can make out the earthy smell of Tartex pâté when they kneel beside the coffee table. Their dad follows with a wine glass and a small bottle that I recognize. It's the bottle with the Viking ship on the label.

'There are two kinds of people in this world,' he says, sitting down right on the edge of the chair. He's going to teach me something. 'There are old souls and new souls. Do you know how you can tell the difference between them?'

I shake my head.

'You can't,' he says, wrapping a fist around the screw cap. It crackles as the perforated metal seal breaks against the threads at the top of the neck. The smell of trouble wafts out.

'It's not visible from outside,' he adds. 'A child's body can have an old soul.' He places a hand on my sister's head and she grins, her teeth covered in Tartex. 'And a fully grown adult can be the vessel for a soul that's never been here before. That's why some people are so lost – like your mum. She's never been here before. New souls need to be guided by the old to find their way in this world.'

I nod cautiously. The blood vessels have probably by now sealed themselves back up in the dark of my nostrils, but I remain lying down and keep pinching the bridge of my nose to have something to do.

'There's nothing but buzzing in her head.' He taps his own temple with the tip of his index finger. 'Surely you've noticed?'

I may have done.

'That's why she's always cleaning. She cleans to delude herself that she's in control of something. And she doesn't know how to do anything else. She dropped out of school – did you know that? Your mum doesn't have an education. She doesn't know a thing. Not a thing.'

I've never heard him talk for so long about anything other than himself. He just keeps running off at the mouth. Time passes. My brother falls asleep on the rug and a while later the wicker chair my sister is lying on with her legs folded over the armrest stops creaking. I fall asleep on the sofa. We sleep there like dogs, spread out in the glow of the kerosene lamp.

I can hear his voice up there at the surface as I sink to the bottom of myself. The bottle has been emptied and his language has become simpler, but he's still talking about her.

She's as dumb as a bird. Easily deceived. Anyone can have her. Anyone.

Day two with the Plant Magician. He's the first out of everyone to get up and locks himself in the bathroom. The tap runs for ages.

'He's turning into a soldier,' says Little Sis.

She's right. When he emerges from the bathroom, he's shaved his face completely bare and gathered his hair into a tight knot. I forgot that he sometimes does that after a spell of intoxication. The transformation usually only lasts for a few hours, but they're dull hours because the whole pigsty has to be tidied up and everything that can be folded needs to be folded. It's not like when Mum cleans and all you have to do is make sure you're not in the way. When the Plant Magician cleans, he sets everybody to work.

'Fall in!' he shouts, snatching the duvets off us.

After cleaning, we go to Linköping to have dinner with the Plant Magician's parents. He takes the back roads like usual – I suppose he still doesn't have a licence – and I start to get hungry in the back seat of his new car, which is a white Volvo Amazon with a home-made air freshener made from dried lavender dangling from the rear-view mirror.

It's only when I kick off my shoes in the hallway that I remember that only grown-ups are allowed into the Plant Magician's parents' dining room since his mum doesn't like children. Mum told me that the Plant Magician's mum never wanted him and that it was only when he got older and became more reasonably sized that she learned to tolerate his presence. This is the first time I've met her since she stopped being my grandmother and I learned about her incredible coldness. This new knowledge makes me alert to her movements.

She receives her son with a kind of one-armed hug, just a single hand touching a shoulder. She's hugging him like bronze medallists hug the person doling out the prizes on television. She receives me in turn by placing a hand on my head as if quickly measuring me. She's wearing house shoes with thick heels.

The Plant Magician's dad is the mellow one in the household. He's a military man who then became an engineer at Saab. There's a framed photograph on the hall wall showing him as a young man in uniform at the garrison in Vaxholm. He's the one who pilots us to the room where we're to wait while the grown-ups eat.

We're lined up on the edge of a bed and each given an apple.

Lying on the floor is a box of toys. There's a unit of tin soldiers in the box and I'm overcome with faint sadness when I realize that the Plant Magician has played with them. Once upon a time, long ago when the world was black and white and crackling, he sat on the floor and lined up these soldiers of Charles XII in front of him. The kneeling ones in the first row, the upright behind them. He made shooting noises with his tongue extended to the front of his palate. He let the dead fall and felt disappointment if they didn't lie in the right position.

On the way home, we stop at a hot-dog stand on the outskirts of Linköping. The Plant Magician gets us hot dogs and mashed potatoes and I wonder whether it's truly necessary to hate him.

I think about the tin soldiers we cast when he was still my dad and how handsome they were before I painted them. I think of the steam engine he gave me and the rush in my body when I got to ignite the methylated spirit tablet. The way the wheel spun as the pressure rose never captivated me in the same way that the burning tablet in the boiler space did. I could see it alive in there. I had the flame in a cage. A pet of fire.

We make one more stop – this time out on the back road. The Plant Magician wades into a corn field, disappearing for a while. When he returns he has a bunch of corn clasped to his chest and is running with his knees excessively high, as if he is the baddie in a cartoon.

'Start the car!' he yells, and I have already made an effort to heave myself towards the ignition key before I realize he's joking.

He says I can take one of the corn cobs home if I like. I would like.

I resolve to hug him with both my hands when we part. But when he pulls up onto the kerb on Gamla Rådstugugatan to return the son that was never his, I refrain after all. I don't want Mum to see me hugging him. Her young soul might get ideas.

It's as if he's being smuggled in piece by piece – like a do-it-yourself dad kit. He's a coat in the hall, a pair of jeans in the laundry basket, a voice in the kitchen at night. He's something she's slowly assembling under cover of darkness and will show us just as soon as she's got him working. I still don't know how dads begin and end, but if this is a dad then I reckon he's now begun.

The day that I learn the Thief is a thief begins with a misunderstanding: I believe myself to be home alone.

Mum has started cleaning for a health farm on the other side of Bråviken bay and has to get up so early that the sounds of her morning routine leak into my dreams. It's the summer holidays and I'm dreaming of misplaced car keys.

(Oh, that's right, she's got a car again. Or perhaps she's only borrowed it. She doesn't seem to know for sure herself, but at any rate it's the same model of Saab as the one we abandoned not far from the ferry quay last summer.)

As I decant my cereal I still believe myself to be home alone. As I still do when I open the fridge and discover that we don't have any milk. There are a handful of ten-krona notes on the draining board and I divine a causal relationship although there is no note to confirm it. I discontinue Project Breakfast and wriggle under my bed. I coax the magazine free from its hiding place and settle cross-legged by the hamster cage, where my scalped friend is rooting about in the sawdust.

The first pages are creased and brittle after a winter spent behind the electrical cabinet, and the women on them look in poor health. Their bodies are pale yellow and sooty with blotches of magenta. The one I'm looking for resides further into the magazine where everyone is healthy.

She isn't the cutest of them all, but she is the one showing the most. She's twisting and turning herself with the care of a child counting her mosquito bites. There's even a picture of her in which she's showing her bumhole and pointing at it. Here's the bumhole. I'm not all that interested in her bumhole – I've got one of my own, and while I may never have seen it I've also never wondered what it looks like – but it's good that she's thorough.

My sister's golden hamster stands on its hind legs, its front paws resting on the lattice, and fixes its beady gaze on me. I glance towards the cage and imagine a scene in which the hamsters – in a fairy-tale outburst of loquaciousness – tell Mum about everything they've seen. It's a preposterous idea but I rotate anyway: a quarter-turn towards the bed so that I'm sitting with my back towards the cage.

There's a big close-up of her front bum. (The boys at school usually laugh their heads off when I say front bum, but that's the term I was taught by the Plant Magician and it will be a while before any of the other words catch on with me.) This thorough woman uses two fingers with white-polished nails to hold her front bum open like the note compartment of a wallet. The inside looks both grotesque and comfy, and I daydream for a while about being transformed to the size of a teaspoon and settling down there. Not inside the hole but in the slit. I want to lie there like a tin soldier in a peapod and allow myself to be enclosed when she takes her fingertips away. Only my head would peek out.

I think the same thing every time I look at the picture, but this time is the first time I'm interrupted in the thought.

'Are you reading about ladies?'

I swallow a chunk of air and look up. I want to hurl both the magazine and myself under the bed, but I'm unable to move. He's leaning against the door frame. He's not wearing the leather jacket or the cowboy boots, but I still understand. This is the man who is a little special. And ill but kind.

'Don't worry,' he says, grinning. 'I'm not a snitch.'

I've never heard the word snitch before, but I realize right away what it means.

He remains in the doorway, narrowing his eyes and biting his cheek. He looks like the singer from A-ha. Is it the singer from A-ha? Mum did say he was special, and that would definitely be special. For a brief moment, I'm almost certain that it's the singer from A-ha before I remember that A-ha are from Norway.

'I promised your mum I'd buy milk and bread before I bugger off.'

Nope, he's not speaking Norwegian. This is someone else.

'For you, that is. I don't eat breakfast.'

He doesn't appear to eat much at all.

'Why don't you come with me to the shop?' He nods towards the hall as he says that.

I don't want to go with him to the shop but my bargaining position is dire. He's seen things that could destroy me. So I shrug and let him decide what I want. The man who looks like the singer from A-ha but is someone else decides that I want to come with him and now there are just minutes left until I learn that he is a thief.

We walk along Trädgårdsgatan towards Östra Promenaden and traverse Drottninggatan at the crossroads where tram routes two and three part ways. It's there – at that crossroads – that I catch sight of our two figures in the window of the hobby shop and I reluctantly admit it.

He looks exciting in that creaky leather jacket and those tight-fitting jeans that were black once but have now faded to the colour of an oyster mushroom. His hair appears to be swaying wildly in a headwind, and slung over his shoulder is a sailor's duffel bag the shade of a giant puffball mushroom, replete with a coarse drawstring. The wallet in his back pocket is tethered to his hip by a chain that jingles in time with his gait.

You can tell he lives outside the system – but not in the vegetable-dyed kind of way. It's more like the posters you find in the middle of *Okej*. I suppose it's really only the boots – more precisely the serrated coins behind the heels – that mar his appearance and embarrass me slightly.

I wonder whether the people we encounter in the street think the man with the spurs is my dad. I hope they think so.

Apparently he does too, because on the way into the grocery store he puts an arm around me and says something unexpected. I don't know whether I'm meant to hear it – he says it quietly, as if to himself – but the words are caught by the downdraught between the sliding doors and gust down to me.

'I'm a dad and you're my son.'

We quickly find the milk and bread, but then he wants to take a look at other stuff too. We wander around for a long time looking at other stuff. We look at meat and razors and batteries and he's keen that we do so together.

'Keep up so we don't lose each other,' he says whenever I lag behind or drift towards the comics, as if it were possible to lose someone with heels and spurs in a labyrinth of tiled floors.

Something is off.

As we approach the queue at the checkout, there are still only milk and bread in the basket. I become alert to his movements. He has long, pink fingers with ragged nails and peeling cuticles. They grab a chocolate bar which disappears inside the leather jacket. He sees that I've seen, grins slightly, shushes me even though I haven't said anything, and pushes me towards the queue for the checkout.

'Don't worry,' he whispers, running his hands through my hair.

But I do worry. My cheeks are burning. I hold my breath to smother those first flames, but it only gets worse. My whole face catches fire and the smoke is billowing towards the ceiling. I can feel every pair of eyes in the shop trained on the plume of smoke by checkout two. Everyone is wondering why there's a boy standing there on fire.

The Thief notices that I'm dying and hands me an empty plastic bag, telling me to go and stand at the end of the conveyor belt to pack our shopping.

I do as he says and walk to the end quite normally. Arms glued to my sides, head centred and fixed between my shoulders. Not too fast and not too slow. I walk past the cashier like a Lucia choir boy.

When I reach the end of the belt, I turn around and meet the Thief's gaze. He looks innocent, and I wonder how that can be – is it something you pick up over the years? About a week ago when I was at home on my own with my siblings, my little brother climbed up to one of the kitchen cupboards and took down the tub of caster sugar. Then he opened the cutlery drawer and took out a tablespoon. He settled down on the kitchen floor and began eating right from the tub and we let him do it because it was such a funny sight. But then we vacuumed the kitchen floor and washed his hands and his cheeks. We really did try to save him, but when Mum got home and called out from the hallway 'what's going on here, then?' he ran straight to her and yelled that he hadn't been eating sugar.

It was for the best, because if he hadn't given himself away then I or my sister would have. We were like shaken-up bottles of Pommac, and when we heard his involuntary confession out in the hallway we exploded into hysterics on the living-room floor.

The Thief doesn't look the least bit nervy as he places two cartons of milk and a loaf of bread on the conveyor belt. But he can't see what I can see. Two men have appeared behind him. They're wearing short-sleeved shirts that are the same as the one worn by the woman on the checkout, but one of the men looks more important than the other because he's a bit fat and is wearing a waistcoat with pens in the breast pocket. The waistcoat is a dark shade of reddish-purple, like a burning brittlegill.

On the fat one's signal, they lock arms with the Thief from either side. He flounders but goes nowhere. The fat one searches the duffel bag with his free hand.

'Well, what do you know?'

The Thief is led away. A customer applauds.

'Not in front of my son!' he pleads, making everyone look at me.

A horde of customers and cashiers look on, their eyes filled with disgust and pity.

I can hear the blood vessel bursting inside my nose. It's as if the wall of cartilage clicks as the pressure from within finds a way out.

The cashier rises to her feet and leaves her pen. She hands me a roll of kitchen paper and asks whether I want to go into the back with my dad. I shake my head and tear off a metre of paper, hiding my whole face in it.

'Well, then, I suppose you'll have to . . . wait here for now.'

Wait for what? While I try to work out what's going to happen, a murmur of unfamiliar voices rises beyond my paper mask.

'You can't just leave him there.'

'He doesn't want to go with his dad.'

'Can't you open another checkout?' A soft hand takes hold of my arm. There is a woman's voice right beside me.

'I'll take him home with me.'

The soft hand leads me away, through the downdraught and into the street. I don't know who she is, but I would follow her to the end of the world.

'Can I come to work with you tomorrow?'

'If you want . . .'

'I do.'

'Why?' Mum doesn't know about what happened at the grocery store and I'm not going to tell. I haven't seen the Thief since he was dragged out of the picture, but I have a feeling he'll be back. And I'm now up to my ears in dealings of silence. The magazine is no longer under the mattress – I threw it down the rubbish chute before Mum got home – but the Thief knows what was there. He saw me and I saw him.

'I thought . . . I could help you clean.'

The Saab wakes me up with a scream. Mum forces it to climb up the sweeping gravel approach in first. The health farm is located in the former home of a mill owner, the façade pale and the windows framed in green.

We stay in the car for a while. It was so nice and quiet inside the car when she turned off the engine. The only thing that could be heard was the ticking of the warm engine block and the whistling of her nose. I know mine is whistling too because I've inherited her tight nostrils, but I can't hear my own whistling – I just know it's there because sometimes my classmates get annoyed and ask me to breathe through my mouth when we're hunched over some group work in the classroom. I usually do open my mouth but quickly forget why it is open, before starting to whistle again.

I know I'm the sort of child who makes other people's skin crawl. Everyone – apart from one person – finds me hard to love. And now I've got her all to myself and it's the best. We sit in the car, whistling to each other.

'Time we were getting a shift on.' She thrusts the door open and the sealed silence is broken.

On the way into the grand house, she explains that there are lots of rooms in it but only two types of guests staying in them: the ones who have checked in to get thin and the ones who have checked in to die. Everyone is there to disappear in one way or another.

'You'll notice which kind is staying in this room,' she whispers before knocking on a door. 'You can stay here – I'm just going to open the window and we can come back later and clean when it's had an airing.'

She draws breath and steps inside, leaving the door open and hurrying through the gloom. There's a shadow sitting on the bed. Mum opens the curtains and the shadow gains a nightie and the face of an old woman. It's obvious that she belongs to the dying because someone like this can't get much thinner. She's no more than a skeleton in a skin suit and her hands are stained brown like panther caps.

'Don't open it,' she whimpers. 'I'm freezing.'

I immediately feel sorry for her because I know there is no version of this scene in which the windows remain shut. The world champion of cross-breezes has arrived to get the air moving in here.

Once the windows have been opened as far as the stays will go, Mum wraps a blanket around the skeleton on the bed and suggests she goes outside into the sunshine to warm up.

'There's nowhere I can get warm,' says the skeleton. 'I'll never be warm again.'

We carry on along the corridor and stop by a bay window filled with spider plants and ficus trees. Mum knocks on another door and this time she waits for a reply before entering.

The woman staying in this room is fat and sad. One of those I notice right away, while the other I notice when Mum asks how she is feeling.

'I can't stay here,' she says wanly.

'You couldn't last week either,' Mum says, reeling out a smile that the fat and sad woman refuses to be hooked in by.

'The vegetables are driving me mad,' she says, stepping into a pair of bath slippers. 'I hate vegetables. Hate them, hate them, hate them.'

She shuffles into the corridor but then stops and looks back into the room. She's wearing a capacious dress and the light of the bay window behind her transforms her into a tepee from which a young woman has stuck out her head to say something.

'How can everything healthy be disgusting? It's unreal.'

Mum laughs. I listen for what comes next with bated breath, because I've never heard a grown-up tell the truth like this. But there is no continuation. She's already gone. I want to stick my head into the corridor and call out that she's right, that it's unreal that a god who created so much never once happened to create something that's both healthy and tasty.

Mum sorts out the cross-breeze and tasks me with stripping the sheets from the bed while she goes to get fresh ones. It feels criminal being alone in this room. There is a purple bra hanging over the back of a chair, and it catches my eye because the cups are like gossamer mosquito nets that divulge ambitions beyond those of practicality. It's the kind of bra usually worn by thin women who live hidden under mattresses and I'm dizzied by the thought that it can be worn by someone who is fat and sad in a room like this. The world is so full of secrets.

I hear Mum's footsteps in the corridor and my gaze begins to move about frantically. I don't know where to put my body because the bedsheets are already in a heap on the floor and now my hands are hanging there, empty and guilty by my hips. I stand as far away from the mosquito-net bra as the layout of the room allows and examine a small ceramic bird that might also be a flute.

Once the room with the mosquito-net bra has been cleaned, we return to the first room and this time I go inside too. The skeleton is gone, which is a relief to me. I take a few steps towards the bed but Mum blocks my path.

'It can be a bit yucky in here,' she whispers, removing the covers.

The movement causes a cloud of white powder and the scent of urine to rise up. There's a sheepskin rug in the bed.

It was formerly black, but it's been discoloured by something resembling flour.

'She doesn't like getting wet,' Mum says, her face wrinkling. 'So she talcs her bum instead of showering.'

I lean in close and gag when I see the talcum powder caked into the wool.

'I know,' Mum groans.

Our eyes meet and the yuckiness becomes nice when we shudder together.

We clean a total of four rooms, and before leaving we go to the health farm's dining room and eat lunch: roasted root vegetables and a salad with marigolds in it. I think about the children in Africa but it doesn't help. Mum talks about the imminent weekend and how nice it will be when Little Bro and Little Sis come to stay.

I wonder whether she knows that I've met the Thief. Probably not. If she did, she would surely have asked me what I thought of him. Should I tell her what I think when she asks the question? Probably not.

I look for the fat and sad woman. She's not here, but I will see her one last time and the scene will be categorized as one of the oddest of my life.

We're already in the car driving down the steep slope towards the main gate. The inside of the car is baking hot and the windows are rolled down. I'm hanging out of the car awaiting the breeze that will appear once we reach the asphalt and pick up speed. And it's there, with my head stuck out of the car window, that I see the fat and sad woman for the last time.

'There she is,' I say.

Mum slows down and we look at her together.

She's sitting on the slope a little way away from the road, poorly hidden between a dwarf birch and a rosehip bush. She's got a grilled chicken in her hands, an empty paper bag serving as a napkin on her lap and brown clown lips from the barbecue spice.

Mum stops the car and leans over my knees.

'How are you doing?'

One hand lets go of the chicken and gives a thumbs-up, but the rest of the body is still fat and sad.

'Did you walk all the way to the shop in Krokek?'

The head nods.

'Good for you,' Mum says, leaning back.

We drive on as the fat and sad woman disappears from sight. I pull my head back into the car and meet Mum's gaze. She looks tormented. Her cheeks are inflated, her lips pressed together and pale, her whole face quivering as if her hands are wrapped around a jam jar as she tries to break the vacuum seal under the lid. The quivering is contagious and my sinuses begin to squeak as the laughter tries to claw its way out of my nose. My squeaking makes her squeak. We squeak together and I feel happy when I think how we're going to laugh once we reach the asphalt and no longer have to contain it.

There are just a few metres to go now. I cast my gaze towards Bråviken bay and get ready.

Saturday. Mum is cleaning and I'm sitting on the floor with my hands closely cupped around my hamster. It's nice enclosing him completely because he immediately becomes unexpectedly strong in there. He roots about with his nose, finds a crack between my fingers and forces his way out, stretching his cheek pouches back and baring his small teeth in a grin.

We're waiting for the Plant Magician to come on the tram to drop off my siblings. But he doesn't turn up. The hours slip by and eventually Mum goes to the telephone to call. It's not the first time she's gone to pick up the receiver, but it is the first time she's input the number instead of just letting her hand hover above the dial.

'There is going to be a row,' she says, and there is.

I don't understand what the row is about, but it concludes in some kind of negotiation where the Plant Magician agrees to give her half the children he owes her. He offers to let her choose which one, and when she refuses he says that it'll be a surprise, then.

When she hangs up she's crying. She says she doesn't want to see him and asks whether I can go to the stop outside the town hall to pick up a sibling – it's unclear which one – and I shrug.

Why do we do that?

'He might not mean it,' she says while I'm sitting in the hall tying my shoelaces. 'Take both if you can.'

But I know he means it. This is the punishment for me failing to say no when he asked whether she was seeing any men.

I only manage to bring Little Sis back home. I thought he might give me Little Bro since he's youngest and weighs the least – I thought he'd give me as little as possible – but he chooses to give me Little Sis and tomorrow I'll wonder whether his old soul knew something that our young souls couldn't fathom. You see, without Little Sis, Mum wouldn't have survived the night.

The Thief is back. I hear the heels in the darkness and am immediately wide awake. I wonder whether Little Sis can hear them too. I know she was asleep when Mum carried her from the sofa to bed, but perhaps the heels have woken her again? She's in the room closest to the hall, the one that's made up for two but missing one. I hope she's asleep because I don't want her to know that a man has been here when the Plant Magician asks her whether Mum is seeing any men.

The heels move towards the interior of the flat. They're in the living room now. I assume that they'll get quieter when they reach the sofa, but they don't. The heels are restless and seem to be moving in circles around the floor.

Now I can hear his voice too. The volume is rising and there's something white hot about the tone.

I sneak into the kitchen to listen. I'm not really sure why, but I suppose it's to do with our shared secrets. I don't believe he's here to reveal what was under the mattress, but his voice is on fire by now and you never know with voices that are on fire. Secrets can shoot out like sparks.

I can't hear what he's saying. He's talking too quickly and the torrent of words is diluted by the clacking of his heels and Mum's fruitless shushing.

I tiptoe towards the hall. Past the hob and the cupboard for assorted odds and ends, past the fridge loaded up to sustain four mouths in the household for a spell, past the sink and the slightly sour smell of the cloth draped across the tap.

Now I can hear Mum.

'I just want to help you,' she says.

Is that why his voice is on fire? Doesn't this man who is a little special and ill but kind want her help? This man who steals and has dangerous needles . . .

The kitchen is usually oblong – like a corridor lined with hatches – but tonight it's even longer and narrower than usual. More like a pipe. And at the end of that pipe I see a door open.

Little Sis is awake. Her hair, too curly to ever get long, has been tousled by the pillow and forms a helmet of sandy candyfloss on her head. She looks at me questioningly. I wave at her dismissively and she takes a step back into her room – but only one. And when I take another step forward she does the same, meaning I have to stop and show her both my palms. She backs up again. I take a step forward and she does the same. We keep at it for a while – it's like a dance in the dark.

The whole town is asleep but we aren't. Everyone is awake at 7 Gamla Rådstugugatan in the flat one storey up behind the door on the left-hand side. There's a thief talking too loudly and too quickly, a mum shushing him, and two kids – a boy and a girl – silently dancing with each other on either side of a hallway. The boy is wishing that the sun will suddenly rise and that everyone in the whole town will wake up, because something is off.

He doesn't want to be caught standing in the hall staring, so he pretends he's on his way to the bathroom. That means he only has to make a right turn for a few seconds' clear line of sight towards the living room. He sees the Thief with his back to the hallway, tall and crow-like, and he sees his mum on the sofa, leaning forward with her torso held up by straight arms in front of her – as if she were getting up but got stuck midmovement. That's all he manages to see before he reaches the bathroom door.

Once there, he places a hand on the handle – but only to

maintain the charade. He hasn't thought further than this. He probably ought to push the handle down too, but he doesn't dare because now it's suddenly gone silent in the living room and he can't remember whether the bathroom door is one of the ones that squeaks. He still doesn't want to go in there. He doesn't know what he wants, except for the sun to rise.

Out of the corner of his eye, he sees his little sister step into the hallway and into the midst of the danger to stare. The boy tilts to one side to see whether they've spotted her. The mum has seen her, and now she's seen the boy too.

'It's all right,' she says to her children.

But it isn't all right. The Thief, still with his back to the hall and perhaps unaware of who she is addressing, takes two quick steps towards the sofa and kicks her in the face.

The boy will later reflect that the kick didn't sound like they do in films. He won't remember a sound at all, which will baffle him. He'll think that it ought to be loud when a cowboy boot hits a face, but right now he's not thinking anything.

His sister screams at the Thief to stop. The Thief marches into the hall, picks up the sister and deposits her in her room before closing the door. He doesn't need to pick up the boy to move him anywhere because he's already in the kitchen, where he's engaged in a new dance of bewildered steps. The Thief, who doesn't seem to see the boy, wrenches open the bathroom door and shortly afterwards the boy hears an unexpected sound. It begins as a shrill gushing but is quickly transformed into a more muffled tone. The boy has heard the change of tone before. It's the bathtub being filled with water.

The Thief returns to the living room and now the boy can hear what he is saying because the voice is controlled. Almost caring.

'Time for you to die,' he says. 'I'm going to drown you.'

The mum howls as the Thief drags her by her hair. The boy

performs yet more dance steps in the kitchen but they lead nowhere. He has no direction.

The Thief reaches the hall with his floundering quarry and catches sight of the boy.

'Go to your room,' he says, giving the boy direction.

In his room, he kneels and opens the hamster cage. Hamsters are nocturnal, but this one has overslept. It's sleepy and docile like a warm beanbag in his hands. He presses the animal's back against his cheek and whispers to it.

'There's nothing we can do.'

The boy can hear the mum kicking the side of the bathtub. She's trying to change direction in the bathroom, but she can't get free and now the Thief is pounding her head against the toilet seat. The boy hears that too. Flesh and porcelain.

'There's nothing we can do,' he whispers, never asking himself whether that is true.

He's a cowardly boy – hopeless in every way. He can't play the guitar or chess and he can't draw – all he can do is trace and pretend the lines are his. He's scared of the dark, scared of the ball, scared of a thrashing. He's scared of everything and the master of nothing. He is a boy without any attributes and he is doing nothing to save his mum. He is letting her die.

But she has more than one child, and now there's a different one rushing towards the bathroom. The boy can hear her battle cry as she casts herself onto the Thief and clings onto his back. And then his scream when she sinks her teeth into him.

It's the girl who saves the mum, because while the Thief goes to the girl's room and hurls her onto a bed, the mum slips behind him to open the front door onto the landing. She runs out to get help and she doesn't have to run far because outside she encounters a swarm of uniforms. The custodians of the system.

The boy hears many voices and footsteps and decides to return the hamster to its cage and leave his room. From the kitchen, he can see the Thief on the hall floor with a knee in his back. He looks desperate.

That's the last time the boy sees him.

It's still night, but at 7 Gamla Rådstugugatan in the flat one storey up behind the door on the left-hand side, everyone is awake. Little Sis and I are sitting on a bed in the flat above our own, eating ice cream straight from the tub. A big pack, 2 litres, three flavours. I'll only remember the one I don't want (strawberry).

The bed we're sitting on is in exactly the same spot as Little Sis's bed in the flat below us. In front of us, where Little Bro's bed would be if we were downstairs, is the perfect altar replete with television and video cassette recorder. The woman who lives here – the woman who woke up and called the police when she heard the cries through the floor – has put on a cartoon for us to watch while she sits in the kitchen and talks to our mum.

I can see them from the bed. They're sitting opposite each other at the kitchen table. Mum's crying and the woman who lives here reaches across the table and brushes tears from her cheeks. It looks like they've been friends for a long time, but they haven't. I know them to be strangers and the tenderness seems mysterious to me.

'By the power of Grayskull!' He-Man bellows, and my gaze snaps back to the television. He-Man raises his sword towards the sky. There are flashes of lightning around the sword and He-Man is practically naked. 'I have the power!' he cries, before pointing the sword at his cowardly green pet tiger, which is transformed and becomes brave.

I was the one who chose the video from the tapes on the

shelf. Little Sis offered no objections. She hasn't said a word since she saved Mum – which I know she did since I heard Mum tell her she did.

'You saved me,' she said. She was holding us both in her arms when she said it, but I know the words weren't for me.

Little Sis saved Mum but has nothing to say about it – she's just eating ice cream with her eyes fixed on the screen.

Over and over, my own gaze is torn away from the screen and towards the kitchen and the woman who lives here. The woman who is almost called Harry Brandelius if you say her name quickly. I too once sat at her kitchen table when she found me in the grocery store and brought me home with her. Her body only looks a little older than Mum's, but I assume one of those old souls lives in it.

PART FOUR

The Priest

In which:
a foot needs a plaster cast,
the whole town smells of burnt meat,
and
the devil can be glimpsed in the eyes of others.

He isn't a priest. It's probably just as well we get that out of the way at once so that you don't harbour expectations of an unexpected twist – this story lacks such inclinations. It's only me who thinks he's a priest because he talks about the devil and he wears a fine-knit jumper on top of his shirt so that the collar is only just visible at his throat. And maybe it's because we live next to a church while he's wooing my mum.

But we don't live there yet. We don't live anywhere. We are in motion and it will be some time before we become still and move into the flat where I'll learn that you can see the devil in a person's eyes.

The Saab is heavily laden but there's no camera among our belongings. The camera – the blue-and-yellow plastic one that the Indian gave me – was the first thing I started looking for when Mum told me to pack the essentials, but I couldn't find it. We were in a rush to leave before the Thief was released.

'If I report him then I'll never be rid of him,' she'd said to the old soul in the flat above.

She'd said the same thing to the police, and the police had agreed.

I searched everywhere for the camera, but it was only when I discovered that the guitar was also missing that I realized that the Thief had taken it. He must have been helping himself to something on each visit – I just hadn't noticed until I began to look. I don't mind about the guitar, but it's different with the camera. Mum says I can have a new one, but I'm thinking about what was hiding within the old one.

I suppose the film's been developed by now – either by the Thief or by whoever he sold the camera to. My guess is the latter. Somewhere in the town we're leaving behind there's a stranger hunched over a photographic riddle:

A man mounted on horseback who's so small he looks like a dwarf.

A horse's cock as big as a shin.

A cage big enough to take a person.

A boy in front of a mirror, camera in his hands and a rat on his shoulder.

The camera isn't the only one of our belongings to be missing. We're also down a hamster, but we don't know that yet. We'll only find out when we arrive in Stockholm at our cousins'. The cage is in the boot and Little Sis calls out to our hamsters to tell them they don't have to worry, which she assumes they might do when travelling by car, but only one of the hamsters – the scalped one – can hear her.

As of a few hours ago, Little Sis's hamster resides under a bathtub in Vilbergen, a suburb where we spent the night at the home of one of the many cleaners Mum knows. They sat in the kitchen saying 'bloody men' while we played with our hamsters on the hall floor. Somehow, a hamster got left behind. Not even the woman who lives there knows about it – not yet – but in a few days' time a small chanterelle-coloured head will peek out from underneath the bathtub and peer at her sitting on the toilet.

The sun is setting as we trundle towards the city where Mum's mum and all her siblings are. She's singing 'Moonlight Shadow' to herself, drumming her fingers on the steering wheel. She doesn't know the lyrics and hums most of it.

Little Sis falls asleep. I cross my index and middle fingers and then draw them down my nose. I often do this when my hands need occupying. I'll never cease to be tickled by the illusion of the two noses.

Mum pulls off the motorway and stops in front of a grassy slope. Above the slope rises a huge building, which according to an illuminated sign on the façade is called Stafsjö Wärdshus. When she switches off the engine, I can hear her crying. She stays crying at the wheel for a long time while the motorway roars behind us. You can hear murmuring and clinking from the inn's terrace, but I can't see the people up there – I can only hear that they're there, and I shudder at the thought of all the people on Earth that are somewhere doing something at any given moment.

'For Christ's sake,' Mum says, biting her hands.

I pretend to be asleep.

Everything's exciting at the cousins'. They live in a *fin-de-siècle* apartment by Sankt Eriksplan and everyone has their own room. There are so many rooms and so many cousins that I keep finding new ones. It's like opening doors on an advent calendar – wow, here's another cousin.

The cousins have trendy names and trendy clothes. They have posters of pop stars and the space lizards from the TV series *V*. They have hairdos. Two of them talk on the phone and have breasts.

There's more than one phone, but all the wires seem to be connected somewhere because as soon as someone picks up the receiver in one room you hear a scream from another. The screams are tuned to the dialect spoken by all Swedish children on screen and it makes everything feel like a film. It's the ones with breasts who scream the loudest, and one of them is so beautiful that you can't look at her. You have to look just to the side of her head when talking to her because otherwise you blush.

The oldest boy has muscles – they're clearly visible because he wanders around with his torso bared. I didn't even know that kids could get muscles, but now I know. He's only a few years older than me but the freckled skin on his chest is tensed across two boulders and if you look closely you can see that they're resting atop a tower of stomach muscles like bricks.

His mum says I can sleep in his room. She's already unrolled a sleeping mat and sleeping bag on the floor and I have to strain to conceal my delight from Freckles.

We've fled our town and we're down a hamster, but it's all so exciting here that we forget the awfulness. We squeeze onto the living-room sofa and eat popcorn from big bowls. We watch a film called *Airplane!* and everyone laughs. We watch a film called *Poltergeist* and everyone screams.

'Cover your eyes now, Andrev,' says the most beautiful big cousin as a man enters the bathroom of the haunted house. She says my name as if it's a word like any other and I struggle to breathe. I close my eyes and listen to the echo of her words in my head as those who are looking scream around me.

We go to bed in the middle of the night. I daren't close my eyes after the horror film, but it doesn't matter. I like lying awake on Freckles's floor looking at his belongings. There are dumbbells and a big spring with handles at either end lying by the mirror wall, and there's something white that might be a karate suit hanging from a hook. It's apparent he's a boy with attributes, but I'm not disgusted in the way I am disgusted when Paella draws or Saga plays the piano. After all, the boy who lives here and is master of all this is my cousin. We share blood and somehow his attributes are also my own. I'm a joint owner.

The only thing I don't like about Freckles is that he's got a dad. It feels excessive, somehow, that he gets to have a dad and all these attributes.

The cousins' dad is big but taciturn – bearlike. He's doesn't take charge of the conversation like the Plant Magician used to, but mostly leans back and listens with a sleepy smile. In this family, it's the mum who's in charge and she's the one who talks the most of them all. She's the one they ask for permission when they want to do something and she's the one who shouts at them when they've done something they weren't supposed to. The dad doesn't shout. He's more like a seat for the younger kids.

'Do you want to see the pavement where the prime minister got shot?' Freckles asks me as we're eating breakfast. I do, and I pause for breath to say as much but Auntie beats me to it. She's standing at the hob with her back to the rest of us but she screeches straight at the tiles in front of her.

'Of course he doesn't want to fucking see it!'

Disappointed, I wonder why she's angry. I seek out Mum's gaze but she's still looking down into her bowl. She's chewing muesli as if there was no screech and so are the cousins. It's only Little Sis and I who have shrunk away, our mouths half open and spoons suspended in mid-air.

'Mum, don't swear,' one of the little cousins says without looking up from her plate.

'Shut your face, crotch goblin,' Auntie says, her back still to the table. All the cousins begin to laugh – even the girl who was called a crotch goblin. She's around five years old and has a face that's heavy at the front – all her features slant towards a big, shiny chin. Almost all the cousins have that chin, as does their mother, but none of them have more of it than the girl who was called a crotch goblin. I've already toyed with the thought of cupping a hand over her chin, but I don't know why. I just want to touch it.

'Shut your face, motherfucker,' she replies, the volume of laughter rising.

Little Sis and I stare at each other. We sit up straight and each try out a smile.

It'll be a few days before we learn to talk like the cousins, but the fear is already starting to ebb away. We'll be crude and shrill with each other and it'll feel as if we never lived any other way. By the time we have to leave, we'll feel at home.

'You can still see the blood.' Freckles has leaned in close to my ear and his voice simmers with something secretive.

'What blood?' I say.

'Palme's, innit.'

We go to look at the pavement where the Prime Minister was shot. I won't remember whether we see any blood, but I will remember the flowers and the video shop we go to on the way back.

We rent *Gremlins* and *Beverly Hills Cop*. Freckles has already seen both, but he thinks it's important for me to see them. We also rent a film written down on a scrap of paper by the mums. *White Nights*. Mum and I have already seen it with Little Cloud, but Mum thinks it's important for her sister to see it. It's probably something to do with the ballet man's chest, because I remember Little Cloud purring when he stripped to the waist.

When we return to the apartment on Tomtebogatan, new cousins have emerged from the walls. I can't fathom how there can be so many of them and it will take several more hours for it to dawn on me that Auntie is a childminder.

Only six of the kids are her own; the rest are being minded or are the cousins' friends, who come and go without knocking. You can easily keep track of which kids are members of the household: if she calls one a crotch goblin then it's one of her own.

In the evening, I learn another thing about the cousins' family: the big cousins have another dad. Bear Dad isn't theirs.

This makes me like Freckles even more. I want to stay in his room until the end of time.

During our spell in Stockholm, Mum starts seeing a man. He's a musician and has written a song that's played on the radio all the time. I'll remember the song just fine, since I hate it with painstaking devotion, but I won't even notice that the man who wrote it is seeing my mum.

Only many years later will she tell me. I'll be about to embark on writing a book about my dads and she'll suggest that I include him instead of the Artist or the Thief or the Priest. Preferably instead of all three of them. But I won't count him as one of the dads because the writing has to follow a set of rules and the most important of them will read: a man cannot be counted as one of my dads if he never made me wonder whether I should call him Dad.

And I'll never wonder anything like that about the man who wrote 'ABC' for Anna Book. In order to wonder something like that, you need to see the man for starters. Sight is a basic requirement, but beyond that everything is fluid.

One night at Gamla Rådstugugatan, somewhere in the interval between the Artist and the Thief, I crept into the hallway to listen to the huffing and puffing of one of my classmates' dads. I was going to a Steiner school where all the mums and dads had to help out with the practical stuff, and he was there for a meeting about something practical but then the sun suddenly set and he happened to end up naked on Mum's sofa. I heard him huffing and puffing, but I never wondered whether we'd become a family because he already had one.

I'll never hear any huffing and puffing from the Priest, but I'll still wonder. Or perhaps I'll hope? But you can't hope without wondering.

We return to Norrköping the day before the start of autumn term to stay with Little Cloud while we await a key.

Little Sis wants to go to Vilbergen to look for her hamster. The woman whose flat we left it at hasn't seen it since it peeked out from under her bathtub. She says she tried to coax it out with birdseed. Nothing happened and when she took off the front panel it wasn't there. Little Sis thinks it's escaped into the woods in Vilbergen and we need to find it before winter comes.

'If it's in the woods then no one will be able to find it,' Mum says. 'But it doesn't matter, because hamsters like being in the woods. If it's in the woods it'll be happy now.'

You can tell she's making things up. It probably fell into the drain underneath the bath and died. Or perhaps it lives in the sewers now, lost and unhappy in the great darkness beneath the town and pursued by rats that want to scalp it.

We watch a film with Girl Face and Scary Hand, *Indiana Jones and the Temple of Doom*, but I can see out of the corner of my eye that Little Sis's gaze isn't really fixed to the TV. She's not even watching properly when an evil priest tears someone's heart out of their ribcage. She's not there – she's in the woods.

Little Cloud is sad too. Mum's comforting her in the kitchen. They're talking about Frozen Boy, who's ended up in a fix. I don't catch what kind of fix he's ended up in, but I do hear them say that he takes after his dad.

I glance at Girl Face and wonder whether he's glad that he takes after his mum and ended up on the mums' team, like me. The jaw muscles are crawling about underneath his girlish skin, but I don't know whether it's down to apprehension or exertion. He's clutching a sprung hand strengthener in one hand. My freckly cousin had one like it. It resembles half a pair of secateurs and he squeezes it over and over. I've tried it myself but I didn't manage to squeeze the rubbery handles together until I used both hands.

After a few days, the key we've been waiting for arrives. Mum's got a flat on Plankgatan and we go straight there to take a look. Little Cloud comes with us and test smokes every room.

'The kitchen's too dark,' she says, tapping ash into the sink.

Mum turns on the ceiling light but Little Cloud is already making for the next room. We follow.

'This is going to be your room,' Mum says, groping for the light switch.

There's a click but no light comes on. I look in and see a glowing dot drifting about the room.

'It's too dark in here too,' the glow says. 'There aren't any windows.'

'We've got windows onto the street,' Mum says, heading to the biggest room. 'Just wait until you see the view of the church!'

We follow her but see no church.

'You've only got a view of the cemetery,' says Little Cloud.

Mum shoves her to one side and presses her head to the pane.

'There it is,' she says. 'The Matteus church.'

I tuck my head under Mum's arm and catch a glimpse of a red tower with green copper spires beyond the birches across the street.

'Come on, you can't live here,' Little Cloud says, flicking her thumb against the cigarette filter. Ash falls onto the windowsill and blends into the mottled pattern on the granite.

'It'll be great,' Mum says. 'Won't it?'

She's looking at me now.

I'm looking at the cemetery and at the street below us. I'm trying to remember whether the undead in the film I watched with Little Cloud's sons were able to climb. No, I've never seen the undead climbing and I decide it must be something they can't do.

I also look at the huge expanse of grass between the cemetery and our street. Should an Indian perchance stop by, there will be plenty of room to park the horse.

'It's going to be good,' I say, turning around to look for the aerial socket.

There's a border made from wooden logs hammered into the ground running around the school's sandpit. The border is no higher than the frame around a raised garden bed since its only function is to keep the sand in place, but we give it a new function: we balance on it and wrestle with each other. Whoever falls first has to go to the back of the queue of challengers while the winner remains and gets to call himself the Logmaster.

I'll probably never be the Logmaster, but I sense a chance when Saga, teardrop-shaped and, apart from his piano fingers, just as physically inept as I am, somehow manages to fell Paella just before it's my go.

Paella points accusingly at Saga's feet.

'It's cheating to wear clogs,' he says, but doesn't manage to explain why. His protest is washed away by the hubbub of the school playground and lost in the autumn wind.

Saga is heavyset and steady in those clogs. And he's stock-still, apart from his twitching cheeks. A smile is trying to prise its way across his lips, but he grits his teeth. Victory – his first – has done something to him. His gaze is fiery. And the thought that there's nothing but Saga standing in the way of my own first victory does something to me. For a long moment, we just stand there on the fence with our eyes fiery, lingering in a tense state.

Saga even forgets to narrate what's happening. He should already have said something along the lines of:

'Drunk with confidence, the boy stepped up to measure himself against the Logmaster.'

But he says nothing. The narrator's voice has fallen silent.

Behind us, the others lose patience and start to egg us on. Even Cyclops, with his oxygen-starved voice, chips in.

'Get him!' he yells.

It's not clear who is going to get whom, but it works. I get going. I slide forward with my front foot but not to catch him; I just want to confuse him and tempt him to do something with his arms because I've seen how unsteady he gets when they're not hanging limply at his sides. And there's no immediate danger posed by putting a foot within his reach – the rules don't allow kicking and Saga doesn't have the necessary balance to grab the leg with his piano fingers.

He doesn't move, but the smile deepens.

'The Logmaster could not help but pity the boy who blundered into his shadow.'

This is what he would have said if he were himself, but he isn't. He's become someone else. A ring-bearer. Poisoned, greedy and vigilant.

The crowd groans in boredom. I slide a little further forward on my front foot and it's probably starting to look like I'm trying to do the splits. The stripes of my cords are smoothed out across my thighs, and the crotch creaks. The hat that Mum knitted for me using vegetable-dyed wool – in three shades of autumn leaves – has started to itch on my forehead, but doing anything about that right now is out of the question.

Saga's gaze falls to my fumbling foot before jerking back up again. His upper body sways, his arms extend, his jacket lifts up and his belly is bared.

Saga isn't as knitted as I am. He's unfashionable in a different way. He inherited his quilted jacket from a brother who is so many years older than him that he's already moved away from home to become a lumberjack in Canada, and the synthetic lustre has been lost after a thousand washes. And while he may be wearing jeans, they're too dark a shade of blue for our era. And too high at the waist. He's wearing them like a mum – pulled up over his navel and fastened with a braided leather belt done up so tightly that the loops press into the soft flesh between his hips and ribs.

'Do something!' Paella shouts. He's at the back of the queue of challengers and I suppose he's started to worry that we're going to be called inside from our lunch break before he makes it back onto the logs to ensure he's not the only person to lose to Saga.

'Come on, you stupid twat!' Mouse shouts, having caught sight of his chance to be Paella's sidekick and friend.

I do nothing. I just stand there and wait for Saga's fall. It's close now. His gaze has dropped back down to the logs and this time he hasn't managed to jerk it back up again. He's cut contact with the rest of the world in order to wrestle with himself.

The hope of victory makes way for a new thought: if we're called in immediately after Saga's fall, then I'll get to be Logmaster in the classroom for a whole hour. For the first time since one of the girls in the class yanked open the bathroom door, I'm going to be someone other than the boy who poos like an Indian and has nosebleeds every day. I'm going to be a boy with an attribute.

It's a shame that it has to be at Saga's expense. He was the only one to come to my defence after the revelation that I do my poos with my feet perched on the toilet seat. He proclaimed that he too would start to do his poos like an Indian. He's a good friend. But he's already got his piano fingers. I don't have fingers of any kind. I need this more than he does, and now is when I take my chance.

'No,' Saga says, as if my thoughts have somehow leaked out and reached him standing there flailing.

And he makes his first and last move. He raises a clog and kicks my foot.

I arrive at school the next day on crutches. My foot is in plaster and everyone wants to take a look. They look at the broken foot as if it is an attribute, and the girls draw small hearts on the cast. Paella draws a sword, but the lines don't come out straight on the bumpy surface. It looks like a rubbish sword and Cyclops says as much.

'What a rubbish sword,' he says, pointing to Paella's drawing.

It's a good day.

The next day isn't as good. The drawings have become smudged. They should have used felt-tip pens or ballpoint, but those kinds of implements aren't allowed at our Steiner school. All the small hearts were drawn on with crayons and Paella's sword was drawn on with a pencil. The plaster looks like crap and no one wants to look at it.

But I'm no longer the boy who poos like an Indian – it's impossible for me to climb onto the seat with my cast.

He's got a Saab just like Mum, although his is silver and modern. Well drawn. And fast – you can tell by the black strip running along the chassis at the same height as the bumpers.

I'm standing on my crutches leaning forward and surveying the car from the window. It's been carelessly parked on Plankgatan. I think it looks like the car from *Back to the Future*. Not that it really does, but at any rate I've never seen a car that was a better likeness to the car from *Back to the Future*. It looks like a time machine and I want to sit inside it.

The driver's door is open. He's got one leg out and there's a hand resting against the thigh, but that's it. The weight of his body is still in the car and I can't even see his head. I've never seen it. But now I see the other hand. It grasps the rearview mirror and twists it. He appears to be examining his own reflection. The hand on the thigh disappears from view up towards the head that I've still never seen.

Mum's seen it. That much I'm sure of, because I heard when she rang him to ask if she could borrow five hundred kronor, which is hardly the kind of call you make to heads that you've never seen.

It only took him about half an hour to turn up honking in his time machine. Now Mum is on her way downstairs to get the five hundred kronor.

We're hard up again. Mum's stopped cleaning at the health farm because she doesn't want to go anywhere that the Thief knows she can usually be found. Not now. She wants to lie low but the health farm is high up. We live behind a front door with someone else's last name on the plaque. We're on the dole. The TV is at the pawnbroker's next to the Palace nightclub. We barely exist.

The main door slams. The man gets out of the time machine and holds out his arms. It's an ugly head. It has a moustache. It has glasses. But he's well dressed. The trousers have a crease and at his throat there's a glimpse of a white collar beneath the fine-knit jumper.

Is he a priest? That thought evaporates when I see the five-hundred-krona note being pressed into Mum's hand, but it will be thought again.

We're sitting inside a cavern of leaves beneath the lilacs when Paella opens up like a secret box.

'If you had to shag one of our mums, whose mum would you do it with?'

He grins mischievously and shifts his gaze between us to indicate that the question is directed at all of us.

Cyclops immediately flushes red and his eyes start to flutter. Mouse clenches both his fists in front of his face and emits a low whimper that's reminiscent of the sound you have to make when you take a closer look at a dead animal in the woods and realize there are worms crawling through the flesh. I make the same sound, although I'm not quite sure what it's supposed to mean.

Saga is the only one to answer without blushing or hesitation.

'Mine,' he says.

We roar with laughter. A forbidden answer to a forbidden question. Layer upon layer of forbidden, but Saga keeps a straight face.

'Seriously,' he says. 'You've seen my mum.'

He's got a point. She is remarkable: an Italian demigoddess with big eyes, big breasts and big hair. She has an almost filmic air. What's more, she smells good. She once hugged me at the celebration to mark the last day of school and the smell came home with me. When it was time to go to sleep, it hovered above the bed in the darkness like a ghost.

'I don't know how my dad was able to get her,' Saga says, scoring another point.

His dad is ordinary: a quiet chiropractor who – unlike Cyclops – actually only has one eye following a macabre fishing accident in his youth. The eye was ripped out of its socket by a friend with a casting rod and once you've heard the story it's impossible to step into the hallway of Saga's house without your sphincter tightening. You rarely see him, but you can tell that he's there, upstairs, with his enamel eye.

'I'll have your mum too,' Mouse says.

'Me too,' says Paella.

I find this development insulting. It's too easy. I glance at Cyclops, who at least seems to have the tactfulness to think it over.

Everyone in the leaf cavern knows that it's between Saga's mum and mine. They must know. Cyclops's mum might be unusually kind, but she has grey hair and saggy breasts. The toil of bringing five sons into the world has made her a solitary pine by the sea. And Mouse's mum is fat.

My mum's beautiful. I'm sure of it. It's only me who knows that her red hair is actually mousy. But she doesn't look nearly as expensive as Saga's mum. She's no premium woman. Besides, she worked in the school canteen for a while, and everyone knows it. That's probably why it's so easy for them to choose. There can't be anything filmic about a dinner lady.

I want to choose my own mum, but I can't. When Saga chose his own, he was simply bowing to circumstance. It was a sensible move. If I choose my own then I'll lay bare something grotesque. So I choose Saga's and that leaves just Cyclops.

'I'll have his,' Cyclops says, nodding towards me.

I scrunch up my face in appropriate horror while it dawns on me that he's my best friend.

One day I ask Mum why the Indian left us. Well, it's not really me who does the asking – it's Little Sis. I could never ask something like that and I cast my gaze out of the side window as soon as I realize what her reckless little mouth is up to.

We're at the roundabout where the cars off Norra Promenaden rumble onto Ståthögavägen and I'm staring towards the railway yard where two boys burned to death when they climbed on top of the goods wagons. I hear Mum's hands kneading the steering wheel. She puts off answering, but at last it comes, somewhere in the dark beneath the railway bridge.

'It's complicated,' she says.

'What does that mean?' Little Sis says.

'Difficult,' Mum says.

He's in the kitchen. I'm standing in my bedroom doorway listening. He's come as a surprise. He rang the doorbell without any warning and rustled a bag of buns until Mum invited him in. I heard hesitation in her voice. I can still hear it, even though her mouth is filled with bun.

She says he'll get his five hundred kronor. He says there's no rush and that she doesn't even need to give him his five hundred kronor anyway.

'I don't need it,' he says.

Rich words.

She says he's kind, but that he'll definitely have it next week. I wonder how that's going to work out, since we still don't have any money and there's nothing to suggest we'll have any more in a week's time. Anything that can be pawned is already at the pawnbroker's. Even the knitting machine, which I hope will stay there.

He tries to change the subject, but he's not very good at it. He seems to be the kind of person who has to look around for things to talk about. Every silence is broken by an observation. He spots an old set of Husqvarna scales and asks whether they're made by Husqvarna. They are. He spots the old cabinet stripped of paint and asks if it's old. It is.

His voice is gentle and pleasant, but he lacks a way with words. Nothing he says makes her laugh more than necessary, which is a pity because I want her to like him. I'd also like some five-hundred-krona notes that he doesn't need. I'd like to be dropped off at the school gate in a car that looks like a time machine.

I press the backs of my hands hard against the door frame and count to twenty. I step into the hall and feel my arms rising by themselves. I didn't know whether it would work with crutches in my hands, but it does. My body floats towards the ceiling and a crutch strikes the small table with the telephone on it.

'Come and have a bun,' Mum calls out.

I come. He looks at me.

'You've got a broken leg.'

Yet another observation.

'One of his friends kicked him with a clog,' Mum says.

She laughs as she says it, but the laugh isn't infectious.

'Not much of a friend,' he says.

'No,' I say. 'He's a rubbish friend.'

They look at me. Him with pity, her with a puzzled and mistrustful smile. I set aside the crutches and sit down at the table. There's a bun ring that's already been cut into lying on the laminated surface. He cuts a piece for me that's so big there's an inside curve, and we exchange grins while Mum goes to fetch a glass of milk.

He's got pearl sugar in his moustache. I stare at the pearls until he combs them away with curved fingers. There's nothing else I can do for him. His hair is mad. He has a bowl cut but the bowl is as shallow as a plate and tilted backwards. It's so high that you could fit at least two fingers between the edge of the bowl and his ears.

The hair looks removable – like Lego hair.

They sit quietly and watch me as I wash the first bite down. The dull gurgling from my throat doesn't seem to bother him, so I wash the second one down too. I love to wash food down – to avoid the discomfort as the food grows in my mouth. If I'd done this in front of the Plant Magician then the slap would have come flying by now, but this man doesn't have any slaps in his back pocket. You can tell by looking at him. I wash my third bite down and his breathing doesn't even intensify.

Mum is scratching her arms. She's restless. He hasn't noticed, but I have. There's an uneasy energy in the kitchen and it's coming from her. She's the one leaking. Someone has to say something.

'What car do you have?'

'I've got a Saab nine thousand.'

Goosebumps form on my skin. I take another bite and silently count. I wash it down and conclude that his Saab must be about a hundred times more modern than our ninety-five.

'Would you like to see it?'

'I've already seen it.'

'Oh, you have, have you?'

'But I could take another look.'

We go to the living-room window and gaze out over the Dr Westerlund geraniums. Mum stays in the kitchen.

He says:

'By the way, do you know why this street is called Plankgatan?'

I don't.

'Once upon a time this was where Norrköping stopped.' He points, drawing a line along the join between the asphalt and the grass. 'Right here is where the city limits were. So perhaps you can guess how Plankgatan got its name?'

I can't. He smiles and points towards Folkparken.

'There was nothing but wilderness out there, and in those days that was dangerous. So what do you think they had down here where the town stopped?'

I take a guess:

'A cliff?'

We're having our pictures taken for the school yearbook and I take care to position myself next to her. We're standing in the centre of the middle row, behind the people sitting down and in front of the ones standing on a bench. I extend my arm slightly and place my right hand immediately behind her left hand to make it look like we're holding hands.

We belong together. She is unfortunately still unaware of this, but my thinking is that she'll find out when she leafs through the yearbook and sees how good we look together. Or that someone else will spot that we're holding hands and laugh at us – that's probably the more likely outcome and probably the best one. Before long, the whole class would be laughing at us and we would deny everything while being bonded together by their malice.

It's a high-stakes game, but I have to do something about her indifference before the boys with attributes realize she's the best-looking girl in the class. So far, I seem to be the only one who sees it.

Cyclops, Mouse and Paella think Cecilia is the best-looking girl, but that's only because she's blonde and wears jumpers with prints and is tanned all year round. And because she's called Cecilia, which is what good-looking girls are usually called.

Saga thinks Patrizia is the best-looking, but that's only because she looks like his mum and her hair's always nice because her mum's a hairdresser.

They're not looking closely.

If you look closely, you can see that Single Mum's Daughter is the best-looking. She wears joggers and has a DIY hairdo without any spray, but there's something there beneath the transience. The lines are incredible. It's just that she's been badly tinted.

The others are going to find out any time now, but I'm still the only one who knows. It's as if there's a real diamond ring in one of those vending machines you insert a one-krona coin into before turning the wheel to get a plastic trinket. I can see it in there but I don't have a krona. And I'm almost in a state of panic at the thought that Paella might realize. That's why I have to take a chance.

When the yearbook arrives, I'm afraid to look at first. I'm sitting at the kitchen table with Mum's head hovering over my shoulder. I didn't think it through this far. I didn't think about the fact that mums would also see it. I flip through haphazardly, but in the end I have to find the right page.

'Gosh,' she says when she spots me. 'You look . . . afraid?'

I really do.

Single Mum's Daughter doesn't look afraid. She's smiling softly and is so good-looking that she looks like a figment of the imagination. But the boy beside her is true to life and clearly panic-stricken. He's the only one not looking into the camera. His gaze has been dragged towards Single Mum's Daughter, but it's drifting towards a spot far beyond her.

Our hands aren't visible – there's a head in the way. The boy sitting in front of us is the smallest in the class, but he still manages to obscure the reason for my haunted expression.

With my free hand, I crush his little head between my thumb and forefinger. My other one is busy pinching my nose. I decide to try again next year. A drop of blood falls onto the yearbook and Mum's had enough.

I can see Saga's black-and-green wooden palace down on Kneippgatan as we walk from the number three bus stop to the medical centre in Kneippen. Each time I see it, I wish it was mine. Everything inside it too. I want Saga's life – the whole package. The mum, the dad, the palace, the piano fingers. But all I can have is a nose that doesn't bleed.

'This is going to be horribly painful,' the doctor says.

He grins. It was a joke.

'It'll only sting a little,' he says, and we all laugh before he shoves the soldering iron up my nose to kill off the leaky blood vessels.

It's horribly painful and on the way home the whole town smells of burnt meat.

Now he's in the kitchen again. Lying on the table are three glistening vanilla buns and a five-hundred-krona note no one wants to touch.

The coffee maker clears its throat as the last of the water drips into the jug and I wonder whether this is the last time he's going to be in our kitchen. She doesn't want him there. I know that for sure now because I've heard her lie that she's busy when he calls. It's only when he turns up unannounced and rustles bags from the bakery down on Kungsgatan that she has time to see him.

I don't understand. If anyone can have her – even a thief – then why not give herself to a man with pockets stuffed with five-hundred-krona notes?

His moustache is glistening, but he doesn't notice me staring. He's made a new observation. There's a stack of magazines on the kitchen worktop and on top are several old issues of *Okej* that Little Cloud brought with her one day. They used to belong to her sons and now they belong to me. They're mostly about music I haven't heard, but they're also about TV shows and films I haven't seen.

He looks at the magazine on top and whistles, before standing up and taking it from the stack. Now it's on the kitchen table.

Issue 10, 1985. 11.80 including VAT. The singer from Twisted Sister is on the cover. Inflammable hair, lipstick, a full set of teeth bared in a manic grin.

'I think you can see the devil in his eyes,' he says, tapping a fingertip on the magazine. 'Don't you think so?' he says, looking at Mum. 'You can see the devil in there, can't you?'

He rotates the magazine and Mum takes a look.

'Well, perhaps,' she says vaguely.

I've had a hunch, but now I'm suddenly sure of it. He's a priest. He wears a different jumper each time I see him, but always with the same white collar protruding at his throat. And his voice is as gentle as steam. He's a priest and that's why she doesn't want him. Mum likes being naked with men – I've seen it with my own eyes – and priests aren't allowed to be naked just any old way. I've read that somewhere.

I lean over the magazine and fix my gaze on the kohl-lined gaze of Dee Snider. It's wild and now I'm sure of it.

'Yes,' I say. 'I can see it now. I can see the devil in his eyes.'

The Priest starts to flip through the magazine and I see the devil everywhere.

'He's got the devil in his eyes too,' I say, pointing. 'And him. And her!'

The Priest and I find the devil in all sorts of eyes. Mötley Crüe's Vince Neil has so much devil in his eyes that we recoil. Mum is scratching her arms. The impromptu witch trial seems to have made her ill at ease. She's probably afraid that we'll see the devil in her eyes too.

I eat my vanilla bun and point at devil eyes. I lean in closer to the Priest so that I can see properly. He puts an arm on the back of my chair while continuing to turn the pages with the other. I wonder how it looks from Mum's side of the table. Does it look like we belong together?

When it's time for the Priest to leave, Mum goes downstairs with him. She's gone for a long time and I go to the window. They're standing in the street, talking. The Priest is drooping. She gives him a hug before he gets into the time machine and disappears.

I'll never see him again.

Mum gets a loan from the bank. Ten thousand kronor. Granny put up her cottage on Väddö as collateral. It's a secret. We're not allowed to talk about it with the cousins because it might put Mum's sisters in a bad mood.

The loan isn't for anything big or particular. The car trundles along.

'I'm just sick to the back teeth of not having any cash,' Mum says.

She told Granny something else when they were talking on the phone, but she tells me the truth.

'I need to breathe.'

It's just her and me the day the money becomes hers. My hands start to tremble when I see the notes emerge from the slot in the cash machine on Drottninggatan.

'We're rich,' I say.

Mum laughs. She's so happy. She's got springs in her feet and her hair bobs up and down. I have to jog to keep up with her as we make for the shops in the town centre.

Domus. Linden. Spiralen.

We're there for hours. I get a jacket. Mum gets scarves and a dress from Indiska. We stay at Indiska for a long time because it's Mum's favourite place in the whole world. Me and my siblings hate Indiska – there's nothing more boring than shifting your weight from foot to foot, your skull filled with incense, while Mum groans in the fitting cubicle – but today that doesn't bother me. I've got a jacket that no one has worn before me and soon we're going to a Chinese restaurant. I've never been to a Chinese restaurant. Nor has she.

She'll be dogged by that loan for years to come, but right now she's free and I have her to myself. On the way home, we're going to stop off at the pawnbroker's to pick up the TV.

PART FIVE

The Murderer

In which:
cheese becomes stained,
the first kiss is kissed,
and
the dead resemble jewellery.

Eighteen-thirty-six-twelve. There's a particular melody to Cyclops's phone number. It will be a long time before I discover that it's mathematical, but I already like humming it. And dialling it.

'Meet you at the park?'

'Okay.'

There's no melody to Saga's number, but it sticks in your head anyway because it's so simple – like the number for a government agency.

Ten-twenty-ninety. But he's got to do piano practice.

'See you tomorrow morning.'

We live on respective edges of Folkparken. I'm in the six-storey building along the eastern edge, Cyclops lives in one of the small houses along the northern fringe, and Saga lives in the huge and remarkable wooden castle with dragon-scale wall panels down by the river to the south. If we set off from home at the same time, we converge somewhere around the crematorium. But since Saga is busy with his attributes, I call Cyclops back and set a new course for him. We're to meet by the fountain behind the fast-food stand at the northern end of Krematorievägen.

On this particular morning, the entire fountain is buried under a meringue of foam. A park keeper is attacking the meringue with a shovel while another watches and talks to an overwrought pensioner. I hear them say that it's the bloody kids who've poured washing-up liquid into the water and I am unpleasantly affected by the fact that there are bloody kids who have thoughts that grand. I would never have come up with it myself.

Cyclops is already sitting on a bench watching the desperate shovelling. He's easy to spot because his hair is practically white and is as thick as wool. It doesn't hang down – it just grows straight out of his head and makes him look like one of those rag dolls that every Steiner kid has at home.

I sit down next to him. I rattle my crutches and say that someone has poured washing-up liquid into the water.

'How do you know?'

'Look at the foam and you'll see.'

'Will I?'

'Yes. But I guess you don't see so good.'

Cyclops squints towards the fountain. He always squints. The tape that used to cover one of the two windows on his glasses has been taken away, but the light being let in by two openings combined is still only equivalent to having one eye. It's as if the world is too bright for him. Or as if he's squinting out of fear that his power might get out again?

Cyclops has a peculiar gift: he's able to stare accidents into being. Before his family moved to Norrköping, they lived in a forest somewhere up north. There was a military airbase in the forest and Cyclops used to wander across a meadow to stare up into the sky while the fighter pilots did aerial combat exercises. One day he saw two planes crash into each other. The pilots had to eject and their planes crashed into the forest.

Around a year later, Cyclops's family moved to Norrköping. Here there were no planes to stare at, so he went and stood on a patch of grass by the spot where the tram tracks intersect with the E4 trunk road and stared at cars instead. A man in a Saab stared back, Cyclops waved, the man in the Saab rear-ended a lorry and then crawled out onto the asphalt to be sick. Cyclops went home and doubtless wondered whether he ought to stop staring at vehicles, but a few days later he was back at the same intersection – on a walk with his dad and Ronja, the family dog – and he stared again. Ronja escaped from his dad's grip so that she could chase an articulated lorry and then his dad had to go onto the E4 to gather up the dog in a plastic bag.

These days, Cyclops only stares at things without engines, but someone probably ought to warn that park keeper before he cuts his own throat with his shovel.

'We got the school yearbook on Friday,' Cyclops says without releasing the man under potential sentence of death from his gaze. 'Have you seen it?'

I have.

'You looked weird,' he says. 'What were you looking at?'

'I don't know.' I laugh. 'You looked weird too.'

'Didn't I look like I always do?'

'Yes.'

The sun emerges from behind the clouds. Cyclops inserts his fingers beneath the windows of his glasses and rubs his eyes. As he rubs, he says that I was standing next to Single Mum's Daughter.

'Was I?'

'Yes, you were. It looked like you were holding hands.'

I've underestimated the acuity of his gaze. I can't make up my mind whether to confirm or deny the observation, so instead I change tack.

'Who were you standing next to?'

Cyclops falls silent briefly. He scratches at a dried milk stain on his velour jumper. 'I don't remember.'

The park keeper is still alive when we leave. We drift around the park until it's getting dark and a cold, foreign wind gusts in from the Stockholm roundabout. The streetlights come on, we part ways and I hurry home. I'm not supposed to run in my cast, but my foot no longer hurts so I run anyway. There are three cemeteries and a prison in the park – no matter which way you go, you're always in proximity to graves or murderers.

It turns to winter. Christmas with Little Cloud and the February sports half-term holiday without any sport. Mum gets a call from Stockholm and cries after ringing off. I ask why she's sad and she says that someone is dead but that she's actually happy.

It turns to spring. Easter with the cousins and *Over the Top* with Sylvester Stallone at the cinema where Palme saw his last film. Hair grows in armpits. A burial for a hamster in hard earth. It turns to summer and with it comes a new dad.

His hands are dirty, although not like the Artist's or the Plant Magician's. There are no colours in the stains, they're just black. He rubs his hands with a rag and turpentine but the blackness won't go – it merely thins to a membrane drawn over a stringy pattern of more concentrated blackness. He chucks the rag over the handlebars of a motorcycle and extends one of his hands. My hand disappears into it and he says his name.

It's a strange thing to do – taking the time to clamber out of the inspection pit and wiping his hands to greet the cleaner's son.

He's big and smells good in that poisonous kind of way a petrol station does. I can smell it when he's up close, but why is he up close? What am I supposed to do with his ridiculous name?

I retreat into the office adjacent to the garage. He stretches and glances over my head.

'I said you can forget about the windows,' he calls out.

'But you can't even see through them,' Mum calls out in reply.

'There's nothing out there to see,' he calls back.

That's true in its own way – outside there's nothing but drab industrial lots with hangars and cisterns, but Mum keeps on cleaning the window and now she's laughing too. This is her new place of work. Well, one of them. She comes and goes in the Saab, cleaning different buildings.

School's closed today even though it's a Thursday. I'm not sure why – something to do with Jesus. We didn't want to stay at home without Mum, so we came with her. We're regretting that now. It's boring in the office and we're not allowed in the garage because Mum's afraid that we'll get up to mischief with the welding torches and blind ourselves. And we're not allowed to go outside because Mum's heard that the ground on Händelö island is contaminated with heavy metals.

We promised not to eat the ground, but that didn't help. She's afraid of all poisons – except perhaps for the poisons in Little Cloud's cloud.

Little Bro is lying under the desk and making noises. Little Sis is sitting on an office chair at the same desk chaining paper clips together. Hanging on the wall behind the desk are five calendars that I'm careful not to look at. Each calendar features a picture of a naked girl. One of them is washing a car bonnet with a lathered-up sponge. Another is washing herself with a lathered-up sponge. The rest of the girls appear to have completed their duties because they're just lying around and resting on various vehicles.

I'm not exactly sure what the men who work here do, but one thing is for sure: they're meticulous about keeping track of the date.

The man with the black hands enters the office and crouches beside a small fridge, the door of which is discoloured around the handle. The fridge rattles when he opens it.

'Do you like fizzy drinks?'

We do. He lets us choose a bottle each and I reach for a Loranga before Mum reminds us that we're only allowed to drink the see-through ones.

'No colouring agents,' she calls out.

Her voice is distant now. I look up and meet her gaze through the windowpane. She's perched on the windowsill, leaning out to one side with a cloth in her hand. Only her legs are still in the office.

The man stands up and takes a few quick steps. He puts his dirty hands on her jeans-clad thighs.

'Can't have you falling out,' he says.

It's a strange thing to say. The office is on the ground floor. The thistles growing along the wall are slumped against the window ledges, possibly weakened by boredom and heavy metals.

Mum laughs. She's laughing more than necessary and this time while she laughs she glances at me again. This time the look is over in a flash, but I manage to see it. It's the childish look of someone caught in the act. I've never received it from Mum before, but I still recognize it. I've seen it in the school playground. It's the kind of look you get when you're approaching a cluster of whispers. The kind that knows more than the look it gets in return. I don't like it.

There's a sofa in the office and I steer a course towards it. On the floor beside the sofa there's a stack of magazines. It's not until I start digging into the stack that I discover it's a minefield. *Classic bike, Classic racer, Private, Automobil, Cats, Trailer, På väg, FIB-aktuellt.*

I hurry past every cover that interests me, lingering on the boring ones but not really looking at any of them. Not really. My attention is fixed on the man with the dirty hands. He wants to be close to her. She's dodging him, but there's a revealing clumsiness to her movements. Something is going on and it can't have started now – it must have started another day, and it's already high time to wonder what sort of man he is.

He's got wavy, combed-back hair. His hair curling with sweat at his neck. The curls look friendly, but everything else is thick. Thick arms, thick neck, thick gold chain around his wrist. And his belly is so fat it's hanging in a fold over his waistband. Gold and grease and dirt. It's hard to tell whether he's rich or poor, but at least he's rich enough to have the gold on his arm rather than at the pawnbroker's.

There might be five-hundred-krona notes in his pockets. That might mean a TV and a VCR.

I make an attempt to like him, but my body resists. It doesn't want to.

In just two months' time we'll be living under the same roof and I'll try again, but my body will still resist each time. Not even when he gives me a fish tank full of fish will my body agree to like him. It will be on its guard from the very first to the very last moment. And once the fish are dead, it'll whisper: Told you so.

I'm inside a denim-blue Volkswagen minibus. Somewhere behind me, Mum and the man with the dirty hands have made up their minds to look for a flat that'll fit us all in, but I still don't know anything about that. I'm heading north for Dalarna. I'm going with Cyclops's family to their cabin in Säter.

Cyclops's dad sticks to the low gears when going uphill because the minibus is too heavily loaded. Six children, two grown-ups, one cat, one roof box and luggage to last the summer. He's playing Dire Straits on the stereo; it plunges you into melancholy and makes you look down at the floor because if you look out of the window it's like an overwhelming music video.

Each time he's finished a Dire Straits cassette, he agrees to play a song we want to hear. It's the same song each time: Europe's 'The Final Countdown'. He plays it at Steiner volume, but it still titillates. It's insane that a song can be that good. When we left Norrköping, I'd never heard it but I didn't let on. It's easy to sing along to the chorus and I'm not going to let the world know that I'm less familiar with its timbre than Cyclops's voluntarily TV-less family.

We stop at a picnic area, pee into Lake Mälaren and eat moist sandwiches wrapped in foil. A child vomits over Cyclops's mum and his dad climbs up to the roof box to get a clean top. Cyclops's cheeks turn blotchy and he turns away. One day – many years later – he will tell me that he was ashamed that they had clothes in a roof box made for skis, but right now it just looks like he needs another wee.

He clambers down to the shore. I follow. He stands broad-legged and pees air. I stand next to him and we watch a flotilla of Optimist dinghies. Beneath each sail there is a child, luminescent in their life jacket. They're moving so slowly through the glitter that they appear to be at a standstill. Cyclops lowers his calamitous gaze to the water's edge. After all, they're only kids.

I'm sitting on the big rock next to the boathouse reeling in a perch out of the darkness. It's too small really, but it's the first of the day and the first can never be reprieved. I pry the hook free, press a thumb into the tight mouth and push backwards until the gills burst into bloom like a red-and-white flower and I keep on going until the flower has stopped vibrating. Just like the Plant Magician taught me.

I ready myself to throw the perch towards the woods, but stop myself and hold it up to the sky. I put down the fishing rod and using my free hand I pinch the folded dorsal fin and unfurl it.

It's a stupid thing to do. It's easy to kill a perch as long as you don't remind yourself how beautiful it was when it was alive.

When I return from the summer holidays in Säter, they've moved in together. We live in Oxelbergen now, on the fourth floor of a brick-built block of flats in a shade of hedgehog-mushroom yellow at the intersection of a narrow street called Kungsladugatan and a big, curving street called Storsvängen. If you follow Storsvängen for three minutes then you reach Oxelbergsparken, where there are chimneys sticking out of the rocky outcrop.

'Although they're probably not chimneys,' Mum says. 'I think it's ventilation for the underground shelters down there. The whole outcrop's hollow.'

I wonder what an underground shelter is.

'That's where we have to live if war breaks out,' she says. 'But it won't. Not here.'

'Are there beds in there?'

'I expect so.'

'How many?'

'Maybe a thousand.'

'Is there a TV?'

'I don't think so.'

She wants to show us the playground, but I deviate towards a grey-and-blue lattice door built into the rock wall. The door is guarded by brushwood and shrubs with small barbs that catch my trouser legs. 'No unauthorized access' it says on the pale yellow metal sign. I try to gain access but the door is locked. Buried under a bush in another park are hundreds of keys and I wonder whether one of them might unlock the rock. If this is an outcrop you want to unlock, that is.

I place my forehead against the lattice and see a dark concrete corridor with walls covered in streaks. The space is only a few metres in depth, but once my eyes have adjusted to the dark I glimpse a niche in the wall in the far left-hand corner. I place my cheek against the lattice and listen for a while before realizing that it's a trap. The silence is as terrifying as the thought that I might hear something, and now there's no going back. I've listened to the outcrop and I'm doomed to sleep restlessly for as long as we live near by.

That night I don't even try – I just lie there hidden in the cocoon of the duvet until I'm sure that everyone else has fallen asleep before padding across the hallway, pillow under my arm.

I stand idly at Mum's feet for a while. She'll wake up – she always does, because she's as easily woken as a prey animal. It has to be done quickly. If I'm still moving when she opens her eyes then she'll only get up and pilot me back to my own bed. But if I'm already lying there – small and settled – so she's unsure how long I've been lying there and thinks I've already fallen asleep, then it might work. She can't manage a sleeping child of my size. I've become too heavy for her.

I take a deep breath and then wriggle into the gap between Mum and the other body. It's some good wriggling. It only takes two or three seconds for me to be lying there as if I'd never been doing anything else. She touches me and whispers my name, but I don't answer. I've already gone back to sleep. Unfortunately. This is just the way it is. She sighs and goes back to being still.

I can still hear the rumbling silence of the outcrop from Oxelbergsparken. And from elsewhere too. Beneath the visible, all the world's hidden voids are connected. The outcrop is using the sewers as organ pipes to reach the whole town, but

I'm out of reach now. In Mum's bed, where not even the dark can keep me awake.

I'm about to drift off for real when my luck turns. The other body comes rolling into the gap that I conquered. Skin contact follows. His chubby upper arm folds over my shoulder like warm dough. I twist towards Mum to get away, but the shoulder is wedged under his weight. The movement makes him grunt and something falls onto my thigh. A dirty hand.

The dirt isn't visible in the dark, but I know it's there. Everything he touches becomes dirty. Grey fingerprints on door frames and mugs, grey fingerprints on the cheese in the fridge. Shadows in the milky puddle in the soap dish in the bathroom and shadows on the towel hanging next to mine.

I make a new attempt to free myself. This time he wakes up and sits up. There's a cavity in the mattress around his bum and I have to stiffen my body to avoid sliding into it.

He touches me and whispers my name, but I don't answer. I've already gone back to sleep. Unfortunately. This is just the way it is.

He sighs and gets out of bed. For a moment, I think he's going to leave the room. It's a good moment, but it ends when he leans in close and pushes his dirty hands beneath me. A warm, pungent breeze strikes my face. He drinks booze mixed with orange juice in the evening, but by now there's no fruit left on his breath.

I make myself heavy but it doesn't help. He's like a forklift and soon I'm floating through the hall.

I'm still asleep. I dangle an arm to emphasize this. It would be embarrassing for us both if I woke up in his arms – after all, we don't know each other. We must be spared the shame.

And for that matter, I realize that I don't hate being carried as he walks sideways to make sure I don't hit my head on the frame of my bedroom door. There's a tenderness in that movement – the cautious sideways steps – which makes me wonder what would happen if I hugged him. Obviously not consciously, but in my sleep. I can't help what my arms do when my head is asleep. They might reach out for his neck as he's laying me down in bed.

But they do nothing. Not until he's left the room do they begin to move. They reach for the bedside lamp that he switched off and turn it on again. They tuck the duvet under my body and pull it over my head. They build a cocoon leaving only a narrow tunnel through which to breathe.

'Daddy's going to drive you to school,' he says, and begins to gobble with laughter. He calls himself Daddy almost every day, but it's some kind of joke because he laughs every time.

Sometimes he does it with Mum too. 'Come to Daddy,' he says, pulling her down onto his lap before they both laugh. I don't understand what's funny, but I'm at pains to laugh because otherwise it's as if they have a secret club with its own language, and I don't like that.

He drives an old Mercedes. It's an inedible shade of green, like the sun-bleached velvet on the armrest of an old person's sofa, the one that's closest to the window. But shinier. Perhaps it's more like a green russula after it's rained. At any rate, it's ugly. It's very different from the car from *Back to the Future*. But he drives it as if it were remarkable and sometimes he steers with a single finger.

We hit a red at a pedestrian crossing on Östra Promenaden. He partly winds down his window and makes a strange sound: a series of sighs sucked backwards using his tongue against his palate as if enticing a small furry animal. I lean forward towards the dashboard, but I can't see any furry animals crossing the road. There are just two teenage girls who have already made it over and a few metres behind them there's an out-of-breath boy holding hands with his mum on one side and his dad on the other.

My gaze is fixed on the dad, whose gaze has become fixed on me. It's the Artist.

He's got a Salomon rucksack slung over his shoulder. It's too little to be his own. I wonder whether to say hello, but don't have to make up my mind because he averts his gaze from me and looks at the man behind the wheel instead. Not closely – only for a second or so – but it's enough for me to be asked whether it was someone I knew.

'Mum knows him,' I say. 'He's an artist.'

He puts both his hands on the steering wheel. 'Well, he looked like a bit of a poofter.'

'He's not very good at drawing,' I say.

'Doesn't mean you can't be a poof,' he says.

I nod.

'But maybe you've seen him kiss girls?'

I have.

'Maybe you've seen him kiss your mum?'

I've seen more than that and my cheeks grow hot at the thought of it. 'It was a long time ago,' I say.

He looks at me. 'But you saw it?'

I nod.

'And how old are you?'

'I'm eleven.'

'Then it can't be that long ago.'

We're crossing Hamnbron bridge now. The cranes are standing down by the water like prehistoric animals. The Murderer – who hasn't as yet committed murder, but needs a name until that juncture – doesn't say anything else about the Artist. Nor does he say anything about anything else. He remains silent all the way to school and I wonder whether I've said something bad.

It seems I have, because that very evening Mum has to answer all sorts of questions about the Artist and later in the night the questions turn to shouts. The next day he gives me a bike.

It's a BMX and it's perfect. There's nothing pathetic about it. No mudguards, no bell. It's the best thing I've ever been given.

I'm being watched. Four boys and a girl, too old for the climbing frame they're sitting on and taking care to show it. They've just landed there like birds on a TV aerial.

Oxelbergsparken is almost deserted at dusk. Apart from the kids on the climbing frame, it's just me and Little Sis lingering in the playground. Little Sis is standing on one of the swings, tugging at the chains to pick up speed. When she gets to the highest point, her shadow is cast right out of the park and grazes the asphalt. She's good at the swings, but it's me they're watching.

I'm riding my bike in the sandpit. You can do that with a BMX. I've constructed a jump in the sand and each time I go over it I leave the surface of the Earth – only for a split second, but that's enough to catch their eye. And knowing their eyes are on me is enough to make me cope with being close to the lattice door into the rock even though it's getting dark.

They tumble down from the climbing frame and approach. The girl is leading the way, the sleeves of her synthetic anorak rolled up. I pedal even harder – as hard as I can – leaving the Earth once more. I finish with a skid, kicking up a plume of sand.

They stand in a row beside the sandpit. I glance over and see they've arranged themselves in size order, like the Dalton Brothers with one sister, and I wonder whether it's coincidence. One day, when I write about them, I'll calculate the probability and conclude that five kids can make up 120 different combinations, and I'll decide that it was on purpose.

'You're messing up the sandpit,' the girl says.

This is when it turns sour.

'It's not fair on the little kids,' one of the boys says.

'They'll be gutted when they get here tomorrow.'

He's the tallest of the bunch – standing on the far left – and while his arms are slender, he suddenly looks strong in his sleeveless T-shirt. He's got his denim jacket tied around his waist like a cloak covering his bum.

I attempt a laugh but it doesn't work – they're not interested in laughing.

'You've got to tidy up the sand,' the girl says.

'You can't tidy up sand,' I say, without being sure what I mean. I don't know what any of us mean.

The boy with the bum cloak climbs into the sandpit to demonstrate. He combs the sand with his sole, turning it into a smooth patch.

'The whole sandpit should look like this,' he says, pointing to the smooth bit.

'It didn't look like that before,' I say.

'Yes it did,' the girl says, and the boys attest that she is right.

I turn my gaze homeward, but the building we live in isn't visible from the lowlands of the playground – it's obscured by a ridge of two-storey houses with windows that have begun to glow against the dark end of the sky.

'I've got to go home now,' I say.

I'm already standing over the bike frame and all I have to do is put a foot on the pedal to start moving, but the boy with the bum cloak reaches me quickly and grabs the handlebars. The others follow.

'You're staying here until the sandpit is tidied up,' the girl says.

'Why?' I say.

'For the little kids,' says the boy with the bum cloak.

'Yeah, for the little kids,' the girl says.

Their concern for the little kids puzzles me. I haven't yet learned that kids who want to lord it over others can cultivate sudden commitment to any issue at all.

'The little kids don't care,' I say.

The girl points to one of the boys who still hasn't said a word. 'His little brother plays here.'

The boy doesn't look at all convinced, but quickly realizes that it's true. 'Yes,' he says, pointing to a spot somewhere behind me. 'He goes to the preschool over there.'

I look – not because I wonder where the preschool is, I just want somewhere to avert my gaze.

The girl says:

'You think you know better than him what his brother cares about?'

At this point I give in.

I get off the bike and start tidying up the sandpit. My cheeks are burning. The kids are balanced on the wooden frame that runs around the sandpit like a bench. I demolish the jump I had constructed by kicking it. They find sand drifts in the grass beyond the border and the girl says they have to be scooped up. The boys laugh.

It's at this point I've had enough.

I can't stand the girl. The boys are just boys, but I don't know what she's supposed to be. It's unbearable being afraid of her.

I grab the bike and run – out of the sandpit and onto the grass. I mount the bike at speed and begin to pedal. They're shouting at me, but I don't look back. I need to be prey they have no hope of catching before they reach the stash of bikes by the climbing frame. I pedal as fast as I can until I've rounded the ridge of houses and only when I reach Storsvängen does it occur to me that Little Sis is still on the swings.

Or did she go home when I was surrounded? I never checked. I forgot she existed.

I stop in the middle of the street and put my feet down. Lactic acid is fizzing about in my thighs. I look around Storsvängen and wonder whether I need to cycle back. If she was still on the swing when I fled, she should be on the move by now. She should be on her way home. I can't very well show my face in the playground again, but perhaps I can sneak along the fence of the outermost house and take a look.

I've only just turned around when I spot the girl and her boys on their bikes. I turn back and pedal for my life. The chubby little tyres flicker beneath me, but the BMX isn't built to be quick and each time I look over my shoulder they've got closer.

When I reach our building, I cycle down the steps to the bike store. I scrape my knuckles when the handlebars smash into the concrete wall at the bottom of the steps, but right then I hardly feel it. I yank out the bunch of keys hanging around my neck on a string. Unlike the bunch of keys buried under a bush in Strömparken, this one only has two keys on it – one for the flat's front door and one for both the main door and the bike store – but I still manage to shove the wrong key into the lock and then time's up.

They swarm down the steps. The boy with the bum cloak holds me while the girl hits me. It's a sound distribution of duties. I'll never speak of this.

She only hits me once, but she knows what she's doing. She aims for the tender flesh just beneath the ribcage and completely winds me.

I hate Oxelbergen. I hate the outcrop and the girl and the grey fingerprints on the cheese in the fridge. Nothing's right here. Not even Mum. In the evenings, the Murderer takes her out and when they come back she trips in the stairwell and laughs at things that aren't funny.

One night she throws up in the hall. I see it through a crack in the door. The Murderer laughs so hard that he has to sit down and then she starts laughing too. She's laughing at her own vomit. I stay behind the crack in the door because I'm not really awake. She's standing with her arms outstretched and her palms pressed against the hall walls. She's turned her face away from the yuck and is laughing silently with her eyes closed. I don't know what she's supposed to be.

I usually like it when she laughs, but I don't like this. She belongs to him now. She's joined his secret club where they're happy in their own language. It's the first time I don't like seeing her happy.

Mum comes into the kitchen and draws a sharp breath. I look up from the table. She's frozen to the spot by the draining board in her dressing gown and curlers, staring at me as if I were a flash of ball lightning.

'That expression made you look so much like your dad.'

'What expression?'

'I don't know.'

I pull one. She shakes her head.

'No, not an expression like that. You just looked sort of absent. I suppose you must have been thinking about something. You weren't really here.'

'Like my dad?'

'Like your dad?'

'Well, he's not really here.'

She laughs, opens the cupboard above the hob and gets a coffee filter paper from the shelf of odds and ends. I want her to say more but she doesn't and now the moment in which we are talking about the Indian is about to dissolve. She measures out the ground coffee and fills the jug with water. The tap fizzes as if the moment were already over.

'Maybe I looked like an Indian?'

She turns off the tap and moves towards the coffee maker without looking at me.

'An Indian?'

'Yes.'

She laughs and shakes her head while pouring water into the coffee maker.

'Why would you look like an Indian?'

'Because . . . my dad's an Indian.'

Now she's looking at me again. This time it's as if I'm a maths problem.

'He's not an Indian.'

'He is.'

She tilts her head to one side but not in the caring way. She's trying to understand. To her, I'm long division.

'Why would he be an Indian?'

'You said he was.'

She gropes for the on-switch on the coffee maker and presses it without taking her eyes off me. I try again.

'You said my dad's an Indian.'

The coffee maker begins to titter. So does Mum.

'I've never said your dad's an Indian.' She comes over to me, crouches and strokes my cheek. The moment has been restored.

'Maybe you thought he looked like an Indian?' she says.

'No – I've never seen him.'

'You've seen pictures.'

'No.'

'But of course I've shown you pictures of your dad.'

She hasn't. I'm almost sure of it, but now I want the moment to end because it's turned so strange.

'I must have forgotten that you've shown me,' I say.

Mum leaves the kitchen. I hear a closet door open and the creak of a stool. When she returns, she's carrying a box. It's smaller and more solid than the banana boxes we usually pack our stuff in when we move.

I can't remember having seen the box before, but I recognize the first thing she removes from it: an issue of *Veckorevyn* from a summer long before my birth.

Inside the magazine there is a three-page article about her, headlined, 'I want to save elms and people!' She's shown me the pictures in which she's riding a bike, talking on the phone and watering a bush behind the statue of Charles XII. She's read aloud from the story which is about her being nineteen years old and never sleeping – at night she guards trees in Kungsträdgården and by day she works as a telephonist and hates automobilism.

She likes flipping through that magazine, but this time she puts it to one side with gentle hands.

Then two photo albums follow, and then a bundle of the kind of papers you never need but can't throw out because you feel they need to be there. These are ensouled papers with stamps and structure and a certain rigidity. One of these papers states that I'm a dual citizen, but I still don't know anything about that. And Mum's forgotten. She won't think of that until seven years later when I receive a brown envelope covered in a lot of stamps. Inside the envelope will be a call-up for military service in another country and she'll run and retrieve the same box from a different closet in another home. She'll rifle through the contents until she finds the paper and then put a hand to her forehead as she reads it aloud.

But right now it's 1987 and she sets the bundle of ensouled papers to one side in order to keep digging.

'Here he is,' she says, handing me a black-and-white photograph.

There he is. Immortalized for all eternity with dark eyes and a circle of beard around his mouth. He's wearing a knitted hat and from beneath the hat long hair spills into a hood. It's the winter where he is, and it feels weird to see an Indian in a winter landscape. But that's not the weirdest thing. The weirdest thing is in his arms. He's holding a corduroy footmuff and protruding from the footmuff is a tiny head wearing a trapper hat.

'That's you.' Mum points to the little head.

The little head is smiling at me, but I'm too dazed to smile back.

My hands are holding the answer, but my mouth still asks the question:

'Have I met my dad?'

The doctor is concerned. There's something wrong with my foreskin. It's too tight and the string of tissue underneath is too short. The foreskin can't be retracted and he's suggesting a simple procedure. He wants to cut me.

'It doesn't have to be done now,' he says, 'but if it isn't addressed then over time there can be issues with . . .'

He's searching for the words. He looks at Mum as if she might be able to help him. She can't.

'He may have issues in the fullness of time when he becomes . . . sexually active. Penetration may be painful.'

There are no scalpels within reach, but if I'm quick I can probably grab the pen from the doctor's breast pocket and stab myself in the throat.

'He's only eleven,' Mum says.

Now they're looking at me. Both of them. I look at the doctor's desk. If I stand up and headbutt the edge of the desk as hard as possible, it should kill me.

'Of course, we can always leave it for a year or two,' the doctor says.

I clasp my hands and hold my breath under the covers. I really go for it so that my body is hot and sticky in the oxygen-deprived cocoon, but it doesn't help. I can't remember him carrying me over the snow. I can't remember him at all. But if he was there from the beginning and then some, it has to be possible. He must be in there, somewhere.

If the day when the old cabinet was stripped of paint is the first one I remember, then the Indian is lost, because I know for sure that it was the Plant Magician who shooed me away from the smell and danger with an orange rubber glove. But do I know for sure that I've arranged my memories in the right order? Might another day be the first?

I remember a jetty over a stream. I'm lying on the jetty and staring between the boards. There are perch and a crayfish down there. I've got a hook and line and on the hook there's a kneaded ball of bread. The perch don't care about the bread ball, so I try the crayfish. It cares, but it tugs the bread away as soon as it gets close and anyway I don't want the crayfish. At the top of the slope behind my sun-warmed back is a red house and I'm almost sure that we live in it. But who are we? Who gave me the hook and line? Presumably a dad, because Mum doesn't fish. Presumably the Plant Magician, because he likes fishing. But I don't know for sure.

I remember a never-ending nightmare. Witches are circling the house even though Mum is sitting on the edge of the bed and says that I'm awake. I can see them outside the window. I suppose I must have a fever. My pyjama top is sodden and clinging to my chest. I scream loudly and soon enough Dad wakes up too. But which dad?

I remember a porch in the countryside. There's the smell of manure. I'm sitting on the bottom step and see three older children – two boys and a girl – emerge from the house. The girl slips a key under a flowerpot before they leave. I don't recognize them, but I still get up to follow them. They say I can't and I return to the step. Once they're out of sight, I pick up the flowerpot, take the key and throw it into the bushes.

When the kids return, they somehow know what I've done and they force me to crawl into the bushes. I want Mum or Dad to come. I'm looking for them, but which dad am I supposed to be looking for? I can't remember. All I remember is that none of them come and the kids get angrier. They take me to a tank and tell me to climb up a ladder. I stand on the ladder and peer down into a yellow-and-brown mire of faeces generated by the cows in the barn. There are patches where the surface has stiffened into a hard crust and the boys say you can walk on the hard bits.

The girl says I'll die if I do. The boys say I'll die if I don't. I raise my gaze from the inside of the tank and look towards the house with the porch. It's far away now. I'm crying and want to call out, but who for? How can a memory end at its most vivid moment?

I clasp my hands and hold my breath but it doesn't help. I can't find him. I give up and let my thoughts run wherever they please. They run down the stairs and out onto Storsvängen. They run towards the lattice door in the rock and wriggle between the bars.

It's Monday 31 August 1987, but I don't know that. I never know what the date is – only the year, and sometimes the day of the week – but I'll remember what we're watching on this particular evening, and one day when I come to write about it I'll find the date in an old TV schedule.

We're on Little Cloud's sofa watching the first episode of *Moonlighting* on TV2. The Murderer isn't there. A job up north came in and he and a few other men from the garage on Händelö island went off to do it. They were supposed to repair a cracked district heating pipe and come back on Sunday, but they're still up there. They can't find the crack. They're digging in the wrong places. I'm cheering for the crack.

Moonlighting is about a detective who plays basketball in the office and talks fast. He's incredible. The mums are purring. He's always quarrelling with the owner of the detective agency, Maddie, but not in a dangerous way. He quarrels in a fun way. He's a rascal and you can tell she wants him even though she says he's awful.

The mums are laughing so hard they're struggling to breathe. It's wonderful. It's like when we were in the fish car on the Autobahn. They're laughing like they laughed when they were doing freewheel and couldn't get enough of saying 'SELMA SCHLAMP'. But there's a difference too. In the fish car, I didn't understand what was funny about the funny thing and I was mostly laughing because the mums were laughing. Now I no longer have to wait for their laughter. Our laughter begins at the same time, and it's wonderful in a new way.

Once, I even start laughing before the mums. It's not on purpose, and I'm overcome by heavy unease when I hear that my mouth is the only one laughing. I deeply regret it but there's no going back. It's like realizing that you're the first to jump off a jetty when there's a row of bodies who agreed to jump at the same time. You're alone in the air above a lake in Säter and it's terrible. But then the water begins to bubble with bodies and the terribleness becomes a victory.

My body is still harbouring laughter when we emerge into Knäpingsborgsgatan and set off towards Oxelbergen.

It's a little after eleven o'clock in the evening and the temperature is 5.7 degrees Celsius, although I don't know that. I never know what the temperature is – only whether I'm cold or not – but equipped with the date and time, I will one day find the temperature on a sheet of readings taken at a weather station 5 kilometres north of the street we're walking along.

We turn right onto Östra Promenaden and walk south beneath the lime trees, a barely perceptible breeze on our tail. 3 metres per second. Too weak to make a flag flutter, but strong enough to set the lime trees' dry helicopters in motion.

1,280 kilometres away, Arsenal concede a cheap penalty against Luton Town and a player called Danny Wilson is about to take it. 8,380 kilometres away, a plane – Thai Airways flight 365 – has crashed into the sea and the wreckage is sinking to the bottom. Everyone is dead. Some float to the surface. Danny Wilson sends the penalty into the top right-hand corner and equalizes. 9,500 kilometres away, an elevator full of South African miners is buried under the rubble at the bottom of a shaft 1,367 metres deep. The people digging for survivors can still hear cries from the depths.

We cross the tram tracks and walk east along Lindövägen through the sweet stench from the chocolate factory where they boil skeletons by night. We'll be home soon.

'We can't miss the next episode,' I say.

'No,' Mum says, although you can tell she's not sure what she's answering.

She's not really there.

'The detectives,' I say, taking her hand. 'We can't miss the next episode.'

This time she looks at me and smiles. 'No, we definitely can't.'

She's back.

We go up Odalgatan towards Storsvängen and I start to look for the girl. We're in her hunting ground now, and I'm only just certain that she wouldn't hit me if she caught sight of me holding hands with a mum.

We're approaching the outcrop and the playground. The darkness needs to be filled with words. I ask Mum whether she thinks the Murderer will like *Moonlighting*. She thinks so. I ask whether he's got a TV where he is at the moment. She doesn't think so.

'Then we'll have to tell him what happened in the first episode,' I say.

'We will,' she says. 'But . . . we don't need to say where we saw it.'

I don't ask why, but she answers anyway.

'He'll only get all sorts of ideas into his head. There's no need for that.'

I'm guessing that it's to do with Little Cloud's brother. I'm guessing that the Murderer doesn't like the Artist since the Artist has slept in Mum's bed and he might get it into his head that Mum's seen him if he finds out that we've been to his sister's.

'We can say we saw it at home,' I suggest.

She squeezes my hand.

I've solved the girl problem. I just won't go out – at least not in Oxelbergen. I sleep over at Cyclops's as often as possible and when that's not possible I stay in bed and read a book called *Lone Wolf: Flight from the Dark*.

Paella let me borrow it, and it's not really a book – it's a game where you face different choices and your decisions take you to different pages. I have to leaf back and forth to follow the pathways that my choices lead to. Sometimes I end up on a page where it says that I've unfortunately died and then I flip back and choose a different pathway. I'm cheating, but who's going to catch me? I've already played my way through the book twice and I'm starting to learn where death lurks.

The Murderer enters.

'Is there something up with the bike?'

I shake my head. It's Oxelbergen and its wicked children there's something up with, but I can't say that. I say:

'There's nowhere to ride it here.'

I don't suppose I can say that either, but we're here now.

The Murderer goes over to the window – as if it were necessary to gauge the statement. He's an idiot who needs to check whether the streets are still there. He's wearing threadbare joggers – like he always does. I suppose he wants to look like Sylvester Stallone in *Rocky*, but he just looks like a grotesque preschooler with his big belly and his dirty hands.

'There's someone cycling,' he says. 'Seems to work.'

I can hear the grin. He thinks he's got me now, but his little charade by the window has given me time to think.

'My bike's a BMX,' I say. 'It's built for rough terrain.'

My mouth has never said the word terrain before, and when I hear it say it I become uncertain whether the word exists. It sounds crazy. Terrain? My whole jaw suddenly feels alien and detachable.

'You can ride your bike on the outcrop,' he says, pointing towards Oxelbergsparken. 'That's rough terrain.'

I linger for a moment on the information that the word exists before the pressure rises again. What does he want? Why do I have to be interrogated? Why doesn't he go out and ride it himself if he thinks it's so important? I'm tempted to go down to the bike store and get my bike to throw at him, but instead I just go down to the bike store and get on the bike. I sit there for a long time before I go back up to the flat. It may have been an hour. It may have been two. Or half an hour. I never know what time it is – only whether it's light or dark. Right now, it's dark.

'Did you ride your bike on the outcrop?'

'Yes.'

'Was it all right?'

I shrug. 'It's not a good outcrop.'

'Aren't there any other outcrops near by?'

I say there's a good outcrop by Cyclops's house. The next day, he lifts the bike into the Mercedes and drives me to Röda Stan. I don't know whether he notices that there are no outcrops and hills in Röda Stan, but that's how my bike ends up at 53 Bergslagsgatan.

It's as if I'm being smuggled in piece by piece – like a do-it-yourself son kit. I have a jacket in the hall, a bike in the garden shed, a spare bed always made up for me in Cyclops's room in the attic. They already have five sons and it's presumably neither here nor there if there's a sixth one in the attic sometimes.

I asked Single Mum's Daughter if she'd be my girlfriend and she said yes.

Well, actually, this is what she said:

'Okay.'

So now we're a we.

My ears suddenly felt blocked up when she said it. The playground hubbub became distant and dull, like the cries at the swimming baths when you duck underwater. That lid remained in place all day, but now it's evening and sound is beginning to regain its edges. I'm lying beneath the sloping ceiling in Cyclops's attic bedroom thinking about the word she chose.

Okay.

Is that the same as a yes? It doesn't have the same energy. There's something feeble and breakable about the word okay that bothers me. It's like a yes but with a right to cancel. I'm starting to feel unsure whether a relationship that begins with an okay can last a lifetime.

I avoided the choice of word when I told Cyclops. As far as he knows, there are no ambiguities. I now have a girlfriend.

'I expect she can tell that we belong together,' I say.

'Why would she be able to tell that?' Cyclops says.

He's no more than a voice in the dark because he's turned off his bedside light and the glow of mine doesn't reach him.

'Because we're so alike,' I say.

'But you're not.'

'Well, we've both got brown eyes.'

'So does practically everyone else.'

Cyclops begins to reel off brown-eyed people. He begins with Saga, Paella and Mouse. He's unusually touchy this evening.

'I don't mean how we look,' I say. 'I mean that neither of us has a dad.'

It's a stupid thing to say, but I never have to think ahead when I'm talking to Cyclops. He's a half-blind prey animal at the bottom of the food chain and nothing I say or do will make him choose someone else. I can never be more stupid than my best friend, and there's something restful about that knowledge.

'Her dad's dead,' he says.

'I know,' I say. 'He killed himself.'

Cyclops's bed creaks. 'How do you know that?'

'She told me.'

That's not quite true. The truth is that I heard the mums in the school kitchen talking about it when my mum was a dinner lady, but I want Cyclops to recognize that Single Mum's Daughter and I have a special bond. She might have told me. She probably will do, now that we're together.

Cyclops turns on his bedside light and reaches for his glasses. He needs to see me to believe what I'm saying.

'How did he kill himself?'

'He hanged himself.'

'Did she say that?'

'No, but that's how you do it.'

'You can shoot yourself with a rifle.'

'Only people in the country have rifles. People in towns hang themselves.'

The radiator clanks. Cyclops flinches, takes off his glasses and turns off his light again. That's how evenings in his room almost always end. A clank, a flinch, lights out. It's Cyclops's dad whacking the pipes downstairs when he thinks it's time for us to stop talking.

After the clank, we usually lie in silence for a while before we start whispering. This time it's Cyclops who breaks the silence and I can tell he's been thinking long and hard.

'Can you kill yourself with a bow and arrow?' he whispers.

I have to pause for thought before I answer. 'I don't think so.'

'I do.'

'How?'

Cyclops explains how and then we giggle so much we have to bury our faces in our pillows.

The Murderer has found something. He says it's a surprise and grins secretively as he jostles us out onto Storsvängen where the Mercedes is parked. At first I think it's in the boot, but he tells us to get into the car.

He opens the back door and points with a finger snap to get me to hurry up. He opens the front passenger door and unfurls his palm towards the seat to show Mum where she should sit. Once he's closed the door behind her, he does a funny walk around the bonnet. He's showing off, walking like Mickey Mouse with his arms bent and swinging along at his sides. He stops by the hood ornament – a three-pointed star inside a circle – and pretends it needs polishing with his sleeve.

'Where are we going?' I say.

'I don't know,' says Mum.

The car sways as the Murderer thuds down into the driver's seat.

'Where are we going?' says Mum.

He doesn't say anything. All he does is start the engine.

We drive down Nygatan towards the town centre and I wonder whether it's going to be a VCR. He turns left by the library and my hopes for a VCR evaporate. He pulls onto Södra Promenaden, past Kungsgård High School where I took six guitar lessons, past the home ground of IFK Norrköping who have just finished second in Allsvenskan and are due to play IFK Göteborg in the play-offs, but I don't know anything about that because I've never seen a football match, past the medical centre in Kneippen and on towards the green expanse of Himmelstalundsfältet. He just keeps driving and driving until we run out of town and once we're on the motorway heading for Linköping he shakes a cassette tape out of its case and shoves it into the slot above the gearstick.

He plays Carola's *The Runaway* and drums his fingers on the steering wheel. My hands want to drum too, but I don't because Mum says that the Murderer has bad taste in music. She thinks Carola is the crappest thing you can listen to.

The Murderer thinks Carola has a hot voice.

Mum doesn't think it helps.

'You've got to tell us where we're going,' she says, but he doesn't.

I reach for the cassette case lying in the bowl between the front seats. Carola has a boy's haircut. There's a white dove perched on her hand.

We drive along the motorway for about three Carola songs and have just crossed the Göta Canal before the Murderer takes an exit. Only one or two choruses later, he pulls onto a steep gravel track and stops in front of a two-storey red cabin with white corner joints and a broken roof.

The Murderer throws open his door and lets in the birdsong and the distant roar of the motorway.

'What are we doing here?' says Mum.

The Murderer puts a hand on her thigh. 'We live here.'

Cyclops and I are attributeless in different ways.

He swings the rounders bat with one hand, because like a girl he's only able to move one body part at a time. Once the left hand has thrown the ball up it falls back to his hip while the right hand swings. He almost always misses and the exceptions never go far.

I swing like a boy. The left hand throws up the ball and then keeps the right hand company in a two-handed grip around the bat. It looks good – it must do – when my whole upper body rotates on my hips just like when Paella and Mouse swing. But like Cyclops, I miss almost every time. It's as if I understand what it feels like to have the attribute – it's just that I don't have it.

Saga misses the ball too, but he's in the third category of boys: the ones who are weak but like weak boys in books and films they've been granted an attribute in return. He can play the piano.

No one would write a book or make a film about boys like Cyclops and me.

The Plant Magician is going to die. It's Little Sis who tells me. She and Little Bro have just returned from a few weeks with their dad. They stayed for longer than usual because Mum had her hands full moving to the house that's three Carola songs outside of Norrköping.

'Is he sick?' I say, perhaps a little shocked.

'No,' she says. 'It's just that he's realized he's going to die.'

We're at the kitchen table eating sandwich wafers. I've sliced away the edges of the cheese so that we don't have to swallow shreds of the Murderer's fingerprints. Around us, empty banana boxes float in a sea of crumpled-up newspaper. Little Bro is eating his sandwich wafer while sitting inside one of the boxes. Mum's putting crockery into the cupboards.

'He was going to live for ever,' I say.

'I know.' Little Sis grins. 'But now he says that it's impossible. He says that everyone has to die – including him.'

'So he's not immortal any longer?'

'No.'

I wonder whether this means that the Plant Magician has stopped all self-care that might grant him eternal life. All the herbs, fasting, steaming, sinus rinses and enemas seem rather unnecessary if they don't make you immortal.

I say:

'So is he going to be normal now?'

Little Sis shakes her head. Her mouth's full of sandwich wafer and there's time for a certain degree of tension to develop as she swallows and drinks after the recommended order of things.

'He's still going to get very old.'

'How old's he going to get?'

'Four hundred years old.'

'Four hundred years old?'

'He says so.'

'Why four hundred years specifically?'

She shrugs. Her lips narrow and stiffen, her eyes glisten, the freckles on her cheeks are consumed by her blush.

I say:

'Does he still poo like an Indian?'

Her sinuses squeak and the laughter erupts. We laugh for a long time and draw Mum's curiosity, but we can't breathe enough to explain. It's wonderful laughing at the Plant Magician and I never want it to end, so when it begins to ebb I climb onto the chair and crouch.

I don't have to say a word. Little Sis's face contorts. It looks like an invisible hand is trying to strangle her. This new laughter is silent. Tears follow.

'Are you struggling to breathe?' I say, my voice attuned to the Plant Magician. 'Should I get you some cucumber water?'

She slips off her chair and vanishes beneath the edge of the table.

We've discovered a new genre and we're never going to stop laughing. For as long as we live, we'll amuse each other with our parents' repartee. We've acquired a language and, in time, it's one that Little Bro will also learn. This is how we'll defeat them. This is how we'll love each other.

One grey-black morning we hit a red light at the intersection where Cyclops's dog was run over. It's just me and the Murderer in the Mercedes. A tram with fogged-up windows crosses the road ahead of us, packed with swaying shadows. Between the tram and the car bonnet there's a stream of children flowing in the same direction. Some are wearing duffel coats with wooden buttons and carrying battered plastic instrument cases. You always see them here, dragging their attributes between the houses in Röda Stan and the music classes at Haga School.

A woman is using the crossing in the opposite direction, wading upstream through the stream of children on her long, thin legs clad in ribbed tights and leather boots with folded tops. The Murderer drapes his wrist over the steering wheel and points at her.

'Check out the pair of legs on her.'

I already am. She looks like a beautiful pirate.

'Go to hell,' he says, beginning to shift uneasily. Something needs to be done, but he doesn't know what. He grumbles and fiddles with the hub of the steering wheel. The pirate has already made landfall on the pavement on my side of the car by the time he realizes.

'Wind it down,' he says, pointing to my door.

I do as he says and with my eyes on the crank I don't see him insert his fingers into his mouth. The wolf whistle hits me like a knitting needle to the ear. The woman looks over her shoulder, but by then the Murderer has already released the clutch and spat his fingers onto the gearstick. It's me she's looking at, with a sort of smile, and I die on the spot.

The Murderer chuckles all the way to the Stockholm roundabout, ruffling my hair and rubbing his knuckles against my thigh.

'She was a looker, wasn't she?' he says.

I want to shrug, but reply with words so that he won't look at me. 'I don't know,' I say.

It's a lie.

He says:

'Maybe a bit too old for you?'

'Yes.'

Another lie.

It is with increasing frequency that I think about the risk of being sexually exploited by an older woman and mourn the fact that the chances seem to be so slim. Cyclops sees red whenever we talk about it. He says there must be women who want to shag kids and that it's unfair that only certain boys get to grow up in their proximity. He reckons it's just as unfair that some people are born in Ethiopia. One night, I promised him that the paedophiles were out there – possibly even in Röda Stan – and he climbed up into his window and did a sexy dance. Something insane dwells inside him that only I get to see.

'What kind of girls do you like?' asks the Murderer, and when I hesitate with my answer he begins to describe the various models and their qualities.

The blondes are the prettiest.

The brunettes are better in bed because they have to be.

You have to keep a particular eye on the redheads because they're insatiable.

'I think they're all quite pretty,' I say.

The Murderer laughs and slaps me on the thigh. 'Now you're lying!'

But I'm not – not this time. I think almost all girls are pretty. Some are prettier than others – Single Mum's Daughter is a case in point – but there are more or less no ugly ones. I'd be with every single girl in my class – at the same time or one after another – including the few ugly ones if that was the cost in some sort of all-or-nothing deal. Anyone can have me. But there's only one I belong with and now she's said 'okay'.

Single Mum's Daughter wants me. The only question is what for? We haven't touched each other since we got together. We haven't even spoken. We used to, but the verbal agreement that we belong together has made us strangers to one another. Sometimes she seeks out my gaze, but I avoid hers and take detours around the classroom to avoid passing within range of her desk. It's not that I don't want to be close to her – I want that all the time, except when it's possible, because I don't know what I'm supposed to do. At least not when everyone else can see.

Maybe if I could have her all to myself in a room or by a rock that's been in the woods for ten thousand years? But I've no idea how we'll get there. Is it even my job to know? Haven't I done enough by asking the question and giving us direction? I'm still worn out. It's her turn to do something.

I'm awaiting instructions.

Instructions arrive. Single Mother's Daughter intercepts me in the school playground. She's got her best friend with her. They're intertwined and move as a single life form. I don't like the friend. She has a repugnant self-confidence manifested in the most severely sprayed hairdo in the class. Her fringe is stiff and arched like a mudguard fitted over her forehead. Her eyelids are purple, and her lips are pale with balm and contourless like those of a fish. Every time I look at her fish lips I get angry because I'll never forget how they fluttered with laughter when she yanked open the bathroom door and saw me doing a poo like an Indian.

'We were wondering . . .' says Single Mum's Daughter, hesitantly, before the other head of the life form takes over: '. . . whether you want to come round to mine after school tomorrow?'

For a brief moment I wonder whether they're suggesting that I should be with Fish Lips instead. I definitely don't want that – at least not right now. Single Mum's Daughter notes my confusion and explains that she'll be there too. Fish Lips has asked Moussaka to be her boyfriend. It'll be the four of us.

'No parents,' Fish Lips adds, leaving her mouth open for a bit. It looks rehearsed. Provocative. The slightly retarded expression usually worn by grown women pointing at their bumholes.

I run the back of my hand along my upper lip but it doesn't get bloody. It's been a year since the doctor shoved the soldering iron up my nose and I still haven't got used to being able to feel my heart pounding away without anything leaking.

The Murderer is pacing back and forth in the kitchen pulling a long face every time he passes the window towards the driveway. He doesn't like it when Mum's late. He's worked out how long it takes to drive from her work to our home. I heard him telling her the times – different ones for different routes since she cleans different places each day. She said he had to keep it together. He said it was thoughtfulness. I heard him talking about the motorway, the dark and the freezing rain until she promised to come home on time. But now she's late again.

The Murderer goes to the phone and fidgets with the receiver.

I'm sitting at the kitchen table with my hands steepled beneath my chin and my gaze fixed on the advent candle tray. It's got a bed of star-tipped cup lichen and is decorated with small wooden amanita and felted woodland spirits. An underworld illuminated by two lit candles.

I imagine that I've shrunk to the size of an ant and am clambering between the white branches of the lichen on my way home to a humble burrow at the foot of the third candle where Single Mum's Daughter is waiting for me. She's shrunk too. We live there together and lie side by side at night. We don't wear any clothes when we're asleep and there's nothing strange about that. We're underworld dwellers and don't need any instructions.

'I was just wondering what time she left?'

The Murderer is on the phone now. His voice is soft and

carefully unconcerned, but as soon as he's hung up it turns hard.

'Shit!' he bellows, returning to the window.

I'm wrenched out of the underworld. The Murderer pulls back his hair with a double-handed grip around his scalp. I want to ask whether something has happened, but I don't dare disturb him because I'm not sure whether he's worried or angry.

For a minute or so, we're silent at either end of the kitchen. My gaze is fixed on his back while his is staring into the December darkness until a sharp light pours in over his shoulders and sets him in motion.

He goes into the hallway and then on into the living room. The sound of his footsteps stops somewhere around the sofa. I stay at the table. Mum enters the kitchen with a supermarket carrier bag in each hand.

I ask if I can sleep over at Cyclops's tomorrow. I can. I don't mention anything about going to Fish Lips's house before I go round to Cyclops's.

'If that's okay with his parents,' Mum adds, putting the bags down in front of the fridge.

'It's okay,' I say. Not that I've asked, but they never say no.

Mum caresses my chin in passing and sets down a jar of pickled beetroots on the table. There's a snap-on lid and a handwritten label on it.

'Isn't it beautiful?' she said. 'Makes you not want to even open it.'

'No, it doesn't,' I say.

Mum laughs because she knows how I feel about beetroot. She moves the jar to the far end of the table closest to the window where the Dr Westerlund geraniums are staring into the pine forest. She puts it next to the advent candles and the two flames make the liquid inside the jar glow with a reddish hue.

She says:

'I don't want you lighting the advent candles when you're home alone.'

I say:

'I'm not home alone.'

Mum asks where the Murderer is and I point towards the living room. She calls out his name but there's no response. She unpacks the groceries before going to look for him. I don't warn her.

Further instructions. Fish Lips explains what's going to happen while she arranges her small, windowless room for the proceedings. She lights tealights and incense on the chest of drawers by the mirrored wall, switches off the ceiling light, takes the alarm clock off the bedside table and sets it in the middle of the floor.

'We'll start at exactly the same time,' she says, kneeling in front of Moussaka, who is sitting on the floor and rubbing his thighs. He's been overcome by a slight air of seriousness and it makes his face alien in the same way that Cyclops's face can be alien when he takes off his glasses. Moussaka usually laughs at everything and it suits him. His eyes are round like orbs and only shallowly fitted into their sockets, sort of bulging out of his skull, which makes him look hysterically happy whenever he laughs. When he isn't laughing his features become incongruous. Sitting there on the floor, he looks sick while waiting for the starting shot.

'Remember to breathe through your nose,' Single Mum's Daughter whispers into my ear. The warmth she exhales into my cochlea makes the back of my neck short and leaves it covered in goosebumps. We're sitting on the bed, each with a foot on the floor and a leg folded onto the mattress so that we're brought face to face. I want her to do it again.

I whisper:

'What did you say?'

Fish Lips snaps her fingers to get everyone's attention.

'Tongues have to be in the other person's mouth at all times.'

She puts a thumb to Moussaka's chin and presses. His lower jaw drops and she beckons his tongue into the room.

'This is just a demonstration,' she says. 'The competition hasn't started yet.'

She leans forward, takes his tongue in her mouth and shoves her own into his. She closes her eyes but Moussaka's orblike eyes remain open, which makes the kiss resemble a mortal struggle, although it's obvious they've been rehearsing.

Fish Lips detaches herself from Moussaka's wild face and asks whether we're ready to lose.

We are.

My first kiss lasts for two minutes and five seconds.

The winning kiss lasts for six straight minutes and while we quietly watch the performance before us she leans in close again.

'I'm not really fussed about the competition.'

I'll remember the whisper better than the kiss.

Mum's late again. The Murderer is still at the kitchen table, but he's glancing at the clock on the wall and breathing through his nose. Any minute now he's going to get to his feet to start pacing back and forth between the phone and the window looking out onto the driveway. It's unfortunate that someone who is so particular about timekeeping has moved in with someone who's never arrived on time for anything.

I make myself three sandwiches and leave the kitchen to eat them in front of the TV. Children with attributes and Lilla Sportspegeln tops tucked into their jeans are throwing balls into a variety of holes in the wall. Little Sis wants to try my sandwiches. I say no. She gets up and heads for the kitchen. I stop her and give her one of the sandwiches.

A boy misses the smallest hole and his whole upper body droops. He's exaggerating and looks like a disappointed cartoon character so we understand that it's unlike him to miss.

The Murderer is on his feet. I can hear him on the phone. He seems to have called his own place of work – the garage on Händelö where Mum cleans one day a week. He's asking when Mum left. He's silent for a moment, then angry.

'Got it, boss!' he bellows before slamming down the receiver with a clang.

Little Sis whispers:

'He doesn't like his boss.'

I want to shush her, but a rattling sound from the kitchen tells me that won't be necessary. The dial on the phone is rotating again.

Little Sis whispers:
'It's because Mum's been making love with the boss.'
I whisper:
'No she hasn't.'
'Yes she has.'
'You don't even know what making love is.'

Little Sis looks at me as if I'm dim, makes a circle with her thumb and forefinger and then inserts her other forefinger through it. I shudder. The Murderer's boss has a van that's a shade of bitter bolete brown – it's a Chevrolet serial killer model – and each time he opens the sliding door, two German shepherds leap out. I wonder if they're in there, in the serial killer compartment, together with the dogs.

I whisper:
'When?'
'Before.' She nods towards the kitchen. 'Before him.'
'How do you know?'

She turns her gaze towards the TV and shrugs. We sit in silence for a while. The Murderer is talking to someone – it's not clear who.

Little Sis whispers:
'Everyone at the garage wants to make love with Mum.'

I look at her and try to understand what she means. The fact that she knows this stuff is brand new to me and apparently she now knows more than I do. She's sitting there like a mini oracle describing the course of history. It's uncomfortable. I decide not to ask any more questions.

'Because she needs to come home!' the Murderer suddenly shouts, and both Little Sis and I start on the sofa. This shout is followed by a series of tinkling blows, a brief silence and then another blow, louder and in a different key.

We don't do any more whispering. We just sit there waiting until we hear the sound of an engine and see a transomed beam of light on the roof. The Murderer goes outside and shuts the front door behind him. I can hear his muffled screams from the courtyard as I stand up and sneak into the hall. From there, I can see the wall in the kitchen, red and blotchy. It's like a murder scene where the body has been blown up and small pieces of flesh are scattered in pools of blood.

I take a few more steps forward before I spot the shards of glass and the snap lid and realize that the victim is the jar of pickled beetroots.

There's still a week or so to go until Christmas Eve, but the Murderer can no longer wait. It's apparent that he's got a guilty conscience.

'I've got a guilty conscience,' he says as I kick my shoes off in the hall. He grabs my arm and leads me into the living room. There's the smell of wet paint as we pass the kitchen door.

In the living room, the ceiling light is off but there's something glowing in the darkness.

'What's that?' I say.

'It's a Christmas present,' he says.

Standing on a low table beneath the window is a fish tank. I rush forward and fall to my knees. A new underworld inhabited by living underworld dwellers in constant and glimmering movement. The Murderer crouches next to me and unfolds a handwritten note. His fingers are dirty in a new way: white stains cover the chronic skin of blackness.

'Neon tetra.' He reads the note and points to a small, blood-red, almost luminescent fish of which there must be at least six or seven in the tank.

'Catfish.' He searches for a while before finding it at the end of the tank where it's suckered onto the glass with its unpleasant mouth.

'Goldfish,' I say, pointing to a golden fish with fabulously billowy fins.

The Murderer looks down at the note and shakes his head. 'No, fantail.'

I try out the word – it tastes improbable.

'And finally . . .' He taps on the glass and the fish he's about to name flicks away and vanishes between the aquatic plants. 'Zebra fish.'

It's striped the wrong way round and ought to be called something else, but I don't say anything about that. It feels like I should hug him. It almost feels like I want to.

'The old biddy in the pet shop said that zebra fish can handle pretty much anything. Basically immortal. But try to keep the others alive too, won't you?'

The Murderer opens a small plastic tub and shows me the flakes that the fish are to be fed with. 'Once a day,' he says, without looking at the note. I feed the fish and feel powerful as they rush to the surface. The Murderer stays until all the flakes have been devoured and then he stands up.

'There's going to be a surprise when your mum gets back. Tonight Daddy's going to sort out dinner.'

He laughs to himself and goes into the kitchen. I stay and stare into the underworld until Mum gets home. She's brought both Little Sis and Little Bro and we stare together until the Murderer shouts that food's up.

He's laid the table with five plates and five glasses, but no cutlery. He's bought five ready-grilled chickens at the supermarket and he places a whole chicken onto each plate. Mum looks doubtful, but that's probably only because there aren't any vegetables on the plates. There are no accompaniments whatsoever – just five room-temperature, golden-brown birds.

I've never had grilled chicken before. My eyes water when I taste the seasoned skin. It's the tastiest thing I've eaten in my whole life.

After dinner, I return to the fish tank and stare at my fish until my eyelids are heavy. I fetch my duvet and pillow from upstairs and make my cocoon in the glow of the underworld's electric sky.

'Sleeping with the fishes,' the Murderer says, laughing loudly as he explains to Mum why that was a funny thing to say. She shushes him, but it doesn't work. He's had a few and needs to drown out a buzz that only he can hear.

Mum turns off the light in the tank. She says the fish need to sleep too. Once she's gone, I turn it back on.

A brush with disaster a few days before Christmas Eve. It's just me and Little Sis at home. I light the advent candles and sit down to stare at them. I sit there for a long time before I hear the front door slam and I go into the hall. Little Sis's shoes are gone. Her coat too. I open the door. She's off.

'Where are you going?' I call out.

'Down to the stables,' she calls back.

The stables are next to one of the neighbouring farms and she likes to go and stare at the horses. I'm not interested in horses but there are girls there.

'Wait for me,' I call out.

I dress quickly but when I step onto the porch she's gone. She didn't wait. I take a few creaking steps onto the thin layer of snow, hesitate briefly and then turn back. I kick off my shoes in the hall and go into the living room to feed the fish. As the fish fight for the flakes on the surface, I dip a moistened fingertip into the tub and place a flake on my tongue. It tastes bad and I go into the kitchen to get a drink.

The curtains are alight in complete silence. It looks imaginary. There's something about the silence that makes the scene dreamlike and for a moment I just stand there staring. The miniature landscape in the candle tray has already been burnt to a crisp – all that remains of the lichen are small convulsing glowing embers. But the fire is on the move and the flames that have got furthest are licking their way along the curtain pole.

I fill a pan with water and before I've turned around to hurl the water at the flames I begin to think about what might have happened if she'd waited for me.

1988 arrives and winter breaks. It's neither warm nor cold, just dark. We're into a new and hitherto unknown season that smells rancid. Sometimes solitary snowflakes sail down to Earth but they don't inspire any hope because it's clear they're not freshly printed. They're just the dross being released from a celestial pipe. The machine up there is at a standstill. And Single Mum's Daughter is no longer mine.

She doesn't say it in as many words, but I notice on the very first day of school after the holidays. It's as if she's forgotten that we kissed for two minutes and five seconds. She's not even avoiding me. She greets me as if we've never been anything other than classmates who greet each other, and I have no choice but to do the same.

One playtime, I find Moussaka in the dark and slush and ask whether he's still with Fish Lips. He shakes his head.

'I don't think so.'

He doesn't look unhappy when he says this, but I don't know for sure whether he can look unhappy with his orblike eyes.

I fall asleep unusually early in the evenings, crying in the cocoon so that I forget to fear the dark. There's something intoxicating in the tears and on occasion I cheat and think about my hamster, but only to get myself going. Once they're flowing I hurry back to thoughts of Single Mum's Daughter and stay there. All you have to do is swallow the tears and more follow. I'm so affected by the salty taste. That's what unhappiness tastes like.

The Murderer is unhappy too. Worried, at any rate. He seems

to miss Christmas, when we were gathered under one roof and he could sit on the sofa with his booze and orange juice in one hand and Mum in the other. It made him soft and caring. He hugged us all, and each time Mum needed to go shopping he'd get up and drive her to the shop in Skarphagen. But then the holidays ended and winter broke.

Mum's driving her own car and failing in her timekeeping.

She's late again. The Murderer calls Little Cloud and finds out that she's there. What's she doing there? He shouts and punches the wall before going into the living room and opening the window.

The boy is sitting on the sofa and sees it all. The hand grabbing all the cables from the extension lead and pulling. The TV going dark, the fish tank going dark, the pump falling silent.

The Murderer crouches and picks up the fish tank from the low table. Perhaps it's heavier than he expected, because he whimpers and spills water on his trousers, but he's strong and once he's adjusted his grip he hurls the tank out into the darkness. The cables rattle across the windowsill and disappear in the same direction.

The boy does nothing to save the fish. He just sits there and lets them die.

The Murderer closes the window and secures the fasteners before leaving the living room. As he passes the sofa, he meets the boy's gaze.

'It's not your fault,' he says.

That night winter returns and at dawn the boy goes outside. He finds the fish under a thin layer of snow, hard and shimmering. They're like gaping jewels.

'We're not going to live here any longer.' Mum fiddles with the ignition. 'I just need . . .'

'I know,' I say. It's not clear what I know. I just want her to be quiet since I'm afraid that the Murderer might hear her and be roused from the peace of a guilty conscience. He's outside the car but still close. I can see the smoke pouring from his mouth behind the open bonnet. The return of winter has made Mum's car be difficult, but the Murderer is helpful. As soon as he heard the starter whining, he came running out of the house. Now he's attaching jump leads to the battery.

'Full choke, keep your foot up,' he calls out.

'I know,' Mum snaps, twisting the starter's rhythmic wail into being while her left foot remains on the clutch. Her fingers whiten around the key. Petrol fumes seep into the car and smell good in that poisonous way.

'Okay,' the Murderer calls. 'Now no choke and put your foot down.'

'I'll choke you,' Mum hisses, putting her foot on the accelerator. Her bum rises off the seat when both her legs are straightened. She doesn't touch the choke.

The car starts with a scream. The Murderer hurries to remove the cables and the bonnet strut before slamming it shut and giving two thumbs-ups. The exaggerated urgency embarrasses me, but I can't help feeling sorry for him when he puts it on.

Mum starts crying once we're on the motorway. I glance at her but say nothing. Her cheek is swollen.

She takes my hand and says she's sorry.

'Sorry,' she says.

'You haven't done anything,' I say.

It has no effect. She's crying so much that she has to turn into Kneippen and pull over for a while. I'll be late for school, but it's not the time or place to say anything about that. Anyway, I'm almost always late when Mum drives me.

'These bloody men and their violence,' she says, gaze fixed on the steering wheel. 'I don't know how they find me, but they always do. They always have done. Have I told you about my stepfather? Have I told you about Ivan Klingborn?'

She has, but I let her tell me anyway.

'He beat me so terribly. He beat us all. He was a psychopath. He aimed his rifle at us. Once he smashed up my mouth.' She touches her lower lip like she always does when she tells this story. 'But I wasn't allowed to go to hospital to get stitches. He stood guard outside my door and forced me to lie in bed all night and it just kept on bleeding. My little brother was given permission to fetch towels, but I wasn't allowed to go anywhere. By morning, the pillow was completely red. It was stuck to my face.'

She falls silent for a moment. Then the name again, quietly, through her teeth.

'Ivan Klingborn.'

She says it as if it were an expression she's trying to understand.

'At least now he's dead,' I say.

The words don't suit the comforting tone, but I know for sure that it doesn't matter to her. It's been a year since the call from Stockholm when she said she was happy after I asked why she was crying.

'He should have died sooner,' she says, wiping her cheeks

with her wrists. 'He crashed every single car he owned, but he always made it.'

She's stopped crying and now the cleaning of her face can begin. She lowers the visor to examine herself in the vanity mirror while she carries on telling me about Ivan Klingborn's special inability to die. I'm listening carefully because this is a story I haven't heard before.

'Once he crashed into a tram on the Liljeholmsbron bridge and wrecked his car. It split down the middle, but he tumbled out onto the asphalt and got to his feet because just like always he had a guardian angel. Not a scratch. It was a miracle. Everyone in Stockholm was talking about it.' She lowers her gaze from the vanity mirror and looks at me. '"Don't forget to thank God's angels for getting your father home," people said to us. They didn't get that we were praying to God for him to die.'

I say:

'Shit angels.'

She laughs and hugs me tightly.

I don't really believe the bit about everyone in Stockholm talking about the miracle. I've heard her lie to dads and I assume she lies to kids too. She means no harm. She lies so that people don't get sad or angry and perhaps sometimes to improve a story. It's no skin off my nose. And for what it's worth, I'll never be quite sure whether she's lied to me. One day I'll be employed as a journalist at *Dagens Nyheter* in Stockholm and with the keys to the newspaper archives I'll spend a whole day searching for the miracle on Liljeholmsbron bridge.

The Murderer heads up north to fix another pipe and Mum changes jobs. It's as if she's taking the chance while he's away, and I can understand what she's doing. She's cutting ties.

Nothing gets packed and nothing gets said, but the movement away can still be glimpsed. We go round to Little Cloud's and watch *The Deer Hunter* but when the film finally starts getting good, the mums go into the kitchen to talk and when the film is over and I'm tying my shoelaces in the hall I see a five-hundred-krona note slip into Mum's pocket. Then we go to Vilbergen and borrow another one off the woman who saw Little Sis's hamster under the bathtub. The movement away can be glimpsed. It won't be long before it's time to leave.

She has to stay at the new job until eight o'clock every evening. For the first two days, I go home to Cyclops's after school and sleep there. On the third day, she picks me up from Cyclops's at half past eight in the evening.

'You've got a new smell,' I say as we drive home in the Saab.

She loosens a strand of her pinned-up hair and presses it to her nostrils.

'Ugh,' she says.

'You smell good,' I say.

'I smell of dripping.'

'I like dripping.'

I'm not sure what dripping means, but it's certainly making my mouth water as I lean close to her shoulder and inhale the smell. She asks if I want to visit her at her new job and we agree that I'll take the bus there tomorrow after school.

Cyclops's dad is crouching in front of my desk.

'Where are you right now?' he says.

'Here,' I say.

'No.'

'Yes.'

'You weren't a moment ago.'

'Then too.'

What's he going to do? I can make myself the size of a teaspoon and scuttle along the frame of the blackboard, I can raid a royal tomb and pry open the brittle skeletal fingers wrapped around the sword. No one knows where I am or what I'm doing there. Nobody can stop me. Their powerlessness in the face of freedom of thought is intoxicating.

'Look at me,' he says, standing up. 'That way it'll be easier to remember what I've said.'

I fix my gaze on his body and let him haul it back and forth along the promenade between his desk and the blackboard. He's talking about prepositions. I stab a sleepy camp guard in the jungle. He writes a sentence on the board, underlines one word and then taps it with the chalk. I'm crawling into the camp on my tummy.

It's raining and I get muddy, but that doesn't bother me. In the jungle, the mud is warm and comes in handy as camouflage. The whole class is trapped inside the camp in cages that have been lowered into a flood, forcing them to cling to the bamboo bars at the top so that they can breathe. Some have already drowned. Fish Lips, for one. Unfortunately, her leech-covered arms could no longer take the strain and it was awful for Single Mum's Daughter to see her friend disappear into the moonlit waters. She's crying in despair because she doesn't know that I'm coming.

I crawl down to the water and swim to the cage. My muddy face makes the trapped children recoil – all of them except her.

'Is that you?' she says.

It is.

I climb onto the cage, open the hatch and pull her out of the water. She's naked. The soldiers must have forced her to undress before they threw her into the cage. Bastards. But right now that doesn't matter – she's too dazed and grateful to be embarrassed. She embraces me and trembles in my arms while the other kids climb up into the moonlight.

She tries to whisper something in my ear but I shush her.

'It doesn't matter,' I say. 'I can never hate you.'

When the school day ends, I follow the path behind the school down to Malmgatan, catch the bus to Norr Tull, the tram to Söder Tull and finally a concertina bus with a number in the hundreds that goes all the way to Söderköping. I sit at the very front and unfold the note from Mum. The whole itinerary is written down on it, and at the bottom is the name of her new job: Rallarns Kiosk.

'I'm going to eat ten burgers,' Cyclops says.

He's sitting on the seat next to me, which is no accident. I've never been on a regional bus before and I brought him along just in case. It's not like Cyclops to cast himself into the unknown, but he was overcome by a thirst for adventure when I told him that Rallarns Kiosk is a fast-food stand and that we can eat as many burgers as we want. I don't know whether that's true, but it's too late to back out now. Cyclops skipped lunch at school and now he's getting weak. His pale little hands are resting on his thighs, shaking.

All food at the Steiner school is vegetarian and we hate most of it apart from the rice pudding they usually give us around Christmas. We're obsessed with meat. Especially Cyclops, who has two Steiner teachers for parents and lives in an almost closed vegetarian universe.

The sun sets while we're on the bus. The plain south of Norrköping is blanketed in a cold fog that makes all light sources glow. When we finally arrive in Söderköping and set a course for Rallarns Kiosk, which stands alone at an otherwise undeveloped crossroads, it's glowing like a small temple filled with secrets.

One night I recount the whole of *Conan the Barbarian* to Cyclops. I've previously described individual and particularly grotesque scenes, but this time I go from start to finish. Cyclops is lying so quiet and still in his bed that I'm sometimes convinced he's fallen asleep, but each time I neglect details he gets annoyed and hisses.

'The thief was chained to a rock?'
'Yes.'
'How did he get free?'
'Conan freed him.'
'And took him with him?'
'Yes.'
'Go on.'

Cyclops isn't allowed to watch violent films if they lack historical merit. He's seen *A Man Called Horse* but his mum told him to shut his eyes when the white Indian warrior was hung up by hooks in his chest. He's seen *When the Raven Flies*, but not the bit with the throwing knife to the throat.

The Murderer returns with a manic grin. He kicks off his shoes in the hall and goes into the living room without saying a word. He's carrying a brown paper bag and when he reaches the sofa he turns it upside down and shakes it. The contents gush onto the cushions and floor. It's like in a film.

I've been watching from a distance, but now I approach. My hands want to touch the spillage: a heap of bundles of cash held together by rubber bands.

He lets us touch the bundles. It's all in hundreds. Some have the goatee guy on them and others have the guy with curly hair, but it says one hundred on every single one.

Mum asks where the money's from and he says that he has been driving a lorry. That's it. He laughs loudly as if the simplicity of the task only dawned on him when he heard himself answer the question. He laughs and says it again:

'I drove a lorry to Stockholm.'

I won't remember anything else of what's said that evening – only the weight of the bundles of cash and a broken feeling that descends upon me towards night-time.

I still want her to leave him, but perhaps it can wait for now? Surely we're not in that much of a rush?

This new dilemma resolves itself at dawn when the police arrive to collect both the Murderer and the cash. I'll never see him again.

It turns to spring and I sleep on things made for other activities. First on Little Cloud's leather sofa, then on a hard velvet sofa in Vilbergen and finally on an air mattress at one of Mum's workmates' from Rallarns Kiosk. She's young and a bit chubby and lives alone in a dark one-bed flat in the outer of the two concrete rings at Navestad. She's got big breasts and lots of tops with Michael Jackson on them. One day she says that I'll be good-looking when I grow up. She touches my face and says I have the right lines.

'You look a bit awkward now because these lines don't suit a kid, but just you wait.'

She's funny and I fall in love but am never disillusioned because she makes it clear she's going to marry Michael Jackson.

Rallarns Kiosk is also a small video shop and sometimes we borrow the Esselte moviebox if it hasn't been rented out when they close for the night at eight o'clock. There are around forty videos on the rotating shelf and we take it in turns to choose. Mum chooses mum films that she's already seen like *Amadeus* and *Witness*. Michael Jackson's wife-to-be and I choose funny films like *Three Men and a Baby*, *Robocop* and *Big Trouble in Little China*.

One time she reaches for *The Color Purple* but only as a joke. It looks so unbelievably boring with its silhouette of a woman in a rocking chair and over time it becomes a joke based on one person taking it off the shelf and remaining straight-faced until the other one starts laughing.

Everything is soft. Everything is easy. Not even when we're stopped by a policeman who looks at the Saab's undercarriage and bans it from ever being driven again does the world get hard. Mum gets a new car before the day is out. The owner of Rallarns has an old Lada 2101 from the Soviet Union in his garage and he doesn't need it. It's cramped and screams like a chainsaw, but it doesn't cost anything, which is exactly what Mum can afford.

It turns to summer and with it comes a new dad. I never see how it starts – all of a sudden he's just there. He climbs out of a red Volvo 240 estate and kisses Mum on the mouth.

A few dads ago, that would have puzzled me, but now it's beginning to dawn on me that dads are like the weather and growing pains. You don't choose when they start or end. Not even mums have any immediate influence over their presence – they just come along and you have to dress right or grit your teeth. They always pass.

And perhaps this one's half used-up already? At any rate, Little Sis is sure the new dad isn't brand new, because she's seen him before. She says she recognizes him from the Händelö garage.

He's got a canoe strapped to the roof of the Volvo. The canoe's long and narrow like a cigarette. It looks fast.

At a quarter past five in the afternoon, Mr Klingborn was driving across the Liljeholmsbron bridge towards the city. While descending the hill, he was obliged to brake heavily due to a motorcyclist. His car then skidded. First, it collided with another car and then it ended up in the middle of the tram tracks at the same moment as a number 14 tram was crossing the bridge towards Liljeholmen. There was a severe collision that resulted in the motor car being caught between the tram and a large iron post. The car was then torn to shreds as the tram passed by. It was assumed by all onlookers that the driver had been crushed to death and it was something of a shock to them when they saw Mr Klingborn calmly crawl out of the wreckage without even a scratch. According to the Liljeholmen Police, this was nothing short of a miracle.

(The front page of *Dagens Nyheter* on Friday 20 January 1956)

PART SIX

The Canoeist

*In which:
there is square-dancing,
old crimes are revealed,
and
virginity is lost.*

It turns to winter, it turns to summer, it turns to winter again. 1990 arrives and soon everything will happen.

Every morning is a battle against the clock and madness. Mum pulls away the covers so that I'm not late for the bus, but I just tuck my legs and arms underneath myself and fall back asleep in my own residual heat.

Mum shouts from the kitchen and I wake up again but stay in bed, furled up like a bud around my morning wood. Only when the Canoeist roars on his way to the kitchen do I unfurl. And then I run.

Round the bend and down towards the lake I go with tripping steps, trying not to slip in the slush, along the footpath that runs like a narrow threshold between the water and the motorway, through the tunnel under the motorway, past the sign pointing in two directions that says it's a long way to Norrköping and even further to Nyköping, under the oaks, over the stream, through the mill and up to the brow of the hill where the home stretch comes into view.

The brow of that hill is the worst. The distance to the bus stop by the inn always comes as a shock and my brain never gets the chance to get used to it since the distance extends by a few centimetres every night. Nobody knows why. Perhaps Stavsjö lies on a hitherto unknown divide between tectonic plates, perhaps it's black magic. It should be investigated, but there's no time to linger on the brow of the hill.

So few people live in Stavsjö that municipal county transit sends a taxi instead of a bus, and it's hard to tell the difference between the taxi and all the regular cars parked down there before the sun rises. It might be there, it might be on its way, it might have left. You keep running towards the answer.

That's the battle against the clock.

The battle against madness starts a little later in Strömsfors, an unusually ugly little village scattered around a trunk road intersection. The taxi ride there takes eight minutes, which is exactly how long I need to learn how to breathe again – but as soon as I get out of the taxi to change onto the number 432 to town, that rediscovered knowledge is snatched away from me.

The 432 is always standing there, waiting, the driver explicitly forbidden to depart without the passengers from the outskirts of Kolmården, which means there's an accusatory energy on board. Getting on is unpleasant. The air inside is heavy with restlessness and contempt and everyone stares out of the window or pretends to be asleep so as not to reveal their thoughts.

But that's not why it's hard to breathe in Strömsfors. It's the girl.

She almost always sits in the same seat, two seats in front of the concertina middle, on the right-hand side in the direction of travel. She's a couple of years older than me and always looks unhappy or perhaps wronged. Sulky? Her face is hard to read because she wears her long, fine hair like a dark hood pulled down over her forehead. She's sort of hidden behind herself.

I think I can see her longing herself away with deadly force. But what would she otherwise be doing? She lives in Strömsfors and I know that for sure because one time – one single time – the taxi got there before the bus and there she was, leaning against the shelter.

That morning it was just her and me for a while. But that wasn't when our eyes met – it was the morning after, when order was restored.

I was clomping down the aisle when I realized she was looking at me. She looked straight into my eyes for more than two seconds. Possibly upwards of 2.4. Of course, she didn't mean to, she can't have; she's older and looks like the product of imagination while I'm little and true to life – but that was still how it started. Not that very moment, but shortly afterwards when I was sitting beyond the concertina middle and staring at the back of her head.

My lungs shrank, my whole chest felt shallow and tight and somewhere down in my stomach a seed burst.

Now madness is germinating inside me.

I seek out her gaze every morning. From the moment I stand on the steps by the driver clutching my bus card, I turn my head to the left and stand on tiptoe. I don't want to waste a single moment of the ten seconds tops that I have before I've passed her seat on the way down the bus.

Her eyes are closed almost every time.

She's so tired and I think it must be because she longs to leave – that there's a darkness in Strömsfors that keeps her awake at night so the sleep she gets on the bus is all she gets.

In my daydreams, I'm sitting on the seat next to her while her head rests on my shoulder. I'm there for her, but never ask her to tell me about the darkness. She doesn't want to – not yet at least. She just wants me to bury my nose against her scalp so that she can sleep soundly all the way to Norrköping. And when she's awakened by the shriek of the concertina on the tight corner off Norra Promenaden to the terminus she looks up and kisses me and says she's glad I exist.

But she isn't glad that I exist. I'm not even sure she knows that I exist and it's that uncertainty that makes the madness rise towards the surface.

I'm so incredibly conscious that she exists. I'm an expert in her existing and it would be deeply unfair if she didn't at least sense my own existence.

One morning, I catch myself sitting down on the seat right behind her. I almost panic when I realize what my body has done. It feels like a crime is being committed, but it's too late to go back. If I stood up to move further down the bus now it would only arouse her suspicion and that of those around us, so I sit there until the panic subsides and my hands are still.

I breathe in. She smells like girls in single-family homes often smell. It's a fresh scent with hints of fabric softener, hair conditioner and a good home. I can't find any notes that reveal the darkness of Strömsfors, but that doesn't mean anything. I'm pretty sure it's there and that she needs me.

She's so close that I could touch her hair.

Little Bro belongs to us now. The Plant Magician has moved to Värmland to build a new family and he doesn't really have time to take care of the remains of his old one. He'd let go of Little Sis before he even left, and now he says that we can keep Little Bro too. Not for ever – but for a year or so. Just as long as we send him to Värmland occasionally so that he doesn't get completely ruined.

I like having my siblings close. It costs me my own room – we're sharing the biggest one and it's rocked daily by border disputes – but it makes Mum slow and sensitive. She doesn't need to be moving constantly and one cross-breeze a week seems to be enough.

Sometimes she lies down on the floor in our room and when we ask her what she wants she doesn't want anything. She just lies there while we do our thing and a while later she's fallen asleep.

Only the Canoeist isn't happy with the new order of things. He hates the Plant Magician and I hear him telling Mum that he's a parasite and probably retarded too. He doesn't even want to be in the house when the Plant Magician calls to talk to his children.

The Plant Magician has been assigned a time when he may call. If the phone rings at half past six in the evening on the dot then the Canoeist picks up the receiver and drapes it over the telephone chair in the hall. He doesn't summon the Plant Magician's children – it's up to them to keep an eye on the time. All he does is slip his feet into his wellies, exhale through his nose and then disappear.

If the Plant Magician calls at other times – as he is wont to do sometimes to oppose the attempts at remote control over him – the Canoeist hangs up and pulls the jack out of the wall. If any of the rest of us answer when the Plant Magician calls at a forbidden time, we whisper that he's not allowed to.

Little Bro is sent to Värmland on the train once every two months and I go along as escort with sandwiches wrapped in foil and juice in syrup bottles made from hard white plastic. I hand him over on the platform at Karlstad, am interrogated about developments in Stavsjö and then get back onto the train.

Every time the carriage shakes and Karlstad station begins to move beyond the window I'm filled with a big, oxygen-rich feeling diluted with just the right amount of horror. There's a small hole in that feeling where the horror seeps in, and it's perfect. Like when you ride a bike without holding the handlebars. I seem to love travelling by train on my own.

A few days later I return to collect Little Bro. He always falls asleep as soon as we've got onto the train home and doesn't wake up until Hallsberg. I never ask about his stays with the Plant Magician, but sometimes he tells me anyway.

One afternoon – somewhere between Hallsberg and Katrineholm – he tells me about seeing a sibling being born and how the Plant Magician buried the placenta in the herb garden.

I look at Little Bro. His lips narrow and stiffen and his eyes glitter. We burst into laughter and laugh so much that people glare.

I say that I want to be the one to tell Little Sis.

'No,' Little Bro says. 'But we can tell her together.'

He looks like the letter Y. His legs are thin and look almost withered in the shadow of his upper body. His arms are thick and his chest muscles are so defined they have upper edges. He probably had squares across his stomach too when he was still competing and became some sort of champion. There are medals on the shelf above the dining table next to the old Husqvarna scales. I've tried to brag about it at school, but it's hard. He's only a plastic dad, and apparently there were two of them in the canoe when he won his medals. It's too contaminated.

Last summer, he even claimed that I could become a good canoeist.

'You've got the body for it,' he said, detaching a finger from his Thermos cup to point.

I was only wearing my swimming trunks. We'd gone up to the Canoeist's cabin in Bommersvik for the weekend. The cabin is really only one room with two wheels and a tow bar, but he's parked that room in a clearing near the water and he calls it a cabin.

I was standing at the water's edge throwing pine cones at the lily pads. His dog was swimming in pursuit of the cones. I'd just learned how to say the name of the breed – Irish Soft-coated Wheaten Terrier – and I was humming the words because it felt like an attribute to be able to say them quickly. Mum was sitting in a beach chair facing the sun. The Canoeist was sitting on a rock beneath the pine tree.

'You've got short legs and a long torso and that's what a canoeist needs,' he said. 'Now you just need a little muscle too, although not on your lower body. Your legs need to be rake thin and you'll be halfway there.'

He glanced at Mum and laughed in that searching way that dull people laugh when they catch themselves saying something funny. I looked down at my legs and tried to make up my mind whether he'd discovered an attribute or a deformity. I laughed too, but only because you're supposed to.

The Canoeist is remarkably dull. We joke about it when he's not around. Little Sis does an imitation that entails sitting quietly and breathing through her nose for a long time before answering a question, and even Mum laughs at it. But there's no contempt in her laughter. 'It's the Norrlander in him,' she says tenderly yet matter-of-factly, as if she's studied nature and learned about its balance.

The Canoeist is in balance.

He's dull but kind and he has skinny legs but strong arms.

He's grumpy in the morning but happy during the day.

He's younger than Mum but he looks older.

He drinks every evening but only ever a medium-strength beer and never so much that he becomes someone else.

He's not rich but he has a proper job as a welding instructor in Katrineholm and he never has to borrow five-hundred-krona notes.

He makes me chop firewood and cut the grass and walk the dog but he never throws fish tanks around and never crawls around the floor naked.

Children should chew with their mouths closed, but there aren't any slaps if you're careless.

He rolls cigarettes while driving but he never ends up in the ditch because he can steer with his knees.

He's scattered showers, cloudy with sunny intervals and moderate wind.

Mum is in her fourth month.

Prisoner exchange on the platform in Karlstad. It's snowing. The wind is whipping flakes under the joists of the platform roof where they float weightlessly around us.

'You really are saddled with that bloke.' The Plant Magician pats me on the cheek – a little too hard for me to tell whether it's tenderness or something else. 'Bloody funny customer, he is.'

The words smell of beer. The train was late and he's probably been killing time in some nearby pub. I say nothing. He comes closer.

'Bossing people about like some little copper. Banging on about times and twirling his little . . . baton. Does he have a little baton? Does he have a little cap with . . . ?'

He waves his hand in front of his own forehead. He's lost his train of thought and screws his eyes shut to find it again. I look around. The platform has cleared and the train we arrived on has become a whisper on the rails making for Kil.

'I suppose he bosses you lot about too? Of course he bloody does. I know his type. You mustn't let him boss you about or you'll be annihilated. Andrev, you must resist.' He presses an index finger to my ribcage. 'You've got to find your inner partisan.'

He straightens up and surveys the station. His breath is billowing like smoke.

'Welcome to Stepford.' He grins. 'Now she's right up to her ears. Now it's all Sunday lunches and guest towels. Who'd have thought?' The grin fades and he looks at me again. 'Do you know she's been in the clink?'

I shake my head. Little Bro does too.

'Ask her,' he says, beaming. 'Ask your mum about when she was in the clink. Ask her how she ended up there.'

I promise to ask. He claps his palms together and rubs them.

'I've never been in the clink. Want a hot dog before you go?'

I eat my hot dog and hug Little Bro before he gets into the Plant Magician's white Amazon. He's allowed to sit in the front, which makes him tall and cocky. He suppresses a smile.

The Plant Magician yanks open the driver's door but stops as he's getting in. He points towards the station building.

'That looks like a gingerbread house.'

I turn around and look. He's right. Karlstad station really does look like a gingerbread house.

'We're just gingerbread men,' says the Plant Magician. 'We're going to drive our toy car and you're going on your Märklin model train.'

When the train that will take me home pulls out of the station, my body starts to fizz. It's the big, oxygen-rich feeling coming back and this time it's so powerful that I have to laugh – not audibly, but enough that I have to turn my face towards the window so that I'm not mistaken for an idiot by the strangers in the carriage.

I laugh silently with my gaze cast out towards the white-powdered miniature landscape.

Somewhere out there, a toy car has skidded on a bend and is now upside down in a field blanketed in snow. It's deep in the snow and the gingerbread men can't get out.

It is spring and the rain is falling as if in punishment. The bus driver has to crawl through the sloping curve on the motorway emerging from the forests of Kolmården and heading down towards the Östgöta Plain. Everyone is looking out of the windows – apart from her.

She's asleep with her head leaning against the window and it's at this moment that I decide to touch her hair.

It's because of the rain. It's falling so hard that it feels like a state of emergency. You can't even hear the drops any longer – the pattering against the bus has been replaced by a uniform rumble. It sounds like when the brush rolls across the roof in the car wash. The world is about to end out there and until its ruin nothing matters. It's overdue. We're beyond Thunderdome and there are no rules.

Her hair has spilled through the crack between the seat and the window, and I know how I can touch it. I have to put my elbow on the narrow windowsill and then extend it. It won't look strange because that's what you do when you're in the window seat – you lean your elbow on the windowsill and choose one of two perfectly ordinary options: either you bend your arm towards your head and put your chin in your hand, or you extend your arm and rest your hand on the rounded corner of the seatback in front of you.

Just like that.

Now my hand is there, just half an index finger away from her hair. My breathing becomes shallow and I open my mouth to silence myself. The rumbling downpour ought to mask the hissing of my stuffy nose, but you never know with sounds and their frequencies. I can hear my own heart.

I conquer the final centimetres in a movement concealed inside another. I glance to the left in a sudden burst of interest in Bråviken bay and rub my shoulder blades against my own seatback as if correcting a point of discomfort. When I return my gaze to the gap between the seatback and the window, my hand is there. I've not made contact yet, but all I need to do is to unfurl my curled fingers to make it happen.

I die on the spot since it turns out her hair is charged with current.

Little Bro was dug out unharmed from an overturned car in a Värmland field, but my heart stopped when I touched a single hair.

Can you feel through your hair? The thought sweeps between the rows of desks while I'm sitting in the classroom, revived yet still exhausted. I touch my own hair and am filled with horror. I try it out in several different spots but nowhere do I get away with it. It's like an impossible game of fiddlesticks where the slightest touch sends a tittle-tattling vibration to the scalp.

It's stopped raining. The great flood has been postponed and the rules of the world have been reinstated. I decide not to touch her hair ever again.

I touch her hair again. I've worked out that it can't feel like it does for me. My hair is so much shorter – only around an eighth of hers – and my hairs are straight as rulers while hers flow down her shoulders in waves and must have some kind of suspension in the curls that muffles the vibrations.

I've decided to only touch her hair sometimes when I really must and when I'm sure she's asleep. Like yesterday and today and perhaps tomorrow, because then it'll be the weekend and in Stavsjö the weekends are as long as seasons.

I don't know the kids who live in the other houses, and the loneliness makes the weekends sluggish. While I'm sitting in my bed playing *Dragonbane* on my own, I can hear time clotting in the clock in the kitchen. I'm cheating when I roll the dice to shape the attributes of the characters. The seconds are dripping onto the floor like honey. The pad of character sheets has almost run out and I've still never played with three or more players over the age of eleven.

It's easier for Little Sis and easiest for Little Bro. Little Bro is only seven years old and seven-year-olds still don't know anything about how embarrassing it is to exist. They stare straight across the fence at each other and suddenly they're on the same lawn talking about the rules of the game. What's more, both Little Bro and Little Sis have enrolled at Stavsjö School, where all the kids know each other because they're all in the same class.

I'm thirteen and thirteen-year-olds aren't allowed to behave any old way. Sometimes I go into the garden but if the kids my age in the village – who go to Råssla School in Krokek – cycle past on the street then I stare in the other direction. Like you're supposed to.

Only on Friday evenings do I get up close to the natives when I go square-dancing at the community centre on the other side of the lake. The Canoeist saw a flyer on the noticeboard down by the inn and suggested that I go along to make some local friends. I shrugged.

The first time he drove me there, I didn't even know what

square-dancing was. It's now been ten weeks and I'm still not sure. It's a completely bizarre activity – a timetabled fever dream where we dance in squares of four couples each while a man in a leather waistcoat and cowboy tie stands on stage and calls moves into a microphone.

'Do-si-do,' he calls out, and I shudder with shame because it sounds like when seven-year-olds speak pretend English.

Time and time again I collide with the bodies in my own square because I can't learn what the different calls mean. And I don't make any local friends. Most of the people dancing are grown-ups and they scintillate with energy that I will one day learn to recognize as unspoken longing for the partner changes.

My body doesn't belong in this community centre, it doesn't want to dance in squares, but when the Canoeist picks me up and asks whether I've had fun I still nod. Unfortunately, I can't stop square-dancing because there's a girl there who's looked me in the eyes.

She looks me in the eyes every Friday and sometimes she touches me. The touching thing is inevitable since the grown-ups push us together when the couples form up. I'm the only teenage boy in the room and she's the only teenage girl not from Stavsjö. The locally grown girls won't let go of each other; they move like an interlaced and giggling organism and prefer to partner up with each other when the dancing begins.

The girl who usually looks me in the eyes comes from Katrineholm. Her parents are wild for square-dancing and drive 80 kilometres down country roads to dance for an hour each Friday. Sometimes while they're dancing they tilt their heads back and howl, making their daughter squirm with embarrassment.

She doesn't move with as much devotion as her parents, but she doesn't seem to be completely normal either. She wears cowboy boots underneath her dress. It's always the same yellow dress each Friday. She smells of horse and sometimes sweat. She doesn't have a hairdo – her long dark hair is simply divided with a crooked parting and her ears serve as loose hair slides. I sometimes get the feeling that she lives in a padlocked basement and is only let out for a few hours a week to dance and that's why there's a hunger in her eyes. There's something off, but she isn't ugly as such, and her hunger seems to be directed at me.

Before the couples are partnered up and sorted into squares, she threads glances between the bodies in the hall and it's obvious it's me she's looking for. I make myself easy to find. They don't even have to push us together any longer. By the time the man in the leather waistcoat and cowboy tie gets up on stage and taps the microphone, my roving survey of the walls has already carried me across the event horizon. I need only look up and pretend to be looking for anyone at all for two seconds before I catch her eye.

It's important to have a wavering gaze on the way there so that it doesn't end up stuck on anyone else. One evening I had to dance with a woman in her fifties – she was fat and jolly and it must never happen again. Since then, I let my wavering gaze sweep a half-metre or so above the heads of everyone else as it makes its way towards Miss Katrineholm.

We look at each other and shrug. Yet again?

Sometimes we try to talk to each other when the dancing is over. It's never more than a few meaningless exchanges as we head towards the exit, but that was how I found out where she comes from.

'I live in Katrineholm,' she said. 'It takes an hour to get home.'

'I live across the lake,' I said. 'It only takes two minutes.'

'Lucky.'

There's no time for us to say any more than that before we

part and set off for our respective Volvos. But I know she's watching me go. One evening, she asked me whether I have a dog and I realized that she had seen the dog in the Canoeist's car the weekend before.

'It's my plastic dad's dog,' I said.

'What's it called?' she said.

I took a deep breath and answered:

'Irish Soft-coated Wheaten Terrier.'

Sometimes I fantasize about her taking my hand and leading me into the darkness behind the community centre, but those thoughts are only fleeting, tucked away into the gaps between the long reveries which are focused on the girl on the bus. Miss Strömsfors. Compared to her, Miss Katrineholm is a series of unlucky rolls of the dice.

I don't really want her – not so it makes my skin tingle – but I'm almost sure that she wants me and I've got a weakness for girls who want me. We might not be far from that being the answer to the question of what kind of girls I like.

My type of girl: a girl who wants me.

Anyway, I need a backup in case Miss Strömsfors never looks me in the eyes again. For it needs to be resolved soon. I don't intend to remain a child for another whole year.

Cyclops turns on the bedside lamp and puts on his glasses. He's got something important to say. I squint towards the light. He's propped up on his elbow.

He explains that I'm at the end of an evolutionary chain where everyone apart from me has done it. I have thousands of forefathers who have done it, and for as long as I haven't I'm the only one in my bloodline who has failed.

'That's why your body is so worked up by your virginity,' he says. 'No one has failed apart from you.'

I grin. He's not grinning. He's as serious as his dad can be when he's leaning against his desk and talking about numerators and denominators.

'For as long as you haven't done it, you're the worst boy in . . . millions of years.'

'What about you?' I say.

'Me too,' he says. 'I'm the worst boy since . . . since life on Earth began.'

I don't quite understand what he means, but I laugh anyway. And now he's laughing too. We laugh until his dad whacks the pipes downstairs.

One day, Cyclops's words about evolution and virginity will come back to me while I'm on stage in Gothenburg interviewing an author. The author will be talking about the placoderms that lived four hundred million years ago and how a fossil found by a Scottish baker taught us that this early relative of humankind had the first cock. On the train home from Gothenburg, I'll think about Cyclops and the chain of lost virginities and with my newly gained knowledge about the origins of the cock I'll work out that at least twenty million boys lost their virginity on the way from the placoderm to me.

But that's later on. Right now, I'm just a boy lying in an attic room smothering a laugh in a pillow.

Mum calls from Rallarns Kiosk and says the old Lada from the Soviet Union has broken down. It's abandoned on the main road between Norrköping and Söderköping, not far from the turn-off for Styrstad. She hitchhiked the last bit to work.

That evening, we go to Söderköping to pick her up in the Canoeist's red Volvo. On the way back, my siblings wave to Mum, who is steering the car on the other end of a tow rope that disappears into darkness. She's only visible when oncoming cars illuminate the inside of her vehicle. One time, she's gripping the steering wheel and baring all her teeth in a manic grin as if she were driving very fast on the Autobahn, and that time I wave too. She laughs silently and disappears again.

By the time we're close to Norrköping it's so dark that the only thing visible is the tow rope extending behind us, black in the red glow of the tail lights. I think it looks like a fishing line, baited with a mum and lowered into a dark lake. I shudder whenever the line careens and vibrates, exhaling every time the lights of the oncoming traffic reveal she's still there.

We drop off the Lada on the industrial estate on Händelö. It'll be declared dead the next day but won't be scrapped because Mum will receive a tip-off that old Soviet cars can be sold in the Port of Norrköping. There's a shortage of spare parts in the Soviet Union and Russian seamen pay more for an old Lada than the scrap merchant.

When I get home from school, she tells me about seeing a seaman use a crane in the port to lift the car off the quayside onto his cargo ship.

'I saw the car flying,' she says.

I ask whether the money the seaman gave her was enough for a new car.

'She doesn't need a car,' says the Canoeist, stroking her belly which has begun to bulge underneath the lavender-blue tunic from Indiska. 'She's going to quit.'

Mum shrugs.

I touch her hair and wonder if it would be possible to steal a lock of it. Why shouldn't it be possible? Surely I just need to bring some scissors with me on the bus?

The thought tickles me briefly before it makes me feel uneasy. It sounds like the kind of thought you have a few years before realizing you're a serial killer. It starts with a stolen lock of hair and ends with being shot by Charles Bronson.

One morning, Cyclops's dad leans over my desk and says he wants a word with me. He suggests I come home with Cyclops after school and I'm immediately worried because it doesn't sound like a suggestion. There's something deep frozen about his tone. It's an order.

I stare at the back of Cyclops's head until his scalp begins to tingle. He turns around and meets my gaze with a pained expression. He knows something.

What? I mouth.

He stiffens his lips and bares his lower teeth – the international distress signal for an impending telling-off. I attempt a smile but he doesn't smile back.

Anxiety gathers around my stomach like a claw.

I know I'll find out what it's about during the first break, but it's a long time until then and I can't bear the uncertainty.

Is it the porn? Has his dad found the magazines in the attic and worked out that I'm a co-owner? I sleep over there so often that his parents have started to refer to his room as ours. 'Time for you two to tidy your room,' has been said. But we hardly have any of the magazines left.

A year or so ago, we had loads. The old man in the newsstand down on Bråboplan accidentally left the key in the lock of the newspaper box chained to a drainpipe outside the door. We took the key and searched the box early every morning but didn't touch anything until there was good reason to draw the man's attention to the fact that a key had gone walkabout. We finally struck when we found bales of unthumbed porn. But we sold almost all of it.

Cyclops prefers to wank in the dark, and when I'm sleeping over at his so do I. Neither of us is bothered by the sound of the other's hand drumming against the covers. But while I may be shameless in his presence in a way I've never been with anyone else, I still don't want him to see me. The room has to be dark because I do it with a weird and ridiculous grip so it doesn't hurt. I don't even want to see it myself.

The concerned doctor – the one who wanted to cut me but agreed to wait a year or two – hasn't been in touch yet. It's been three years and I assume he's forgotten. Or maybe he's died. Anyway, the string of tissue is still too short – my whole cock bends when I pull back the foreskin, but what am I supposed to do? Call him with a reminder? Book an appointment to get my dick cut? You can't do that.

There are three porn magazines stashed in the attic of 53 Bergslagsgatan, tops. It seems unlikely that a dad's voice would be deep frozen by three magazines. I've had porn tellings-off before and they're usually delivered at a different temperature. The tone can even be lukewarm – admonitions diluted with understanding.

But what else could it be about? I decide that it's the porn we're going to be told off for and it calms me down ahead of breaktime.

'No,' Cyclops says once we're in the corridor pulling on our jackets. 'It's not the porn.'

He takes a deep breath.

'He's found the book of mischief.'

In the summer of 1989 we started keeping a log of our crimes. It wasn't my idea and it wasn't Cyclops's either. It was the neighbour's boy – the policeman's son, the one who knew ninjutsu but wasn't allowed to show us since it was too dangerous – who realized that crimes without structure lacked meaning. He sketched it out on a sheet of paper. It was ugly, filled with wonky lines and scattered numbers, but we understood and we agreed.

Cyclops got out a fresh sheet of paper and a ruler. He did it neatly. He ran down to the basement and returned with a hole punch and a stiff ring binder. On the spine of the ring binder he wrote *Book of Mischief* in silver marker.

Once upon a time, the three storeys of Cyclops's house were three different flats and there's a small kitchen next door to his bedroom in the attic which his parents have filled with junk. That's where we hid the ring binder. We squeezed it into a gap in the niche for the old fridge. It was a good hiding place and we only ever got the ring binder out briefly when we had new crimes to record.

There was a points system from one to five and a list of standard crimes and their values. We rarely dared do anything that scored more than a two, but low-scoring crimes could be stacked for a higher score. A stolen bike tyre valve was worth one, while ten valves – five deflated bikes – could be traded in for three points. A stolen tow-bar cover was a two and you only needed five to get a three since motorists (men) were more dangerous than cyclists (women and children).

For an undiluted three, you needed to nick sweets or porn, smash a window or yank the hood ornament off a Mercedes. I pulled three ornaments off that summer and sold them all to Paella, who had become a hip-hopper and needed stuff to hang around his neck.

Each crime was recorded in the tables contained in the ring binder. A date, a concise description of what happened and a score between one and five. We talked about burning the ring binder at the end of the summer, but when it turned to autumn we forgot.

'I'm willing to forget about most of it,' says Cyclops's dad, dropping the ring binder onto the floor between us.

We're sitting on our respective beds in Cyclops's room and we jump when the ring binder lands with a thud.

'Look, when I was a kid I was a hellraiser too.'

I have time to brush past the hope that this will be a lukewarm telling-off but then he lowers the temperature.

'But there's something in this ring binder that makes me feel completely hollow inside.'

We're staring at the ring binder.

'I assume you know what I'm referring to, Andrev.'

I carefully shake my head. I'm not sure why. I almost certainly know what he's referring to.

'If you don't remember what you've done then you can always check the ring binder. It's all in there. Pick it up.'

I reach for the ring binder. There's a weight to it that somehow surprises me. How can it exist?

'Open the ring binder and read.'

I open the ring binder and allow my gaze to slide between the tables for a while, aimlessly, as if I still didn't know which one of the many crimes he wants to talk about. He loses patience, bends to duck under the eaves and taps his finger inside the ring binder.

'Read from there,' he says. 'Read it aloud.'

I gulp. I can already taste salt.

'There are only two words, Andrev.' He crouches and points to one word at a time. 'Verb. Noun. Read it.'

I clear my throat and say it aloud:

'Killed duckling.'

Cyclops's dad takes my chin in a pincer grip and forces me to meet his gaze. He says he's heard the story behind these two words. He's squeezed the truth out of his son and now all he wants to know is why.

'What's wrong with you?'

I don't know.

'Or have I misunderstood everything? Was it self-defence? Perhaps it was a very big duckling. Was it you or it?'

I attempt a smile. It's a stupid thing to do. He slaps his palm hard against the ceiling and looks over his shoulder.

'And what about you, you little swine? You just stood there and watched. And then you wrote it as neatly as you could in the ring binder. I can see that you're the one who's written all of this.'

He throws the ring binder at Cyclops's feet. Cyclops has his whole upper body hunched over his knees. His neck is flushed red.

Cyclops's dad falls silent and stops moving. He's still crouching but now he's looking out of the window. The only thing moving is Cyclops's cat, who struts through our midst, incapable of reading the room. She's black and named Samus after the hero in the Nintendo game *Metroid*. I stare at the cat and the cat loses its sharpness. I'm crying as quietly as I can, but at last I have to snuffle and then he looks at me again.

'Are we supposed to feel sorry for you now?'

I shake my head.

'But you're crying. You're sitting there feeling sorry for yourself.'

I say:

'I cry every time I think about the duckling. I think about it every day.'

He takes a deep breath as if he has something else to say, but the air just hisses out of him. He wraps a hand around my neck and pulls me to his shoulder. He holds me for a long time.

I turn fourteen and the Indian sends me a letter but no present. He writes that I've got too big for presents and that I probably feel that too.

I don't.

He writes that he's never understood the significance of festivities and that they're only celebrated for the sake of commerce and that he doesn't even mark Christmas.

I put the letter back in the envelope without reading to the end. I put the envelope in the box where I keep all communications from the Indian and his mother together with my *Garbage Pail Kids* trading cards. It's a pale wooden box with sharp edges. I made it in woodwork and I was supposed to finish it with sandpaper and linseed oil but I never got round to it before the end of term. I spent too much time customizing it for a shared bedroom. It's got a hinged lid, fittings and a padlock.

'Now you're big enough to go to work and earn your own money,' says the Canoeist while we're sitting at the kitchen table eating the Christmassy rice pudding I requested as dessert for my birthday.

'I go to school,' I say.

'Not in the summer.'

'In the summer I'm in Säter.'

'Not the whole summer.'

He looks at Mum. I do the same and am both betrayed and saved in the course of a few seconds.

'You're really not a child any more,' she says. 'But isn't it a bit late to be applying for a summer job now?'

'Not just a bit,' says the Canoeist, pointing his spoon at me. 'You should have got started long ago.'

He looks ridiculous and now I realize why. He's like the result of that game where you take turns to draw a man part-by-part and fold the paper so that you don't see each other's parts until the drawing is finished and unfolded. He's got an old man's pate – his forehead is comically high and opens into two folds around a transparent tuft – while below the old man's pate there is a boy's face and below the boy's face there is a muscular man's body. He is incoherent.

You look like a folded-up man, I think to myself, but I say nothing. Instead, I agree with him through a becoming nod, wise with hindsight, and I make to stand up. He lays a hand on my shoulder and I get stuck in a challenging position with my bum hovering just above the seat.

'But perhaps you'll get lucky,' he says. 'I heard they're still looking for summer hires down at the inn.'

'Which inn?' I ask.

'Does this village have more than one?' he retorts.

My legs begin to vibrate and I sink back down onto the seat. He suggests that I go there right away. I say it's the evening and he says that inns are usually open in the evenings.

It's Monday 14 May 1990 and I stroll towards Stafsjö Wärdshus with the sun in my eyes. The temperature is 11.6 degrees Celsius and the wind speed is 3 metres per second. 280 kilometres away, the West German cargo ship *Betty* has struck the Soviet tanker *Volgoneft* and 900 tonnes of waste oil are spilling into the sea off Karlskrona. 1,410 kilometres away, half a million people have gathered for a demonstration in the Place de la République in Paris after the desecration of a Jewish cemetery in Carpentras, where the carpet merchant Felix Germon's body was exhumed and violated with a beach umbrella. 7.5 billion kilometres away, the Pioneer 10 space probe is rushing onwards through the void – nothing touched by humankind has ever been so far from human beings.

I get a job as a dishwasher. I'm due to start the week after school breaks up.

In the contract he writes that I'm fifteen years old. I've gained two years in one day.

Once my siblings have gone to sleep, I turn the bedside lamp back on and read the rest of the letter from the Indian. He writes that we must meet. He's written that before, but this time he doesn't change the subject in the next line.

He writes that he has never met his own dad, that he doesn't even know what his dad is called and that his mum refuses to tell him. He doesn't want me to grow up with the same void and that's why we must meet.

He writes that he's planning to fly to Sweden in late August and stay with an old friend in Stockholm. He writes out his long phone number and urges me to call him so that we can decide when and where to meet.

He writes that it's *important for both of us.*

Once the immediate nausea has receded, another messy feeling creeps up on me. An Indian on a plane? That's not right. Indians don't fly on planes. When I try to picture it, he turns into a folded man.

Mum has explained to me that the Indian isn't an Indian – she's told me several times that he was born in Hamburg and only ended up in the USA because his German mother married an American marine – but it's as if the words never sink in for me. Lying in the ugly wooden box is the photograph of him holding me in a corduroy footmuff and each time I look at it, I can clearly tell that he's an Indian. When I took the photograph to school and showed it to my classmates, they could tell too.

'He's an Indian,' I said.

'You can tell,' said Paella, and everyone agreed.

Mum says it's up to me.

'But if it was my dad who'd got in touch and wanted to meet me then I would have done it.'

Little Sis looks up from her plate where her eggy bread lies paralysed in a puddle of apple sauce.

'You haven't met your dad?' she says.

I shake my head before realizing that the question is directed at Mum.

'I have,' says Mum. 'When I was little. But he got a new family and I haven't seen him since . . . well, since I was Andrev's age.'

'When were you Andrev's age?'

Mum extends her fingers and counts silently. She puffs up her cheeks with a trapped sigh when she gets close to the answer.

'More than twenty-five years ago.'

There are only a few days of term left and I bring a pair of scissors with me in my rucksack. It feels like a crime is being committed when I remove them from the sewing box and hide them up my sleeve. Mum's fabric scissors aren't allowed to be used for any old thing, but what I'm going to do can't be done with a pair of blunt scissors. They need to be sharp, otherwise the hairs might stretch and get caught between the blades.

I shudder at the thought of what would happen if Miss Strömsfors were suddenly to wake up at the moment the scissors were attached to her hair and my fingers were attached to the scissors. We would be entwined, her hair would extend and it would cause a throbbing pain in her scalp.

Perhaps she would immediately identify the romantic side of the scene and forgive me for the theft of a lock of hair? Perhaps we would get together? Although probably not. Those kinds of emotions would probably be overwhelmed by confusion and only surface a few hours later. And by then I'd be on my way to the secure wing at the Säter mental hospital to spend my summer with Svartenbrandt and the other psychos. I'd have to live in a small room with barred windows and a view of Lake Ljustern from the wrong side. Across the water, I'd see Cyclops and his brothers swimming off the jetty and catching perch from the big rock next to the boathouse. They'd be as small as insects and completely noiseless beyond the windows. I'd have to spend summer in a fish tank, sitting there fingering the stolen lock of hair.

No, I need a really sharp pair of scissors. I need Mum's Fiskars fabric scissors with the orange plastic handles.

I go into the hall, slip my hand into my rucksack and shake the scissors out of my sleeve like Travis Bickle shook the pistol out of his sleeve holster. They land in my hand with a forbidding chill and I hurry to push them down to the bottom of the rucksack. And then I run.

I run with the scissors.

Round the bend and down towards the lake I go, under the motorway, past the oaks, over the stream, through the mill and up to the brow of the hill where the home stretch to the bus stop heaves into view. The mornings are brighter now and you can already see from the brow whether the taxi has arrived or not.

It's arrived and I keep running.

Past the gateposts at the bottom of the concrete steps up to the inn where I'm due to start work as a dishwasher in a week's time. Past the noticeboard where the flyer about square-dancing in the community centre has become faded and brittle.

It feels good to run. The movement dispels my anxiety. If I think too much about what is to be done then it won't be done, and it needs to be done before the summer holidays because then it'll be over. We might not sit on the same bus ever again.

The Canoeist doesn't like the Steiner school. He's never understood why I need to travel 50 kilometres a day to twirl copper rods and dance the alphabet during my lessons.

'That's enough guff,' he said two weeks ago, and that very evening it was decided that I'll change schools after the summer holidays.

I'm going to start at a proper school with yellow municipal brick walls, an asphalt playground, a sports hall and a smoking area. I'm going to Råssla School in Krokek.

The Canoeist drove me there one evening so I could see it. He pulled into the car park at the end of the sports hall and turned off the engine. There was a herd of mopeds parked along the iron railings in front of the ramp down to the youth centre in the basement. There were two guys leaning against the railings. They were taking turns to drag on the same cigarette and one of them stuck out his bottom lip and drew smoke into his nostrils from his own mouth.

'Shall we get out and take a look around?' said the Canoeist, patting the car door.

'There's no need,' I said.

We sat in silence for a while. The Canoeist rolled a cigarette. The two guys stared at us, stubbed out their cigarette and then vanished behind the railings. The Canoeist lit his own cigarette and pointed across the dashboard.

'That's a Puch Florida. That's a good moped.'

Although I didn't know a thing about mopeds, I immediately realized that he was referring to the ugly old moped wedged between the modern ones with criss-cross tyres and the letters DT on their fuel tanks.

On the way back home, he told me about a moped he's got in the barn at his parents' place in the country and said it can be mine when I turn fifteen next summer.

'The Monark Monarpeden,' he said. 'It's a real cult bike.'

A few days later, I got to see the moped. It looked like it had been built in the age of chivalry, but I still hugged him.

She's asleep like usual, her hair spilling through the crack between the seatback and the window. I'm holding the scissors but my hand is still inside the rucksack.

The colour is peculiar – almost unnatural, maybe like chestnuts dipped in engine oil, and it glistens when the light is broken into waves. It's fairy-tale hair. It's the name of some hitherto unknown *My Little Pony* horse with a serious character.

I pull the scissors out of the rucksack and hide them between my thighs.

I need at least 3 centimetres, otherwise it won't be a lock – it'll just be a pencil brush. The stolen artefact must be long enough to accommodate curvature. I measure the hair with my eyes, rehearsing the movement in my thoughts and feeling overwhelmed with small sorrow when I imagine the lock falling onto the mottled grey floor of the bus.

What kind of sorrow is that? Is it the sorrow of the fisher faced with the beauty of the perch? Or is it merely fear trying to disguise itself as something else in order to be taken seriously?

I hesitate for a long moment before I set my hand in motion.

On my first day as a dishwasher, I smash seventy-seven glasses.

The first seventy-five are lost when I push the dishwasher trolley the wrong way round over the threshold between the kitchen and the dining room. The basket locks are facing me and when the wheels strike the threshold the top four baskets – each one loaded with twenty-five freshly cleaned, warm tumblers – slide off the trolley. I manage to catch one of the baskets before I hear the others exploding beyond the trolley. The hubbub from the lunch patrons falls silent and through the opening left by the missing baskets I see the dining-room floor glittering with shattered glass.

Somewhere in the silence: applause.

It's coming from behind me and I peer towards it.

He's in his twenties and looks like a hard rocker. The Pommac-blond hair is three times the length of his face and held in place by a patterned bandana. He's wearing it pulled down over his eyebrows à la Axl Rose. I've only seen him from a distance until now because he works on the till, but right now he's in the kitchen for some reason, applauding.

For a few seconds, his applause is the only sound in the world. Then the cold buffet manageress behind him starts applauding.

She's in her twenties too, and I've already stared at her a few times. I haven't managed to work out whether she's cute or not. There's so much going on on her face. She's covered in freckles and her skin is so flexibly fitted over her skull that she looks like a vacuum-packed skeleton when the light catches her the wrong way. But where she's standing right now the light is perfect and she's almost wonderful as she laughs.

The applause spreads and soon there's clapping from every direction. Even the lunch patrons in the dining room are clapping.

'Now we're talking,' Hard Rock Guy shouts, shaking a fist above his own shoulder.

I don't understand what we're talking about, but I clench my own fist and show it to him. The applause fades away and Hard Rock Guy fetches a broom. I reach out to take it.

'I'll handle it,' he says.

I say I can do it myself. He shakes his head and presses his index finger against my chest.

'You're a dishboy and the dishboy is king. It all starts and finishes with you. If you stand here sweeping up in the middle of lunch service then the whole chain falls apart. The king's got to be the king and nothing else.'

He ushers me into the corridor leading to the scullery.

'Run along, Your Majesty.'

I work for ten hours and towards the evening I start to thrive in the scullery. After lunch service, the stacks of dirty dishes were unrealistically large, but the giant dishwasher is fast and swallows twenty-four plates at a time. It's like working in a cartoon. The impossible is possible. I can transform chaos into order and there's a crude pleasure in certain moments. Like when I get to obliterate béarnaise sauce using the shower gun hanging over the rinsing sink like a sprung coil. Or when I let myself be enveloped by the steam that billows out each time I open the hood to move the basket on.

It's only towards the end that it starts getting boring again – when the kitchen closes and the pattern is broken. The chefs roll in trolleys laden with canteens and pots that need scraping and scrubbing by hand.

But in the middle of the tedium, he turns up again.

'All right, King,' he says, clinking two bottles of beer.

He pries off the caps using a fork and hands one to me before turning a plastic bucket upside down to sit on. The label on the bottle states that it contains strong beer, which I note with a carefully untroubled expression. The label on the plastic bucket states that it contains 30 litres of strawberry jam, although it doesn't any more. I've been seeing traces of the jam all day. It goes with the pancakes on the kids' menu and what was once in the bucket is now being spread all over the country by hundreds of small couriers.

'Did the boss say anything about the glasses?'

I shake my head in the middle of a sip. I haven't seen the boss since I signed the contract that says I'm fifteen years old.

Hard Rock Guy lights a cigarette.

'I suppose it'll get taken off my pay,' I say.

'Fuck that,' says Hard Rock Guy. 'It was an accident.' He winks at me as if we're sharing a secret. 'Did you manage to break anything else?'

I hesitate. Beneath the counter to the left of the pre-rinse sink there's a grey plastic crate half-filled with chipped or broken plates, wine glass stems and other objects that can't be thrown in the bin because you might slit your wrists and bleed to death while carrying the bin bag to the skip by the staff entrance. Beyond the seventy-five glasses that were lost in the dining room, I've only broken two wine glasses. I point to the crate.

'I broke a wine glass.'

'Nice one,' says Hard Rock Guy with a smirk. 'That's enough for today. But don't forget to break some tomorrow too.' He stretches his upper body and taps ash into an unwashed pot. 'You've got to cost more than you're worth.'

I don't understand what he means, but it feels as if I ought to laugh or at least grin. I opt for a grin. He looks around and lowers his voice.

'As long as they're losing more than they gain by having you here, they haven't defeated you.'

'Okay.'

'You're free.'

'Okay.'

'Do you understand what I'm saying?'

I don't. He looks around again, stands up and lowers his voice to a whisper. 'Check this out.' He unbuttons one of the large pockets on his checked trousers. I'm wearing the same type of trousers because they're part of the kitchen uniform, and in mine there are a few one-krona coins I found on a tray and an almost full tub of sweets I found on another. The Hard Rock Guy's contains a wodge of crumpled fifty-krona notes.

I say:

'What's that?'

He says:

'Kept change.'

The Plant Magician calls at a forbidden time but I'm the only one at home and we talk for a while. He's not drunk or angry – just curious. He asks what month Mum's in and I tell him she's in her seventh. He asks whether she's fat and I say she's fat.

'So is she in love, then?'

'I don't know.'

'Is she still or cleaning?'

'I think both.'

'Mhm.'

I press the tip of my index finger into one of the 550 holes in the rattan of the telephone chair back.

'Now I'm going to teach you something about love, Andrev. Love is about saving someone. That's it. Every single bastard is looking for someone to save and we can't save each other, so there's only one rescuer in each relationship. And over time, the saved person longs to leave because she wants to save someone too. She wants love too.'

'Okay.'

I release my fingertip from the rattan and contemplate the compression-moulded blister. I touch it with the pad of my thumb – it's pale and hard.

It's my fifth day in the scullery and I'm toiling to stay one step ahead towards evening. Miss Katrineholm doesn't know that I've started working at the inn and I don't want her to think that I've missed our last dance for no reason. I need to finish before nine so that I can run up to the community centre before her parents pack her into the car and go home.

I've no plan as such – just a note in the pocket of my checked trousers and the feeling that she's the only one in the world who wants it.

On the note I've written my address so that we can write letters to each other and arrange to meet privately. I wanted to write my phone number too, but that was incompatible with the layout of our house where the phone is fixed to the hall wall and there are no doors between the hall and the adjoining rooms. I would be completely defenceless when I talked and later I'd be subjected to questions of an unbearable variety. The address has to do.

At around seven o'clock there's a blockage in the pre-rinse sink, which is presumably my own fault. On the tiles behind the mixer tap there's a sticker with a warning that albumins will coagulate if the water in the gun is hotter than 62 degrees Celsius. Sometimes I cheat when I feel certain that the dishes being rinsed aren't stained with anything containing albumins, which is a bit stupid since I can't name a single thing that contains albumins. Well, apart from eggs.

I curse myself but manage to deal with the blockage after just a few minutes' work with the plunger. The water recedes and I'm still sitting pretty. Towards eight o'clock, I even have time to go into the dining room and retrieve individual trays from the trolley to guard against ambushes while I await the final challenge: the trolley of pots and pans from the kitchen.

I'm not planning to change before running up to the community centre – I'll just unbutton the white jacket of my uniform to split the formal look with a glimpse of a tight T-shirt. It's a good look. I've tried it out in front of the mirror in the staff changing room. There's an energy in the unbuttoned uniform jacket that can never be extracted from a buttoned uniform jacket, let alone from any civilian attire. It's the energy that radiates from someone who has completed a task.

Hard Rock Guy usually radiates that particular energy when he strides into the scullery towards nine o'clock with two bottles of beer in one hand and his jacket unbuttoned all the way down to his waist. That's how I'm going to look when I'm standing in the community centre car park with the note for the girl.

I'll nod towards the inn and say:
'I've come straight from work.'
She'll look towards the inn and say:
'Are you the chef?'
I'll say:
'Sort of.'
She'll say:
'You kind of smell of beer.'
I'll say:
'I probably do. We usually have a beer in the kitchen once our work's done. It's a bit of a tradition when you work in a restaurant.'

Then there will be some kind of hug, during which the note will be discreetly pressed into her hand.

At twenty past eight one of the chefs brings the heavy dishes up from the kitchen. He pushes open the swing doors with the trolley and lets go of it so that it rolls over to me before he turns around and returns wordlessly to the kitchen.

It's a strange thing to do – he usually carries on across the scullery and says goodnight before vanishing through the door into the changing room – but I can already feel that something is up before I hear the wheels of yet another trolley give away its presence before it reaches the swing doors.

There isn't usually another trolley, but this time there is. It's loaded with frying baskets, fan grills and other stuff I've never seen before. He says these things only get washed up once a week – on Fridays.

Not long after, Hard Rock Guy arrives with two bottles of beer in one hand and his jacket unbuttoned all the way down to his waist. It really is a good look.

I scrub, while he smokes and talks about a band called Poison and how he's never wanted something as much as he wants to hear the record that Poison are releasing in two weeks' time.

It reaches nine o'clock and I know I'll never see her again.

I'm not sure why I'm calling her. I've never called her before. I still want her, but there's almost no girl I don't want. I'm unrequitedly in love with most of them and when one day I come to write about the call I'll wonder whether I dialled her number in some sort of attempt to speak with the headquarters of the female sex. I'm calling the boss of all the girls with a vaguely worded complaint. I want to know why it's all so complicated, but when I ask the question it sounds more like this:

'What are you doing?'

'Nothing much.'

Single Mum's Daughter's reply is curt, incapable of disguising her surprise, but then she is beset by a guilty conscience – girls sometimes are when they realize they're the co-owners of a silence – and then come the words. She spends an entire minute describing the nothing much before she asks me what I'm doing with my summer holidays.

I tell her about the job at the inn and when she laughs for longer than necessary at the thing about the smashed glasses, my cheeks start to burn. I remember that we belong together and I'm tempted to say something big.

And why not? It's the right time of year for it – if I say something big and it turns the mood weird then we have the whole summer to forget about it, and I've got the house to myself since the rest of the family have gone out for a swim. I'm standing in the hall with a view of the porch and the lawn. I'm guarding the only way in.

'Are you going up to Säter this summer?' she asks.

'Later,' I say. 'I've got to work another three weeks.'

The conversation is going the wrong way and suddenly I hear voices and see the Canoeist through the lilac by the corner of the house. They're back.

'I've got to go now.'

'Okay.'

The Canoeist has already reached the steps and it's possible he can hear me, because the front door isn't completely closed. The last one out forgot to give it a push and the wonky bolt ended up resting against the frame. There's a crack where words can leak out, but I say it anyway.

'I love you.'

She says:

'Oh.'

And then:

'Thanks.'

I hang up the receiver and glance towards the front door. The Canoeist is standing on the porch making kissing sounds through the crack.

One evening, I hear Mum telling the Canoeist how the Plant Magician came by the piece of paper that states he's unable to work. They're at the kitchen table. Mum's laughing as she tells the story. The Canoeist is laughing too, but only to begin with. The more he finds out, the quieter he becomes.

She tells him about a professor at the university who was looking for test subjects for a poorly funded study and how the Plant Magician and his best friend said they'd do it for free in return for a particular piece of paper.

The Canoeist can't believe his ears. 'So they were signed off for the rest of their lives?'

Mum sighs and laughs at the same time. The Canoeist stands up.

'They lay in some room taking LSD and answered some questions and now I'm covering rent and food for these bastards as long as they live?'

Mum nods. So I assume. The only sound I hear is the Canoeist's footsteps as he heads for the hall. He jangles the lead and the dog runs after him.

On the hill leading up to the staff entrance there's a small building with a façade made from yellow wooden cladding, three doors on the ground floor, and a fourth one beneath the ridge of the gable roof that is accessed via a steep staircase at the end of the building.

The building is for seasonal workers. The ground-floor rooms are fitted with showers and washbasins and the girls stay there. The attic room contains nothing but two legless beds pushed into the eaves. This is where Hard Rock Guy stays. He's furnished it with two trays of canned beer, a tape player and a duffel bag from which tentacles of summer clothing grope their way across the floor. It's like a dark and pernicious reflection of Cyclops's room and I like being there.

Neither of us can stand up straight in there, but it doesn't matter because all we are doing is lying on the beds, each of us with a beer, listening to Poison. It's after ten o'clock in the evening.

The door to the early summer evening is open and I can see my socks hanging on the banister outside. My feet are pale and wrinkled after my ten hours in the scullery. My whole body aches, but here comes the chorus.

Hard Rock Guy clenches his fist and sings along to 'Every Rose Has Its Thorn'. He looks at me as he does so and I move my lips to show that I'm starting to learn the lyrics. He likes that and I like that he likes that.

After a particularly raucous rendition of the chorus, one of the girls downstairs whacks a wall. Hard Rock Guy rolls his eyes and turns the volume dial down 3 millimetres.

'She's just pissed off because I won't do her,' he says, grinning mischievously. 'Do you know what she did today?'

I don't.

'She grabbed a big knife and held it to my throat' – he shapes his hand into a blade and threatens himself – 'and she said she'd kill me if I didn't do her.'

I laugh loudly to disguise my own despair. I've never heard someone say anything more provocative and I'll never be able to persuade myself that he's lying. The girls at the inn seem to be crazy about him and I can see why. His cheekbones are as chiselled as shoulder blades; his arms muscular in that lean, sinewy way; his wrists wrapped in thin leather straps. He looks like a poster.

I say:

'Why aren't you doing her?'

He says:

'I'm going to. But she's not the hottest and you've got to do them in the right order.'

I don't understand. He explains.

'You know who's the hottest?'

That I do know. She's got Dallas hair and is a permanent member of staff. I only see her occasionally. She's a few years older than Hard Rock Guy and seems to float in an unpredictable pattern between a variety of duties in the restaurant and the hotel's reception. Her name's probably Cecilia.

'Now I'm going to teach you something.' He sits up, tucks a leg under his body and lights a cigarette. He smokes Yellow Blend, which puzzled me at first since everyone knows that Yellow Blend cigarettes are for sad mums, but he manages to single-handedly blow new and delicious energy into the whole brand.

'If the hottest one finds out you've done the second-hottest one then you're toast,' he continues. 'You ain't ever going to get to do the hottest one. But if the second-hottest one' – he points down at the floorboards – 'finds out that you've done the hottest one then it just makes her more into you. It's science. If you put them in the right order then you can do all of them.'

'Are you going to do all of them?'

'No, only the hottest ones.'

He falls back on the bed and I'm gripped by a desire to throw something hard at his face. I want to disfigure him. I enjoy his company, the way he talks to me as if we were brothers and gives me private tuition in hard rock and misappropriation, but the thought that he could – if he felt like it – go downstairs and have sex with a girl this very night fills me with a kind of horror.

He's worse than the kids who get given their child benefit as a monthly allowance. He's living as a god among men.

I say:

'What if the hottest one doesn't want it?'

He says:

'She does.' Smoke rings rise from his beautiful head before breaking against the ceiling. 'It's just taking a little while because she has a boyfriend.' The mischievous grin returns. 'But it's the staff party on Saturday and we're going to have beer and play rounders at Rosenberg. You're coming, right?'

'If I'm allowed.'

'Why wouldn't you be allowed?'

'I'm not that old.'

'How old are you actually?'

Quite, how old am I actually? The boss took care to say that I was supposed to say fifteen if anyone asked, so I don't suppose it would be a flat-out lie to say fifteen. It'd be more like following orders. But it feels wrong to lie to someone who seems incapable of imagining that I'm not to be trusted. On just my second evening in the scullery, Hard Rock Guy told me in detail how he had gone about misappropriating more than 30,000 kronor from the tills the summer before. The trust is almost aggressive and I don't know how to repay it because I don't have any good secrets to offer in exchange. The truth about my age would surely be a reasonable part payment.

'I'm fourteen.'

'Shit. I told them you were seventeen.'

'Told who?'

'Told the girls.' He points down at the floor. 'I mean, it's not like I thought you were seventeen, but they asked and I thought . . . well, I figured you'd like to get lucky this summer too.'

'Who asked?'

He points to the floor again. 'The girls.'

'Did they ask in chorus?'

'You what?'

'Did they all ask at exactly the same time, or was it really just one of them who asked?'

He waves his fingers in front of his own face. 'It was the one with the freckles. She likes you.'

I immediately have difficulty breathing and it must be obvious because he starts to laugh.

'Relax. She's only twenty. You'll be fine. But don't go forgetting that you're seventeen.'

In the winter, you can tell the difference between the haves and have-nots. It's the down jackets and the freckles after February half-term that give it away. Everyone wears their class affiliation like a snail shell. In the summer, the differences are burned off. You don't have to go skiing to get a tan and all you wear are a pair of shorts and a T-shirt. In the summer, no one can know for sure which world you belong to. You're free and enigmatic. I hate winter and I love summer.

Cyclops calls from Säter.
'When are you coming?'
'In July.'
'When in July?'
'First of July.'
'Good. I'm bored.'
'What are you doing?'
'Hanging out on the jetty staring.'
'At the German's breasts?'
'Probably.'
'Most probably?'
'Most probably.'

Cyclops has an ugly aunt who every summer brings a beautiful friend with her from Germany to Säter. They have a remarkably powerful friendship. They're inseparable. They even sleep in the same bed down in the wooden cabin.

The only thing they don't do together is bathe in the lake because the aunt doesn't like bathing. At least, not like the German does. The German loves to bathe. She's indefatigable, like a child, her upper body bare, like a child. She plays with the real kids until her lips turn blue. She cannonballs and splashes water and doesn't seem to notice that everyone is apparently bewitched by her breasts. It's impossible not to be. Even Cyclops's mum occasionally has to stare and that's unfortunate because it's obvious what she thinks. She wants to shut down the performance.

It's as if everyone apart from the German knows that some

of us are no longer kids and I fear that Cyclops's mum might take her aside at any moment to tell her this. All I hope is that it doesn't happen before the end of the month because I'd really like to see the breasts from Germany one last time.

'But she's not always bathing,' Cyclops adds. 'I'm mostly staring at the lake. There was a guy who drowned over on Sågholmen a few days ago.'

'What's Sågholmen?'

'The island!'

'Shit! That's close!'

'Yes. Only a few hundred metres from us. They were heading over to the island in a canoe and it capsized and two of the guys swam back to shore while the third one just disappeared.'

'Did you see it?'

'I think so.'

'You think so?'

'I don't see so good. But I was probably looking that way when it happened.'

After we've hung up, I think about all the accidents that Cyclops has stared into being: the fighter planes that crashed mid-air, the man who rear-ended a lorry and crawled onto the asphalt to throw up, Ronja the dog who had to be gathered up in a bin bag.

Was he there when Saga kicked my foot off the border too?

Yes, he was. He needs an exorcism.

Beer and rounders at the staff party. I swing like a boy. Throw the ball up with my left hand, use a two-handed grip on the bat, and my whole body rotates on my hips. It feels right and a sound effect escapes from my lips – 'douff' – but as usual I miss. Well, more badly than usual since the freshly cut meadow is swaying underneath me.

I drank two beers with the crayfish from the Stavsjön lake, another on the way down to the meadow and three unnecessarily large gulps on my first lap around the bases. I'm overcome by a giggling greed each time I'm called out and now I'm out again.

The first base is usually the base of shame, populated by attributeless children jostling each other while waiting for someone who can hit, but this evening it's just as worthy as any other since each base is a crate filled with strong beers.

I pull a half-full bottle from the crate, wipe the neck with my palm and look for Hard Rock Guy. I want him to meet my gaze and laugh with me, but he's busy with Dallas Hair. They're fielding, positioned unstrategically close to each other with their hands shaped like cornets. Talking incessantly. She laughs, he pushes her, she laughs even more and her breasts ripple beneath the embroidered bodice of her white dress. They're both demigods and I knock back the entire remaining contents of the bottle to wash down the jealousy.

The meadow is full of bodies but I still feel abandoned. I'm tumbling around in the gaps between everything they have in common and laughing to myself. No one's interested in the boy who is supposedly seventeen. Not even Cold Buffet Manageress.

'You should probably take it easy.'

The immediate relief that someone is talking to me is punctured by the look of disgust. He's old enough to be my dad and he's looking at me as if I've pushed my way into the queue for the lucky dip at his kids' party. My cheeks become hot and I turn away, looking up towards the edge of the woods where the sun is glowing between the pine trees.

There are mosquitoes up there. They want to join the game. They come from the woods and use the long shadows of the pines as player tunnels to make their way onto the pitch.

I point and shout.

'The mosquitoes are coming!'

No one replies. Tomorrow I'll shudder with self-loathing when I think about the warning cry about the mosquitoes, but right now I'm already ashamed enough not to shout again.

Douff!

I rush, see Hard Rock Guy's overarm throw out of the corner of my eye, navigate the second base and make for the third where I'm caught out so I hold my arms and turn back. My body feels heavy. There's rumbling within. I laugh and vomit. Someone leads me to the uncut end of the meadow and tells me to rest for a while in the long grass. I fall asleep in the foetal position and wake up on my back. The sky has turned blue-black and the Hard Rock Guy constellation is gazing down upon me.

'Let's get out of here.'

He's standing astride my knees. I take his hand, am pulled up and brushed down. The air has become cooler and the meadow is deserted, apart from Hard Rock Guy and two girls who are shifting from foot to foot not far behind him. One of them is Cold Buffet Manageress while the other is the one who threatened Hard Rock Guy with the knife.

I ask where Dallas Hair has gone. He shushes me and whispers:

'Her boyfriend came and picked her up.'

We walk back towards Stavsjö along the gravel track. I'm still drunk, but my body feels lighter now and I don't feel sick. Hard Rock Guy asks whether anyone has a cigarette, Knife Girl says he's already asked umpteen times and I wonder just how long the party lasted while I was asleep.

'We can smoke cow parsley,' Cold Buffet Manageress exclaims, pointing to a plant with a fluted stem and white flowers on the bank next to the track.

'Always make sure you have a pipe,' says Hard Rock Guy.

'No, you smoke the stem.' She holds up an empty interdigit in front of her mouth and feigns several rapid drags. 'It's hollow. You can smoke it like a ciggie!'

'There are ciggies growing in the woods?!' Hard Rock Guy says, leaping across the ditch to extract a cigarette from the stem.

The girls laugh.

'It only works in the autumn,' I say. I've smoked cow parsley with Paella on the fringes of the school playground. 'The stem needs to be dry first. Anyway, that's not even cow parsley, it's hogweed and you'll burn your hands if you break it. It's like alien blood inside.'

Hard Rock Guy lets go of the stem and rubs his hands against his jeans.

Cold Buffet Manageress turns around and looks me in the eyes, possibly a little impressed. 'Are you a field biologist?'

I laugh to indicate how absurd that would be.

'No, I'm just . . . a druid.'

It's a bad joke but she smiles anyway.

'Like the guy in *Asterix*? The one with the magic potion?'
'Yes, like Getafix.'
She laughs again and this time she touches my arm.
'You doing science at college?'
'No.'
'Well, what are you doing?'

I suppose I should have said yes, but now I'm suddenly unable to think of any college programmes of study apart from electrical comms and I don't intend to play the role of a young man dreaming of cutting cords.

Hard Rock Guy comes to the rescue.

'He's doing humanities. Second year. Hurry up. I've got ciggies in my room and I'm going to go nuts if I don't smoke soon.'

The community centre is at the end of the track. The girls go round the back for a wee and I resist the impulse to say something about square-dancing. We leave the woods and follow the motorway down towards the inn, past Horberget and the Diana temple that's two hundred years old but always mistaken for a vulgar gazebo from the 1970s because of where it's located behind two sand lime brick gateposts in a garden in Stavsjö.

When we cross the motorway, Hard Rock Guy points to the inn's ice-cream stand down in the car park – shuttered for the night.

'That's your real treasure chest, Andrev. That's where you should apply to work next summer because when you're on the ice-cream stand you can eat as much ice cream as you want – it's included! – and no fucker can prove anything even if you do keep the change.'

'Isn't it only kids that work on the ice-cream stand?' says Knife Girl.

Hard Rock Guy doesn't answer because he's begun to run

up towards the small building where the seasonal workers stay. By the time the girls and I round the corner he's already sitting on the steps to the attic, smoking. Cold Buffet Manageress and Knife Girl unlock their doors on the ground floor and go inside but leave the doors open. It's unclear what happens now.

If I leave the party and carry on around the lake then I'll be home in a quarter of an hour, but while we were walking along the gravel track in the woods Hard Rock Guy mentioned something about an afterparty. The word tickled me because I've never been to an afterparty. I've only just been to a party and I don't know where the boundaries are between one and the other. Is this an afterparty?

I'm awaiting instructions.

Knife Girl returns from her room with a bottle of wine in one hand and a stack of white plastic cups in the other. She kicks her door shut behind her and disappears into Cold Buffet Manageress's room. Hard Rock Guy stands up and flicks away his cigarette. It flashes like a shooting star in the darkness.

'You'll have to take off your jeans if you're going to sleep in my bed.'

She kicks off her own jeans as she heads for the basin. There's a plate of flickering tealights on the floor and her shadow moves like a jittery phantom across the plasterboard ceiling.

I wriggle out of my jeans without getting up from the bed, hiding my lower body under the covers. This feels vaguely organized – as if the situation after the party and the afterparty also has a name and a structure that I've simply not heard of.

The same situation is taking place in the room next door and I'm listening for clues. I can hear their muffled voices but not the words – only the cadences. Hard Rock Guy's lines are short and compressed like an untimed bass line while Knife Girl's are longer and burst into laughter at the end. The silences grow longer and longer.

Cold Buffet Manageress examines herself in the mirror and ties up her hair. When she raises her arms, her T-shirt rides up and I have to look away. My heart is beating so violently that it makes my chest hurt inside the cage of my ribs.

I can't close my eyes because that makes the bed start to spin and I can't look at the wallpaper pattern of meadow grass on the wall because that makes me feel sick. I look at the digital clock on the floor. I promised to be home before midnight. I wonder whether Mum is asleep or worrying.

Cold Buffet Manageress kneels and blows out the candles before climbing over me towards the wall. She lingers over my head briefly and seems to consider something before rolling onto her back and putting her hands to her face. She laughs. I don't ask but she answers anyway.

'You're so young.'

'You're not that old either?'

She laughs again.

'I'm older than you think – you just can't tell because I've got a troll's face. I'm always going to look like a little troll.'

'You don't look like a little troll.'

I can tell that the compliment lacks a dimension and I add: 'You've got an amazing face.'

She sieves air through her teeth and cups a hand over my face. The movement is clumsy – violent almost – and I don't know what it's supposed to mean.

I try to say something beneath the cupped hand but she shushes me. She's heard something and now I can hear it too. The sound is coming through the meadow grass wallpaper and the volume is rising quickly. It's Knife Girl moaning on the other side of the wall.

We help each other to tug the covers over our heads. The moaning falls through the octaves and becomes a lowing. We giggle in the hot darkness. Now we have a cocoon.

Silence returns abruptly and just half a minute or so later they start talking again. Light-heartedly, as if nothing special happened.

We stay in the cocoon. Our legs are intertwined. She kisses me, wraps a hand around the crook of my knee and presses my thigh towards her crotch. I slip a hand under her top.

One winter's day in thirty-three years' time – by which point the motorway will long ago have moved to the far side of the lake and the inn will be derelict – I'll return to this room. I'll find the door ajar, forced open by subsidence in the rotting skeleton of the building, and I'll be arrested by melancholy as

I enter. The curling sheets of meadow grass wallpaper will be hanging off the wall and the plasterboard sheets on the ceiling will be discoloured by black mould and flowers of damp. The night with Cold Buffet Manageress will feel distant, almost dreamt, but I'll still feel a pinprick of despair when I'm reminded of Hard Rock Guy's sudden betrayal.

'What's she on about?' Cold Buffet Manageress opens the cocoon and listens.

Room-temperature air seeps in and contaminates the state of emergency. My hand is still under her top – holding a breast. Knife Girl is hammering the wall and shouting again. This time I hear every word of it and so does Cold Buffet Manageress.

'HE'S FOURTEEN!'

The envelope contains 8,400 kronor and I laugh to myself when I emerge onto the inn's terrace. It's morning and the restaurant has just opened but the stone steps down to the car park are already full of bodies and I take a short cut over the ornamental hedge and slither down the slope to avoid wading against the current. I laugh again as I jog towards the foundry.

8,400 kronor. What do you even do with that much money?

The Canoeist has an idea.

'Now he's earning his own money, don't you think it's time he starts paying his way around here?'

He says it to Mum, but he's looking at me. We're at the kitchen table, the envelope of cash between us. Mum is standing at the hob.

'I'd say so,' she says as if it's something they've discussed, but I can tell the thought is new and unfamiliar to her. She would never have suggested anything like it without his involvement.

The Canoeist points to the envelope. 'Half seems reasonable to me.'

I laugh. Biding my time. The Canoeist has such a bad sense of humour that you sometimes don't know for sure whether he's joking or not. And the more confident he becomes as a father figure, the more often he tries to joke with us, which has created a brand-new element of stress in daily life.

'Is half too much?'

I shrug. I still don't know whether he's joking when he

reaches for the envelope. There's only seven weeks to go until he becomes a dad for real and he's growing a beard to get into the mood. The beard is reddish-yellow and dense like a carded mitten. Just the other day, I thought he'd started to look like Chuck Norris, but now I think he's starting to look like a twat.

Of the 4,000 kronor left after paying twat tax, 3,000 buys me a Pioneer HiFi tower including a vinyl turntable, CD player and double cassette deck, a haircut that will soon be known as the Beverly Hills look but is still known as the James Dean look, a yellow PVC wallet with Velcro fastening, and a baggy black T-shirt from Levi's with the words 'REDTAB'S XX' printed in pale grey across the chest so that I can radiate Levi's energy without having to pay for a pair of Levi's jeans.

Then I catch the train to Säter.

Cyclops meets me on the platform. He's leaning over the handlebars of an old lady's bicycle and he apologizes that his dad couldn't bring the Volkswagen minibus.

'It's the triathlon today,' he says, nodding towards the lake.

Each summer, the open water Swedish triathlon championships are hosted in Säter and I've arrived on the very day of it and in the midst of the opening swim, which means that Cyclops's dad, who also happens to own the best motorboat on Lake Ljustern, is occupied with his traditional task of conveying the public broadcaster's cameraman about on the water. This evening he'll open the TV cabinet in the lounge and switch on the sports news so that we can see the part filmed from the boat. The report usually lasts for a minute or so, and that minute tends to represent our collective annual consumption of televised sport.

'I'd give you a backie but apparently this bike has a slow puncture.' Cyclops kicks the back wheel, making it rattle against the chain guard.

'I'm too hungry to walk.'

Cyclops glances across the tracks towards the town. 'Do you have cash?' he says.

'Most probably,' I say, fishing the yellow PVC wallet from my back pocket as if I needed to check. 'Okay, I've got nine hundred kronor on me.'

Cyclops whistles and points towards Salutorget. 'Why don't we get a burger at the Square?'

The temperature is 19.3 degrees Celsius. The cloud cover

above the town is almost complete and a rain as fine as a sneeze falls on us as we cross the tracks. One day I'll ponder how carefully fate's helpers herded my body towards hers, but right now the only thing I'm wondering is why the single-storey building beneath the lime trees has that name.

I say:

'Why'd they call a fast-food stand the Square?'

Cyclops leans the bike against a rough picnic table made from pressure-impregnated softwood and measures up the fast-food stand by eye. The windows on his glasses are pimpled with raindrops.

'Probably because it's square.'

'Probably not, since almost all buildings are square.'

'Probably yes, if the building is unusually square.'

He takes off his glasses and rubs them against his top. Without glasses, his face becomes alien and grotesque. I look away and my gaze falls through the sash window by the counter and lands on the face of a girl. She's leaning forward with her elbows on the counter, looking out at us.

'I think it might be a perfect square,' Cyclops says, stepping forward to embark upon an examination. 'A geometric shape where all the sides are the same length.'

He measures the front of the fast-food stand in seven strides. The girl behind the counter follows him with her gaze until he goes around the corner and disappears. Then she looks at me. I shrug.

She smiles.

I smile.

She lowers her gaze, swallows the smile and looks up again.

She has a big and undulating face. Her cheekbones are as rough as kneecaps, her nose almost as wide as her mouth, and her eyelids are so puffy she looks like she might have allergies. It's a good face. Clear. I want to bite into it, but only tentatively. I want to smell her hair, which is dark bordering on black, like Coca-Cola.

This is how it begins.

'She was a bit like Sigourney Weaver,' Cyclops says once we've made our way around Dalkarlsnäsviken bay and are walking along the gravel track towards the cabin.

'Who's that again?'

'The one in *Aliens*.'

'Have you seen *Aliens*?'

'No, but you've told me the whole film.'

'Only the first one, right? It's called *Alien* because there's only one alien in it.'

'You've told me both.'

'Are you sure?'

'Yes.'

'How can you know what Sigourney Weaver looks like if you haven't seen the films?'

'I've seen her on the cover. And on the poster. When she's holding the kid and the machine gun.'

'It's a flamethrower.'

'That's it.'

I don't know whether I want the girl in the fast-food stand to be like Sigourney Weaver, because I don't quite remember what Sigourney Weaver looks like. At the moment, I can't remember what anyone in the world looks like – except the girl at the fast-food stand. She's drifting around like glare on my retina and I'm thinking about everything I know about her: she's got a summer job at that fast-food stand but has never wondered why it's called the Square, she's exactly a month older than me, she lives up in Åsen with her mum and sister, she's going to the stables after work today but not tomorrow, she'll be at the ice-cream kiosk down by the campsite bathing spot at exactly five o'clock tomorrow afternoon. How can I know all this? How did it happen?

I pick a fireweed from the edge of the ditch and whip Cyclops across the back with it.

'Does that hurt?'

'A little.'

I discard the stem and we walk in silence before I say:

'Is Sigourney Weaver good-looking?'

'I think so.'

'I think so too.'

The cabin in Säter is really four buildings scattered across a verdant hillock on the southern shore of Lake Ljustern.

At the top is the big cabin, a red-washed timber building of two storeys with a gallery facing towards the lake. That's where Cyclops's family stay. Behind the big cabin is the little cabin where Cyclops's grandmother – a hymn writer and retired Riksdag member for the Liberals – sits in a rocking chair and feels cold. If you go in and lie down on the floor she reads you a story. Halfway down the hill towards the lake is the prefab cabin where Cyclops's aunt stays with her beautiful friend from Germany, while over by the gateway and without a glimpse of the lake is the new cabin where Cyclops's uncle – the obvious loser in this arrangement – stays with his family.

In addition to the four residential buildings, there's a spacious shed down by the jetty where the canoes, waterskis, sunloungers and fishing gear are stored. And hidden among the pine trees close to the shore is a boathouse with rails, a cradle and a hand winch where the best motorboat on Lake Ljustern stays during the winter.

Cyclops and I share a small room upstairs in the big cabin. It has woven wallpaper and curtains checked like a picnic blanket. Our beds are built into the wall, one on top of the other like bunks. I sleep on top. I have my own curtain and my own reading lamp. It's the only bed in the world where I can fall asleep with the light off. If I want. But I don't want to.

'Can you finish telling me *The Running Man?*' says Cyclops.

'How far did we get?'

'Schwarzenegger had just strangled that hockey player with the barbed wire.'

'Then there's still a long way to go.'

'Are you too tired?'

'Yes . . . but I still can't sleep.'

'Are you thinking about the Sigourney Weaver of Säter?'

'Probably.'

We're allowed to use the rowing boat whenever we like provided we wear life jackets until we're out of sight.

On this particular morning – the one that develops into the day when I meet the Sigourney Weaver of Säter at the bathing spot on the far side of the lake – we bring fishing rods, a can of worms, a bucket and two of Cyclops's four brothers. We row west, past Björknäsudden point and into Jönshytteviken bay where we land, driving the little brothers ahead of us towards the golf course.

We move, crouching, through the tall grass growing between the shoreline and the green on the eleventh until we've filled the bucket with stray golf balls. Then we row back towards Björknäsudden point to fish under the shade of the deciduous trees.

Cyclops clambers ashore and takes the forest track home. He's uninterested in catching and killing. The brothers stay with me.

We row back into the sun to escape the gnats but cast our lines back towards the trees. The lake is deep and rocky here. Cool. We're hovering above a gloomy slope where the perch thrive and it's the perch we want.

I know where all the fish are to be found in this lake – at least when they're where they're supposed to be. Sometimes they swim to the wrong place, but when all is right the perch are here and the pike are among the reeds in Jönshytteviken bay while the roach, bream and ruffe – the feeble ones – are happiest around Sågholmen in Dalkarlsnäsviken bay, where it's so shallow you can always see the bottom. We don't fish there, or by the hospital pier, where you can end up with eels on your hook.

There's an old hand-drawn chart lying in a drawer in the big cabin and I've examined it closely to learn about every sounded depth in Lake Ljustern. Around ten oar strokes off Björknäsudden – only a stone's throw from where we are now – is where the lake is deepest: 36 metres. We once lowered a line with a jigger sinker on it at that spot. It was at my suggestion – so I got to hold the harp and let out the line until it hit the bottom. My eyes can still fill with horrified tears when I think about the weight of the line and the vibrations in the joints of my fingers. If I had felt a tug from the underworld I would have thrown the harp overboard in a flash.

'You've got a bite!' the little brothers hiss one after the other.

It's me they're hissing at but I've got my chin resting on my shoulder and am looking the wrong way – towards the bathing spot on the far side of the lake – and when I turn my gaze I see that the float has disappeared. I lift my rod and a perch is yanked out of the aspen crowns in the reflection of the woods. It sputters but is incapable of gaining our sympathy because it lacks vocal cords. If fish could scream then I never would have fished.

I break the perch's neck, bait the hook with a new worm, cast out and then return my chin to my shoulder. I can see the ice-cream kiosk from here. I could see it from the golf course too. I've been able to see it all morning.

Last night, I longed to be there. Now I'm hoping for a storm to come and make it all impossible.

Her tongue is cool. It tastes of soft ice cream and white Prince cigarettes. Her eyes are closed but mine aren't. I know they're supposed to be, but I want to see it all. It will be many years before I kiss another peeper and realize how insane it looks.

Cyclops is walking along the water's edge with his joggers rolled up and his upper body hunched over his feet. He's pretending to look for something, but I know he can see what we're doing because his cheeks are blotchy. We're sitting on the grassy slope above the beach and now I'm hers. That's clear.

'You're mine now,' she says, tucking her left arm under my right so that the tender insides of our upper arms make contact. We're soft as cats' bellies there and for a short while I can't exhale, only inhale.

There's something restless and determined about her movements – a stern tenderness that speeds proceedings up. Not long ago, I wasn't hers. Then we were just sitting here and squinting towards the evening sun burning through the narrow chink between the clouds and the woods beyond the mental hospital on the other side of the lake. Cyclops pointed towards the jetty where a small dog was barking at the boys on the diving tower. He said something about the dog being ugly and then she said something about it being cute. It was a bulldog, but she said 'bylldog' because she speaks with a thick Dalmål accent and we became wild with laughter.

We imitated her, taking turns to say 'bylldog' and each time it was my go she touched me and demanded that I stop. So I kept going until at last she knocked me onto my back on the grass and – as if there were no other way to silence me – kissed me while I lay there.

Now she lays her head on my shoulder and says:

'I'm glad you came and saved me from this shitty summer.'

Then she raises her free hand and pulls my head down towards hers. She's wrapping herself up in me. She's wrapping us up together.

'The summer's still pretty shitty,' I say.

It's a bad line and I'm forced to show with an artificial shiver that it's the weather I was referring to. She sits quietly for a while before prising herself free and standing up.

'My guy friend drowned a few weeks ago.' She points towards Sågholmen. 'Right there.'

There are tears in her eyes and I'm struck by a dash of jealousy. I don't believe in guy friends. And I know that the guy who drowned was two years older than her, so they can't have been in the same class. I fancy he was something else.

'How terrible,' I say.

I stand up and gaze towards the island. In my mind's eye, I can see the hand-drawn chart that is in a drawer on the other side of the lake. I want to say that it's only 2 metres deep where he drowned and that I've wondered whether he reached the surface with his hands and could feel the air up there while he was standing on the bottom being filled with water, I want to say that I've thought about him, but I say nothing.

Cyclops has noticed that our bodies are no longer intertwined and now he comes stomping up the beach with his dark gift hidden behind a grin.

We ride home on our old ladies' bikes. I lead the way

because mine has a headlamp connected to a dynamo on the front fork and powered by the wheel. The lamp flickers on the uphill parts. Sometimes it goes out completely and we shriek with fear because we're pretending that there are evil creatures in the woods that can't bear the light.

On Sunday 8 July 1990 my childhood ends.

I sneak out via the gallery, shoes in my hands, slipping along the wall of the house so that my footsteps don't make a sound. At the bottom of the steps, I sit down on the rough-hewn, cool stone step and prise my feet into the shoes. There's a metallic rumble from the lounge behind me and I have time to wonder why before I hear a happy shout and remember that Cyclops's aunt's German friend was going to come up from the prefab cabin to watch the World Cup final between West Germany and Maradona.

When one day I come to write about this evening, I'll look up the particulars of the World Cup final, note that the only goal was a penalty in the eighty-fifth minute and calculate that the time must have been around 21:40 when I sat down on the doorstep to put on my shoes. I'll be moved by the precision of the timing and write a long paragraph about how a penalty kick can stand like a surveyor's rod in time. Then I'll delete the whole paragraph and return to the past. Which is now.

After putting on my shoes, I run with tripping steps along the path through the jungle of ferns on the lake side of the hillock. I fetch a life jacket from the shed, slip my arms through it but don't fasten the buckles.

The lake is so still and shiny that it feels as if I am breaking something when I push the rowing boat into the water from its spot drawn up in the gravel of the beach.

The rowlocks whine, so I quieten them by rowing with small movements. I'm not sure why I'm sneaking about – there's no prohibition on leaving the big cabin and going out onto the lake after dark. However, I don't want to answer questions about my business.

2,060 kilometres away, there are only minutes left of the match at the Stadio Olimpico in Rome and in an act of pure desperation, the striker Dezotti receives his second yellow card after wrestling the centre back Kohler to the ground. The Argentine players swarm around the referee while Dezotti trudges towards the touchline and then Maradona gets a booking.

I set a course between two rocks and leave the bay that has always been too small and too indistinctly drawn to have its own name. I row through a cloud of gnats, spit, peer over my shoulder and adjust course. I'm rowing towards the diving tower in Säter.

Halfway to the town – where the lake is 26 metres deep – I pull the oars into the stern and let the hull glide almost silently across the black abyss while I wriggle out of the life jacket and stow it under the thwart. I look over my shoulder again and now I can see her, a small blob of darkness on the jetty between the beach and the diving tower. The blob is waving the flame of a cigarette lighter and I wave in return before turning my back on the town to start rowing again.

It's 13 degrees Celsius and West Germany are the football World Champions.

When I reach the jetty, I make an attempt to moor the boat but the Sigourney Weaver of Säter tells me not to bother. She gets down into the boat and pushes away from the jetty, making us drift into open water before she straddles the thwart and gestures to me to do the same.

We're sitting face to face. I'm becoming cautiously obsessed with her clearly defined face and now I'm touching it. She likes that. She kisses the hand, lifts it off her face and guides it to a breast under her hoodie. She's not wearing a bra. The hand is warm since it's attached to a body that has been rowing across a lake, the breast is cool since it's attached to a body that's been waiting on a jetty.

She says:

'It's so nice being with you.'

I pull her close and ask whether she's cold, but that's not what she means.

'It's nice being with someone who doesn't know who you are, because then you can be who you want to be.'

It's not the first time she's said that, and it makes me wonder whether there's something wrong with her that everyone in Säter knows about but I don't. I don't know very much about her. She says we've got all sorts in common, but it's hard for me to know with as much certainty as she does because she doesn't tell as much as I do.

When I said that I was going to meet my real dad for the first time in just a few weeks, she asked me to tell her everything about him. So I told her everything I had found out from Mum and the letters.

I told her how my dad was born in Hamburg a few years after the war and that the house he was born in was the only one on the street left standing after the firestorms. She asked what a firestorm was and I explained that a firestorm was the only kind of weather that humans could create themselves.

I told her that my dad had never met his dad and that his mum, my grandmother, refused to say who he was. He believes his dad was a football star since he has early memories of his mum's brother, who is dead now, calling to report on all the goals his dad had scored.

I told her that my dad was adopted as a seven-year-old by an American marine who married his mum and that he grew up on different military bases around the world: Frankfurt am Main, Okinawa, Vacaville and finally Tucson, Arizona, since my grandmother needed to live in the desert because of her asthma.

I told her that he deserted during Vietnam and ended up in Sweden where he found my mum chained up to an elm tree, but that he now lives in Brussels and is a taxi driver.

She listened carefully, as if dads really interested her, but when I asked her to tell me about hers, all she said was:

'He lives in Falun and he's sick. He can't be a dad.'

Is she sick too? Is that why she's sitting opposite me on the thwart and saying that it's nice to be with someone who doesn't know who you are because then you can be who you want to be? Or is it just the mental hospital on the eastern shore that makes me suspicious of everyone who lives here? Sometimes I think the madness within is leaking into the ground water and making everyone in Säter sick.

I say:

'So who do you want to be?'

She thinks for a while. 'I want to be someone who gets picked up by a boat in the middle of the night.'

'You are.'

'Not yet. You have to row away first. I haven't been picked up until you've taken me away from here.'

She gets off the thwart and sits at the very front of the boat.

'Row,' she says.

'Where?' I say.

She thinks for a while and then replies:

'To a bed.'

I laugh and am about to ask what she means before it dawns on me that only a child would ask that question.

A while later, I pull the boat onto the gravel beach and cast a long, wary look up towards the big cabin. All the windows facing the lake are dark, but I know with almost absolute certainty that Cyclops is awake and awaiting a report.

We creep along the beach and up to the shed. The full moon is casting small wisps of white light through the cloud cover. I open the shed and point to a sunlounger within. It has yellow cushions and a backrest that can be reclined completely horizontally, making the lounger like a bed.

She shoves me into the shed and pulls the door shut behind us. It's like having your eyes gouged out. I grope for the light switch and set canoes hanging from the roof swaying before remembering that there's never been a light in the shed. I push open the door to let in a strip of moonlight. She's already unbuttoned her jeans – the 510s from Levi's she bought with her first pay packet – and now she's rolling them down so that they gather in a heap around her feet.

I'm awaiting instructions.

'Lie down,' she says.

'I did it.'

'What did you do?'

'It.'

Cyclops turns on the bedside lamp and puts on his glasses.

'Tell me about it!' he snaps so tersely that the words are merged into one.

I want to but I can't. I'm lying on my back in a cross on the floor trying to regain control of my breathing. I rowed like a madman when I crossed the lake for the fourth and final time that night and then I ran all the way up the hill and up the stairs to the gallery. I ran because I was afraid that the details in my short-term memory would evaporate along the way.

'Tell me about it!'

He's trickled down onto the floor and is now kneeling next to me. He grabs my face, shakes me, and then slaps my chest like a dejected field doctor in pyjamas.

'You've got to tell me!'

'Wait!' I pant.

But he doesn't want to wait. He begins without me and he does so in a tone that reminds me of the one his dad attunes himself to when telling us about Odysseus's wanderings.

'You're not a virgin any more. You rowed across the lake and dropped off your virginity. You've known a woman and can never unknow it.'

I begin to laugh. He sinks to the floor and lays his head on my arm.

'Tell me about it.'

I tell and Cyclops is lying so quiet and still in his bed that at times I'm convinced he's fallen asleep, but each time I neglect details he gets annoyed and hisses.

'How? You're still wearing your underpants . . .'

'No, they're down.'

'Who pulled them down?'

'Uh . . . I did.'

'Go on.'

Once I've told him everything, we lie there in silence for a long time until he flinches.

'What happened to . . . did it hurt?'

Apart from the doctor and Mum – the ones who knew but forgot – Cyclops is the only person aware of the design flaw that was never operated on.

'It's fine,' I say. 'My cock's indestructible.'

The soreness says otherwise, but it'll be another five years before it breaks. On that night – also the first and only night of my life with Single Mum's Daughter – I'll spurt blood and faint in my own bed. But even then, I won't go back to the doctor. I'll wrap myself up with a sock and wait out the pain.

And once I remove the sock, it'll dawn on me that the operation has finally taken place.

PART SEVEN

The Indian

In which:
a boy catches a train to Stockholm,
and
a dad awaits him by the main entrance on Vasagatan.

The Indian calls to go over the details. It's the second time we've heard each other's voices and just like the first time I'm disgusted by my own inability to speak English to someone who speaks English. I thought I knew how, but the words get stuck in my teeth like toffees and my tongue feels swollen and numb. Besides, Little Bro is semi-concealed behind the doorway to the living room, smirking away.

I clench a fist and show it to him. The grin disappears but only to make way for something worse. He starts to mime that he has a square American jaw.

I hiss that he's going to die.

'What's that?' says the Indian.

'It is not . . . anything,' I say, shuddering at my sentence structure.

Little Bro starts to move sideways like a crab, back and forth through the doorway. He's shaking his head – perhaps trying to dance like MC Hammer. I aim a kick at him and he jumps out of the way.

He knows he's going to get beaten up as soon as I hang up, but that doesn't bother him. On the contrary. He teases me almost daily and rarely stops until I've hit him. It's starting to resemble a ritual, and deep down I understand what he's doing. He just wants to be with his big brother and I can't hit him unless I'm with him. That's it.

I'm a bad big brother, but it'll be many years before that begins to bother me. Right now I'm in far too much of a hurry to leave to see how lonely he's become.

The Canoeist doesn't like him, and that's not just because of the Plant Magician. The Canoeist goes to bed at nine o'clock every night and after that everyone has to be quiet and if you're watching TV then the volume has to be turned down to a whisper. Little Sis and I know more about how dangerous dads can be if they lose their temper towards night-time and we're good at being quiet, but Little Bro is completely useless. He just can't be quiet and sometimes I have to wrestle him onto the sofa and press a cushion over his face. My eyes fill with tears of hatred as he laughs through the cushion. He's putting us all in danger.

'See you soon,' says the Indian once we've agreed the details.
'Yes,' I say.

A few days ago he got into the car and drove all the way from Brussels to Stockholm. Tomorrow, I'll take the train to Stockholm and he'll be waiting for me outside the main entrance to the central station on Vasagatan.

He says:
'I love you, son.'

It doesn't sound as dramatic in English as it does in Swedish. In English, words are like monopoly money, but it still makes my body tingle when he says it.

At first it feels like when you're riding a bike and let go of the handlebars. Then it feels like when you're riding a bike and let go of the handlebars and put your hands in your jacket pockets.

The boundary between freedom and horror snaps on the train to Stockholm. Around Vagnhärad, where the countryside is at its ugliest, I wish for a storm that would bring everything to a standstill. I wish for the power he described in a letter.

In the summer of 1943, the British dropped so many bombs on Hamburg that they created a new type of weather. It was an artificial type of weather the world had never seen before – a firestorm that transformed stone walls to glass and people to stick figures in the streets. The fire swirled and screamed as if it had a soul and it destroyed practically everything except the house on Lindenstraße where my paternal grandmother lived together with her mum and an escaped Belgian prisoner of war whom they were hiding in the attic.

The man in the attic was called Arthur Marcel Delhaye and it was his last name that I took when I was born. The Indian still uses it, but only because he doesn't know what he should really be called. He was supposed to take the last name of the American marine, but the adoption was never quite signed off. Arthur Marcel Delhaye refused to renounce paternity because he said there was no paternity to be renounced. The Indian became trapped in no man's land. He's still got the same name as the man in the attic even though he's never belonged to him, just like I've got the same name as the Plant Magician while I await instructions.

The Indian and I don't have the names we should have. We're not quite rooted in the world.

He thinks we need each other – he writes as much in his letters and I feel sorry for him when I read it. It's tragic that he doesn't realize it's too late.

I press my forehead against the window.

There's a man leaning against a car smoking on an industrial estate in Södertälje. He's probably used to the train rushing past because he doesn't even look up towards the embankment. I see him for two or three seconds and then I'll never see him again.

It's fantastic – a whole person was just standing there and his life had been going on since he was born before it brushed by mine and now it'll carry on until he dies.

It's been ten seconds since I saw him and I can imagine what he's doing now. He's taking another drag. Not long after, he throws the cigarette onto the asphalt and steps on it before getting into the car and driving away. Or perhaps he goes into the building made from corrugated metal sheets to do whatever it is they do there. I never saw what it said on the sign.

It's been thirty seconds since I saw him and it's now getting hard to guess what he's doing. All I know for sure is that he's doing something, because everyone does all the time. That's what's so fantastic.

It's been a minute since I saw him and I feel dizzy when I think about all the people I've ever seen – and all the others, for that matter – who are all somewhere doing something right now. Even the dead ones who are underground being dead. Every person is somewhere, doing something, every moment.

I used to think: What's my dad doing right now?

I would think that thought several times a week, but now I almost never think it and that's how you know it's too late.

He's standing outside the main entrance on Vasagatan, but I'm not ready yet. I go to the newsagent's on the concourse and buy a bag of Djungelvrål liquorice.

Standing in the queue by the till, I open my wallet. The Velcro fastening has already become shaggy and stiff, but still makes a ripping sound.

In a narrow compartment that opens into the fold there is a stack of black-and-white photographs. Most of them have been cut by hand from the school photographers' thumbnails. There's Single Mum's Daughter, the Sigourney Weaver of Säter, Cyclops, Saga and Paella. There's also a portrait of the Indian that he sent in a letter so that I'll be able to recognize his forty-year-old face when we meet.

I study it one last time. The long hair has become short and he doesn't look one bit like an Indian; he looks more like a taxi driver, and this might come naturally to someone who drives a taxi by day, but it'll be many years before I get used to it.

I replace the stack of faces in my wallet and pull out a note to pay. The change goes straight into my jeans pocket because I'm keeping a lock of hair in the coin pocket.

I catch sight of him through the window of one of the entrance doors and immediately recognize him from the photograph in my wallet. He looks anxious, combing his hair with his hand and breathing with his mouth shaped like an O. I watch him for a moment before I tackle the door with my shoulder.

Now I'm gone. The camera lingers on the door, which swings several times before coming to a stop and then there's the sound of an organ rising above the hum of the concourse. It's the beginning of a song. It's 'Nevermore' by The Soundtrack of Our Lives and this is a bit strange because it won't be recorded for another eleven years, but it's so perfect just here.

When the drums start in the fifth bar, everything turns black and then the credits start to roll. Partway through the credits, you're shown old photographs of how everyone looked in real life and then a knot forms in your stomach.

We're a little uglier but still beautiful.

'So you don't ever see the dad?'
　'Only through the window, blurrily.'
　'That's crap.'
　'Yes.'